Young Digger

Anthony Hill is a Canberra-based writer, former journalist and speechwriter for the Governor-General. In addition to this, Anthony Hill and his family ran an antique shop for five years in a small country town in New South Wales. The experience formed the basis of his first two books, *The Bunburyists* and *Antique Furniture in Australia*. His first children's book, *Birdsong*, was published in 1988, followed in 1994 by his award-winning novella *The Burnt Stick*, illustrated by Mark Sofilas. The two combined again to produce *Spindrift* in 1996 and *Forbidden* in 2002.

Soldier Boy and *Young Digger* are the products of Anthony Hill's extensive research and travel to the Gallipoli peninsula and the battlefields of the Great War.

PRAISE FOR ANTHONY HILL'S SOLDIER BOY *(Winner of the 2002 NSW Premier's Literary Awards' Ethel Turner Prize for Books for Young Adults)*
'This book is a model of historical writing for young (and old) readers . . . a significant contribution to the nation's culture . . .'
(Judges' report)

Also by Anthony Hill

The Bunburyists
Antique Furniture in Australia
Birdsong
The Burnt Stick
Spindrift
The Grandfather Clock
Growing Up and Other Stories
Soldier Boy
Forbidden

Young Digger

ANTHONY HILL

Penguin Books

artsACT
ACT Government

The author expresses grateful thanks to the ACT Cultural Council and the ACT Government for the generous assistance which enabled this book to be completed.

Penguin Books

Published by the Penguin Group
Penguin Books Australia
250 Camberwell Road
Camberwell, Victoria 3124, Australia
Penguin Books Ltd
80 Strand, London WC2R 0RL, England
Penguin Putnam Inc.
375 Hudson Street, New York, New York 10014, USA
Penguin Books, a division of Pearson Canada
10 Alcorn Avenue, Toronto, Ontario, Canada, M4V 3B2
Penguin Books (N.Z.) Ltd
Cnr Rosedale and Airborne Roads, Albany, Auckland, New Zealand
Penguin Books (South Africa) (Pty) Ltd
24 Sturdee Avenue, Rosebank, Johannesburg 2196, South Africa
Penguin Books India (P) Ltd
11, Community Centre, Panchsheel Park, New Delhi, 110 017, India

First published by Penguin Books Australia, 2002

10 9 8 7 6 5 4 3 2 1

Cover and text design by Cathy Larsen, Penguin Design Studio
Map illustrations by Pat Kermode, Purple Rabbit Productions
Quotation from *Sagittarius Rising* (First published in Great Britain by Peter Davies, 1936) reproduced with kind permission from Greenhill Books/Lionel Leventhal Limited
Typeset in 11.5/16pt Bembo by Midland Typesetters, Maryborough, Victoria
Printed and bound in Australia by McPherson's Printing Group, Maryborough, Victoria

National Library of Australia
Cataloguing-in-Publication data:

Hill, Anthony, 1942– .
Young digger.

Bibliography.
ISBN 0 14 100062 7.

1. Tovell, Henri, d. 1928. 2. Orphans – France – Biography.
3. World War, 1914–1918 – Biography. 4. Adoptees –
Australia – Biography. 5. Children and war – Germany. I.
Title.

940.40092

www.penguin.com.au

To the memory of Honoré 'Hemene' Tovell,
the family who cared for him,
and all children visited by war

The air was our element, the sky our battlefield.
The majesty of the heavens, while it dwarfed us, gave us,
I think, a spirit unknown to sturdier men
who fought on earth.

CECIL LEWIS
Sagittarius Rising

AUTHOR'S NOTE

The story of how No. 4 Squadron of the Australian Flying Corps smuggled home their boy mascot Henri Hemene Tovell, called Young Digger, was once described by the military historian Arthur Bazley as 'one of the most extraordinary incidents of the First World War'. He was right.

Much of Young Digger's tale survives in the public arena: in newspapers and journals I consulted; in files at the National Archives of Australia, the Australian War Memorial, the Public Record Office of Victoria, and elsewhere; in E.J. Richards' squadron history *Australian Airmen*, and especially in the chapter *Henri* from Norman Ellison's 1957 book *Flying Matilda, Early Days in Australian Aviation.*

I was also privileged to speak to members of the family of 2nd Air Mechanic Timothy Tovell, who brought Digger back to Australia. Tim Tovell's daughters, Mrs Edith Lock, Mrs Nancy Elliot and her children, Marilyn, Rick, Rob, and Sally, generously shared their memories and family collections with me, for which I am deeply grateful. His son, Mr Edward Tovell, also kindly helped with my enquiries.

The records differ on many points, particularly about Henri's background. As the text indicates, I believe his true Christian name to have been Honoré, and it is as such that I dedicate the book to his memory. There are at least five different spellings of his supposed French surname 'Hemene', none of which appear in today's telephone directories for the region. There are many families with the name Herman or Hermann however, especially in the Lille-Armentières district where he was found. It is possible – perhaps even probable – that his real surname was a form of this, misspelled by the child writing in 1919: but at a distance of more than eighty years, it is unlikely it will ever really be known.

Wherever possible, I sought to resolve the many differences in the narrative by documentary or photographic evidence, by adopting the most commonly accepted or plausible version, and ultimately by relying on Tim Tovell's expanded account as narrated to Norman Ellison.

Even so, there were a number of gaps in the story, especially with No. 43 Squadron (one of three Royal Air Force units said to have cared for Henri before the AFC), and the precise role played by the officers in the smuggling operation, over which a very discreet veil had been drawn. I could only account for them by making certain assumptions – which I hope are not inconsistent with the known facts, although future research may reveal new evidence.

On the other hand, this is a biographical novel. Thus I have claimed some artistic licence in the psychologically crucial scenes at Mons and the placement of Tim's dark dream. In a book such as this, the story is vital. But for those readers who prefer a more conventional approach, I have included a set of endnotes showing my principal sources for each chapter and where assumptions have been made.

Anthony Hill
Canberra, 2002

CONTENTS

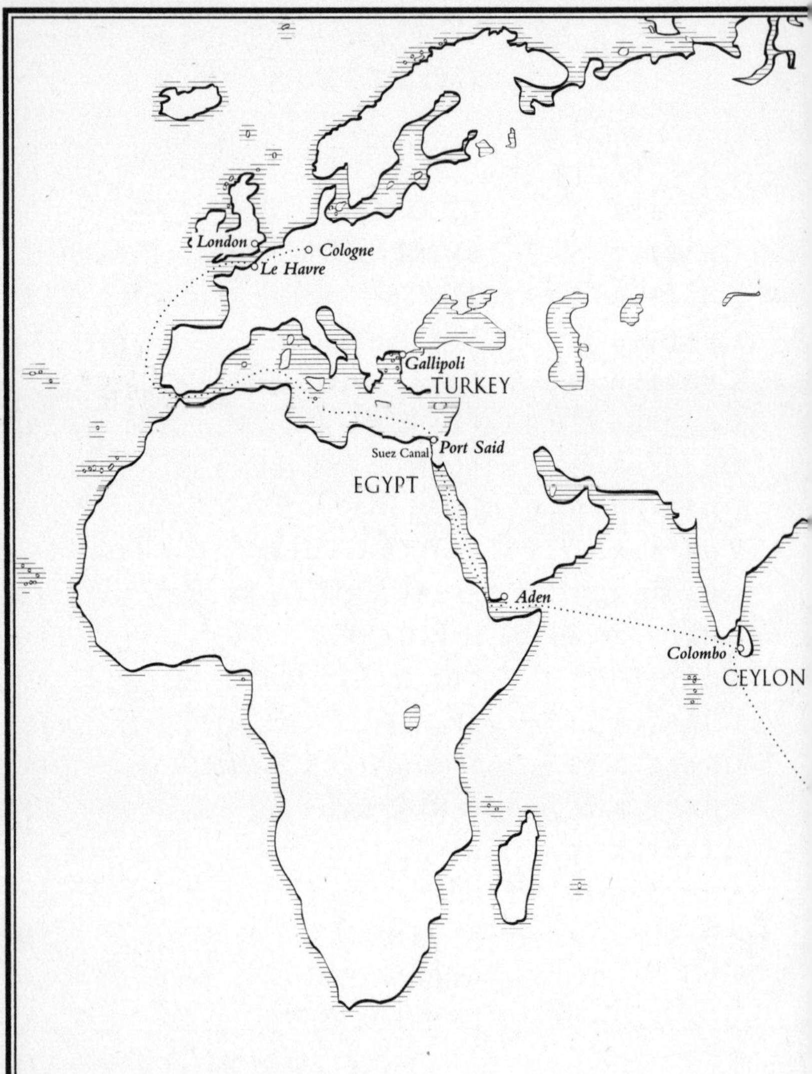

MAP OF THE WORLD

Showing Henri's route from Europe to Australia

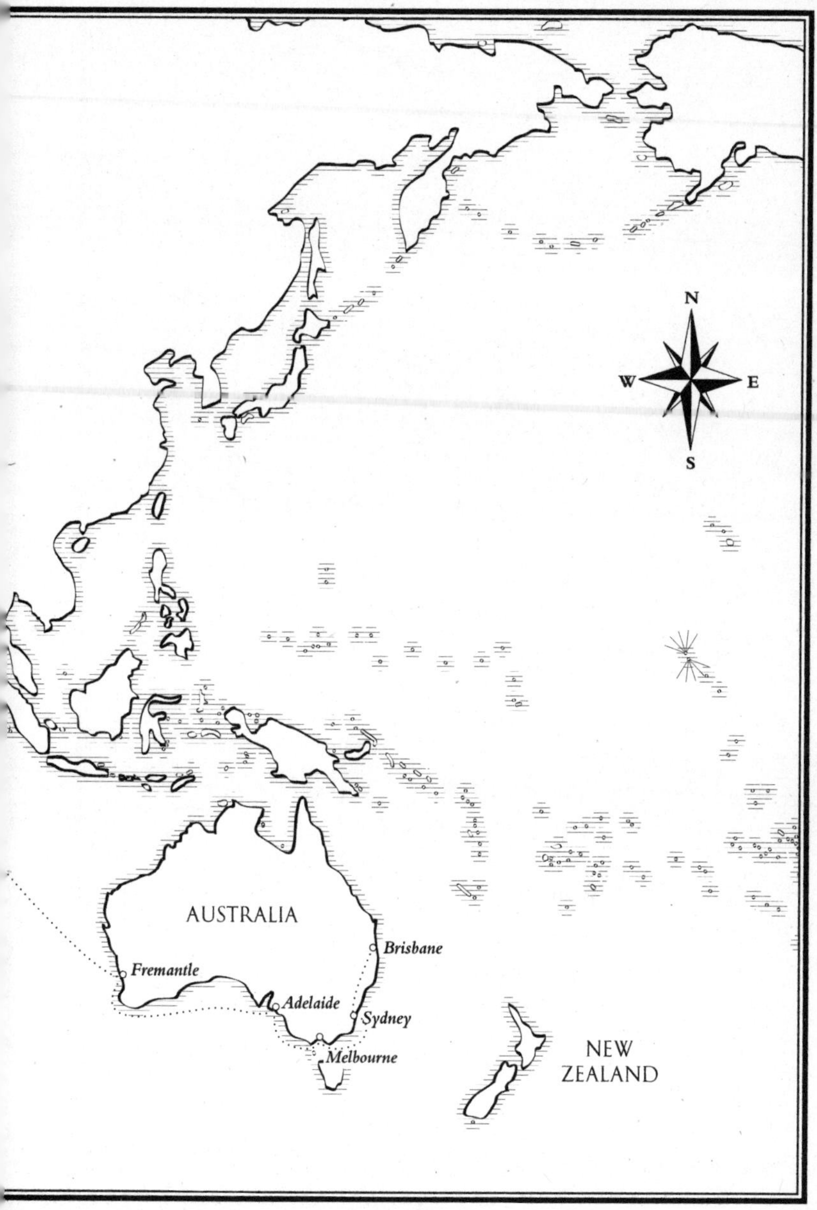
N
W
E
S
AUSTRALIA
Brisbane
Fremantle
Adelaide
Sydney
Melbourne
NEW
ZEALAND

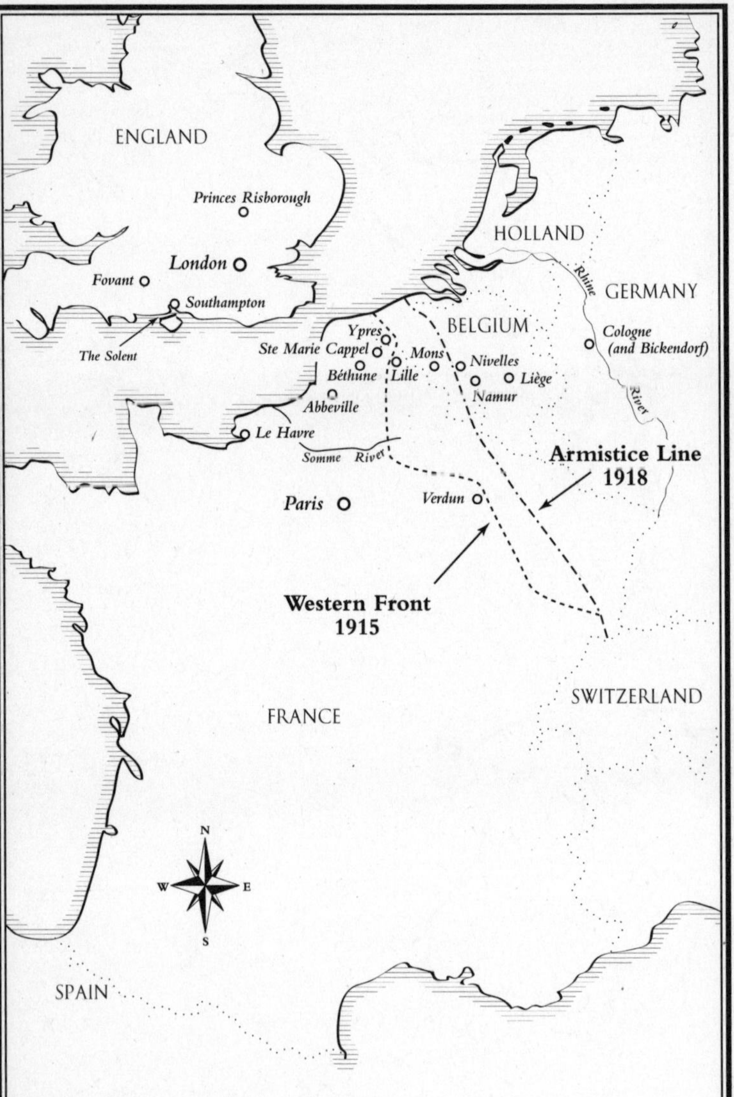

THE WESTERN FRONT

Showing the Front in 1915 and the Armistice line 11 November 1918

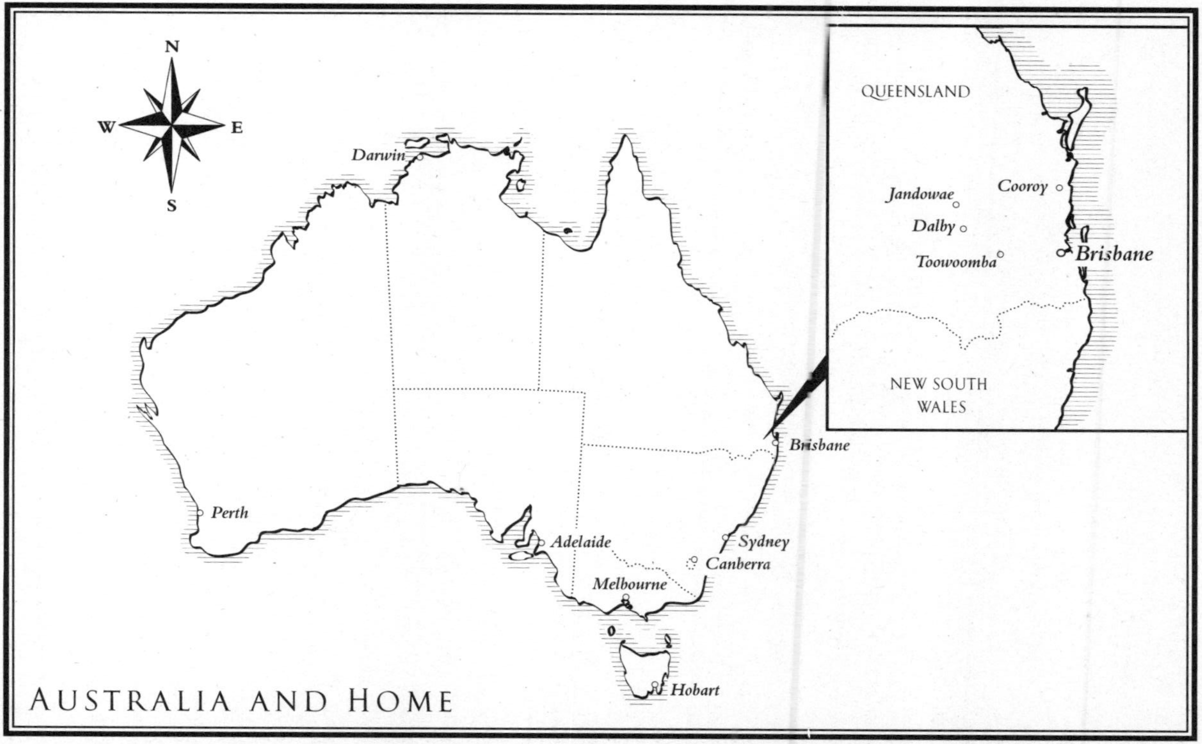

AUSTRALIA AND HOME

1: Orphan Boy

A young French war orphan – a boy of eight or nine – stood by the gangway on the deck of a troopship berthed at Fremantle, waiting to step for the first time onto Australian soil. It was just after lunch on Monday, 9 June 1919.

In one hand the boy held a disembarkation pass, giving him leave to remain ashore until ten o'clock that night. His other hand was clasped by a tall, uniformed soldier – one of the Australian Flying Corps, returning home in HMT *Kaisar-i-Hind* after the Great War in Europe.

'I'm so excited, Tim!' cried the boy, who was himself dressed in a miniature soldier's uniform, complete with slouch hat and a Rising Sun badge. At that time, the Flying Corps was still part of the army, and the airmen wore the same uniform as every digger. 'I can hardly believe it! We got here!

Home to Australia! You and me and Ted!'

'Hold your horses, Young Digger,' said the soldier called Tim. The boy twisted away to look at the khaki line of men moving slowly down the gangway. 'We're not there yet.'

'No,' added his younger brother Ted, a solid, fair-haired Englishman standing behind them. 'And by the look of that customs man on the wharf, we may have trouble before we *do* land.'

The boy shrugged his shoulders in a very French manner. 'It's only a man with a list of names. Everybody knows I'm Henri Hemene – the mascot of 4th Squadron. You just tell them.'

'It may not be as easy as that, son.' 2nd Air Mechanic Tim Tovell dropped his voice and spoke softly into the boy's ear. 'You forget: you're not *supposed* to be here.'

'They don't even know you're on board the *Kaisar-i-Hind*,' murmured brother Ted.

'I've got a pass!'

'That was a friend of ours on the ship,' said Tim. 'The disembarkation officers are on the dock – and *you're* illegal.'

'But . . . but . . .' The war orphan suddenly grew afraid. 'We've come so far . . . all the way from Germany. And you said . . .' The boy turned to Tim and pleaded. 'You *promised* you'd take me home with you . . . to Queensland and your Gertie. You said she'd be my new mum and . . . You won't let them stop me *now!*'

'Hush . . .' soothed Tim in a fatherly voice, squeezing the little fellow's hand. 'The family is still waiting for you. We'll get you there. Somehow. You'll just have to be a brave, clever boy for a bit longer.'

'Quiet as a mouse, Henri,' added Ted. 'Let *us* do all the talking, like the other times. Remember . . . ?'

'*Oui*.'

The boy pulled himself together, thinking of similar occasions when he and the Tovell brothers had sneaked past customs men on the way home. His eyes lit, and he looked at Tim again with a dimpled smile.

'They were good adventures. Will the men be just as surprised this time?'

'They will be if they find out, Digger. But we don't want them to . . . not yet.'

'And when they do . . . ?'

'I don't know . . .' Ted looked at the men filing past the civilian official waiting with the military. He turned to Tim and said dubiously, 'I'm not sure about this. That chap's asking too many questions. It's risky. Perhaps we should stay on board and not go ashore . . .'

'Oh, *please* . . .' Henri whined. 'You promised . . .'

'I think we must try,' Tim replied. 'We've got to buy Digger some new civilian clothes for later on. He'll stick out like a sore thumb in his uniform. We've been lucky so far. Let's hope it holds. Anyway, it's too late. Our turn now . . .'

The shuffling line moved forward. Henri stepped onto the gangway, with the Tovell brothers on either side of him, and began the slow descent towards the wharf.

The *Kaisar-i-Hind*, carrying seven squadrons of AFC airmen, had docked in Fremantle at noon to a huge welcome from crowds waving flags, cheering, and blowing kisses to loved ones coming home – some of them after four years or more away at the war.

The troops leaving the ship in Western Australia had already disembarked, carrying their kit bags, their war souvenirs, and the enduring comradeship of their mates: those still living, and those who would forever lie beneath the scarlet poppies of Flanders fields. Now it was the turn of the airmen travelling on to other Australian ports to take shore leave for a few hours and embrace once again the pleasures of home.

Tim and Ted Tovell, in charge of the young mascot who wasn't supposed to be there, moved with the queue. They had hoped the officers would have tired of checking names and let them disembark quickly, for there were more than 1500 troops on board the ship.

They had no such luck. The disembarkation officers were conscientious. The name of everyone coming ashore was carefully ticked off against a list of the *Kaisar-i-Hind*'s boat roll.

Step by step, the orphan boy in his soldier's uniform came down the gangway, holding Tim's hand tightly. Tovell felt him trembling. Henri didn't look at the customs official waiting for them with his papers. Rather, he stared at the sunlight playing on the harbour water, at the tin roofs and the watching faces on the pier of this strange, new land Young Digger had been promised would be home.

Step by step. Closer to the bottom of the gangway.

'Names!'

'Tovell, Timothy William.'

'Tovell, Edward John.'

They presented their passes to the military disembarkation officer.

'All right. Go ashore.'

Their names were ticked.

'And who's this?' asked the customs man, looking at the boy.

Tim took a deep breath.

'Hemene, Henri.'

Digger held out his pass, shaking ever so slightly.

'Hemene . . . ?'

The official consulted his list.

'I don't see any Hemene on the boat roll.'

'He must be there . . . the boy's been with us all the time.' Tim tried bluffing in his best English voice. 'Have you the correct spelling . . .?' He and Ted leaned forward to crowd the official shuffling his papers.

'Henri Hemene, did you say? . . . No . . . I can't find that name . . .' He turned to the military officers with him, but a boy was not *their* responsibility.

'But surely . . . sir . . . there must be some mistake!'

Tim spoke quickly – a little too quickly. It betrayed an edge of nervousness. The customs man looked up sharply.

'Who *is* this boy?'

'Nobody. I mean . . . he's . . .'

'Not some young stowaway is he?'

'No! That is to say . . .' The brothers spoke together. They were starting to sweat. To fumble. Tears were already beginning to pool in Henri's eyes. Things were going wrong, and they shouldn't have pushed their luck.

'No! He's with us . . . the Flying Corps . . . No. 4 Squadron. He should be on the list . . .'

And the boy was getting ever more upset. His lips were quivering. Any second now, and the truth would come out! Much longer, and Digger would blurt the whole story! And what then . . . ?

'Tell me who he is.' The customs official spoke severely. 'I require an explanation.'

But at that very moment, help arrived.

'Ah! Excuse me! Perhaps I can assist . . . ?'

The voice of Major Les Ellis, the Tovells' Squadron Commander, rang out behind them.

He was a tall, fine-looking man, with his clipped moustache and Sam Browne belt – only young, but with a Military Cross to prove his valour. Coming down the gangway, Les Ellis heard the commotion in front. He saw that his squadron's little mascot and the boy's two guardians were about to be sprung. Quickly, Ellis hurried forward crying, 'Perhaps I can assist . . . ?'

The Tovell brothers sighed with relief when they heard his voice. The awful look of anxiety faded from Henri's face. Surely the Major would set things right, as he always did.

'And who might you be, sir?'

The civilian official had seen much khaki, and wasn't overpowered by uniforms. But Ellis had a bearing of authority, and briefly introduced himself.

'I heard you questioning my men. Is there a problem?'

'This boy. He's not on the roll.'

'Isn't he? How extraordinary! Let me look . . .'

Major Ellis didn't wait to be asked. He snatched the papers from the man's hand, and made a great show of leafing through them muttering, 'Dear me!' and 'How strange!' and 'Yes, I can see you're quite right!'

But before the customs man could regain control of the situation, Major Ellis called to a couple of his officers standing with a group of airmen on the wharf . . .

'Captain Jones! Lieutenant Ellison! See here . . . Acting Corporal Hemene's name has been left off the disembarkation list!'

The whole party joined them, everyone talking at once, passing around the papers, mobbing the officials, and creating a splendid diversion. Tim and Ted Tovell, holding Young Digger, eased themselves to the rear.

'We don't understand this, sir!' the airmen babbled loudly. 'What could have happened? There must have been a cock-up! Has the ship's master heard of this . . . ?'

'Captain Palmer knows about the boy, does he?' The customs man struggled to assert himself.

'Certainly he does!' Major Ellis waved the list in his face.

'Perhaps we should ask him.'

'Good idea. He'll be coming ashore himself soon, I dare say.'

'And in the meantime?'

'Why . . .' Major Ellis glanced up the gangway. 'Here's someone else you could ask.'

Besides the airmen, the *Kaisar-i-Hind* was carrying some distinguished passengers. The Surgeon-General. A couple of other generals. Their wives. And the Honourable Thomas Ryan, Premier of Queensland, who, even as Major Ellis spoke, was coming down the gangway with his wife and two children to see the sights of Perth.

The customs man may not have been impressed by the military. But, like every good public servant, he stood mightily in awe of a politician – especially a Premier. When the family stopped to enquire what was happening, and Major Ellis introduced the official to the Honourable Tom and Mrs Lily Ryan, to Miss Jill and young Master Jack Ryan, the man was so flattered he almost forgot his questions.

'Henri Hemene?' boomed Tom Ryan. 'Young Digger? Mascot of the Flying Corps? Lovely boy! Know him well!'

The crowd of airmen applauded. The customs official simpered. The military disembarkation officers relaxed. And Tim and Ted Tovell, screening Young Digger, took this as their cue to steal away.

Quietly, they merged themselves among the soldiers milling about on the pier. Rapidly, they slipped along the passenger sheds, and around the corner where a goods train stood blowing steam. Quickly, they hurried out of the *Kaisar-i-Hind*'s sight: past the cranes and derricks; behind the bales of cargo; swiftly, down the last of the wharf, until they stood in the street beyond.

Not far away a footbridge crossed the main railway line to

Fremantle station. Walking – half-running – with the boy, the soldiers mingled with the passers-by. They crossed the road, dodging cars and lorries and horse-drawn wagons. Over the bridge. And ten minutes later, all red of face and puffing, they were sitting in the refreshment room at the railway station, waiting for the steam train to Perth.

It was only when they were sipping glasses of lemonade that they allowed themselves to relax.

'Ho! Tim!' gasped Henri. 'That was exciting, wasn't it?'

'It was more than that, Digger. It was a blooming close shave.'

'Too close for comfort,' panted Ted. 'We nearly ruined everything!'

They took off their slouch hats, mopping the sweat from their brows, and fanned themselves. But the boy, fascinated at this first experience of a new country, drank his lemonade and stared out the window at the other passengers on the platform.

In one way they seemed much the same as people anywhere else, absorbed in themselves and each other. But in this bright, southern sunlight, they were also different: sharp-edged and unknown. The orphan boy wondered if he would like them. Even more – would they like *him?* Especially, would the family waiting in Queensland like him and accept him? Tim's Gertie. And young Nancy. Would they love him, as he had come to love all that he'd heard of them during the long journey home?

Henri's mouth formed the word he'd been practising over and over again. He held the lemonade glass to his lips, and silently breathed onto the cold surface . . .

Mum.

The two men were also thinking of Queensland. Of the wives that waited for them in the small bush town of Jandowae, out on the black soil plains, thirty miles from Dalby. Ted's Emily. And Gertie, who waited for Tim with their little daughter Nancy . . . grieving for loss, and their menfolk so far away at the war.

Would they still want them and love them? Would they take to their hearts, as the airmen had, the young orphan who had come to them last Christmas? They'd risked so much to bring him home. And they'd almost lost him when the customs man had just about nabbed him at the wharf.

Stupid! They wouldn't do that again.

'We've got to think of something else,' Tim muttered at the refreshment room table. 'We're not home yet!'

'We're ashore,' Digger said.

'Yes, son. But only for a few hours. There's a long way to go before we reach Queensland.'

'We've got to return to the *Kaisar-i-Hind* tonight when we've bought your new clothes in town,' Ted reminded.

'And we can't just walk up to the ship like this again,' Tim went on. 'Digger could be seized and sent all the way back . . .'

'Non!'

'It's all right, Henri. We'll think of some plan.'

'What about a kit bag, Tim?'

'Won't work. You know that . . .'

They went outside and sat on a platform bench in the warm sunshine. Thinking. Wondering. Reliving their recent fright . . .

'If it wasn't for Major Ellis . . . !' Tim exclaimed.

'*Bravo* for the *Majeur*,' cried the French boy.

'He's solid as a rock,' Ted murmured. 'Always has been. From that first day, remember . . . ?'

'We can't rely on Les Ellis to be there every time . . . We have to use our own wits.'

'That, too. But the Major's seen us through, so far.'

'And Captain Jones, don't forget!' Henri laughed. 'He's been there from the start, as well. Don't you remember, Tim? The look on his face at Christmas! And on *your* face, too, when I said . . . *Mes amis!* My friends! We've come such a long way together, since then. *Such* an adventure . . . We'll think of something!'

The early afternoon sun was making them sleepy after their exertions. As the boy nestled between the two airmen on the railway bench, their thoughts moved in many directions.

To the families waiting for them at Jandowae . . . The new clothes they would buy Henri in Perth . . . Trying to form a half-decent plan to get the mascot back on board the *Kaisar-i-Hind* when they returned to the ship . . .

But mostly, in their drowsiness, memory was taking them back to the beginning of their extraordinary adventure together. To that Christmas Day last year at Bickendorf aerodrome near Cologne, in the Rhineland. And to that moment when the little boy they called Young Digger first wandered into the airmen's mess.

2: CHRISTMAS DAY

Christmas 1918 was something to remember. The first Christmas of the peace. The first Christmas since the Armistice had been signed on 11 November, and the victorious Allied forces began rolling into Germany as an Army of Occupation.

For the Australian airmen of No. 4 Squadron, recently arrived at Bickendorf – war-weary, triumphant, but far from home – it was a Christmas worth celebrating. They arranged an old-fashioned, slap-up Christmas dinner that no one would ever forget.

The mechanics all contributed. The mess room walls were hung with flags, and painted with pictures of wattle and distant horizons under sunny skies. There was beer and wine, Christmas trees and streamers. The officers had been invited, a German band engaged, and everything worth eating bought up for miles around. Goose and roast beef! Plum pudding and brandy sauce!

As lunchtime and the hour of feasting approached, such delicious smells wafted from the cookhouse. They were irresistible, and drifted over the aerodrome in the frosty December air . . . enticing ever closer to the mess one small, hungry orphan boy.

'Get away, you little Hun! There's nothing for you here.'

An airman, arriving late, saw the young beggar. Taking him for another German war waif, the man hissed as he slammed the door in the boy's face. 'Go on! Scram!'

But the child didn't. He shrank deeper into the shadows, drawing his thin coat around him, and, limping a little, crept nearer. He couldn't help himself. Such aromas! They carried him instantly to some almost forgotten place in his memory, called home and Maman.

Closer the lad moved. Through the window he heard the band playing Christmas carols. 'Joy To The World!' and 'Silent Night'. There was laughter and the clink of glasses as the airmen drank to each other.

'There'll be no silent nights with my missus, when I get home!'

The boy pushed the door open, just a fraction, to peek inside.

They knew how to enjoy themselves, these diggers. The squadron was one of the few Australian units to enter Germany after the war, and the boy had seen them flying their Sopwith Snipe biplanes over Bickendorf aerodrome as if they'd been born with wings. The men played hard: only this morning he'd watched them at rugby and soccer against teams from neighbouring British squadrons of 11th Wing of the Royal Air Force. And here were the cookhouse doors opening, and stewards coming in with bowls of steaming soup. So rich and tempting . . . The boy opened the door a little wider and peered around it. If he could only wheedle his way in, perhaps they might let him share a morsel! The child squeezed through, and stood inside.

But suddenly there was another tall, determined airman, a moustache bristling on his lip, trying to shoo him away. Tim Tovell was mess sergeant that day. Spotting the urchin, he came marching over, waving his hands and shouting, '*Imshie! Imshie!*'

It was bit of Arab dialect the Australians had picked up in Egypt, meaning 'Go away! Buzz off!' Strange that they thought German kids might understand Arab slang, but it seemed to work with all foreigners. The little Hun waifs, who hung around the Bickendorf kitchens, were constantly being told to '*Imshie!*' – and they usually did buzz off for a while.

So it was with the ragged boy shivering at the door during Christmas dinner.

'*Imshie* you!'

But instead of turning tail, the little chap stood his ground. He looked up at the airman through sore eyes, his brown hair lank and his face dirty. A smile edged into the corners of his mouth. And he said in the cultivated voice of an English officer, with only the hint of a French accent, 'Who are you talking to?'

'Eh? What's that?'

Tim took a step back. Astonished. This Englishman, who'd migrated to Australia only a couple of years before the war started, knew good form when he heard it.

'How does a German boy like you speak the King's English so well?'

The child's manner changed. Outraged. He drew himself to his full height, though he didn't reach much above Tovell's waist. As the band wheezed to a halt, men nearest the door heard the boy exclaim, full of scorn:

'I'm *not* a German! I'm not one of *les Boches!* I'm a Frenchman, *monsieur*. One of the glorious Allies. I'm one of *you!*'

'Well! Blow me down!'

Tim wasn't sure what to do next.

The airmen burst into laughter. They banged the tables and cried, 'Good on you, sonny! You tell him.'

'That's the kid I buzzed off as I came in,' said the man who was late. 'Come and have a drink, chum.' He held out a glass of beer.

The fuss caught the attention of the officers. Captain George Jones DFC, commanding B Flight to which Tovell belonged, called out, 'Is anything wrong, Tim?'

Glad of someone else to take responsibility, Tovell waved away the beer and led the boy to the top table. Ripples of laughter spread as they walked across the room.

'Another new recruit, eh? Is that one of yours, Tim, come out of the woodwork? You told your missus yet?'

Tovell ignored them, and continued his stately escort: the soldier and this funny little kid, pathetic in his threadbare clothes, toes sticking through his shoes, but every bit as dignified.

'Well, Tim, who have we got here?' asked Captain Jones, as the band struck up again with tunes from 'The Merry Widow'.

'The boy pushed his way in, sir. I thought he was just another little Hun and was going to boot him out. But he speaks good English. Says he's French. One of the Allies.'

'Is that so?'

The child's face softened with his dimples. 'But certainly,' he said. 'I've been with the British Army throughout the war. First with the field artillery, then with the air force. It's with 48th Squadron that I came to Bickendorf.'

'Don't talk nonsense!' Captain Jones didn't like fibs. 'Tell me the truth.'

'Hang on a moment!' Major Ellis interrupted. He was seated at the same table, looking quizzically at the boy. 'I believe I've seen this little fellow around No. 48's hangars these past few days. You're their squadron mascot, right?'

'*Oui, Majeur.* But I'm with 48th Squadron no more. I've gone to the 43rd instead.'

'Why?'

'Because they're nicer to me.'

The boy spoke in an engaging way: one designed to flatter and to charm.

'A child? As a mascot with a fighting unit?' Captain Jones was unconvinced. 'How come?'

'I have nobody, monsieur.' The orphan spoke to their sympathies. 'My father and mother were both killed when the war began. So I've been told. I don't remember them, though sometimes I think about Maman . . . But the Tommy soldiers saved me, and I became their mascot. I helped to bring them victory. *Vive la France!* God Save the King!'

He spoke with such emotion that the airmen found themselves surprisingly touched. His words seemed to stir their gentler feelings, suppressed by years of warfare, and they softly voiced assent. 'Hear, hear! Good lad! Well spoken . . .'

'And what do you want with us, young man?'

'I'd like to share your Christmas dinner, Captain.'

'Why not with your friends from 43rd Squadron? They're celebrating Christmas. They told me after soccer. Why come to us?'

The orphan's attitude changed again. He had a variety of parts, each one of which he played in turn. It was the lesson of survival. So, now, he spread his hands, raised his eyes, and uttered a little French laugh.

'It's true the Tommies are having Christmas lunch. And what are they eating? Boiled mutton and cabbages! But you diggers are having a banquet! It's the talk of the aerodrome. Roast duck and apple sauce. Fruit and custard. I come to you because the Aussie Christmas dinner is so much *better!*'

The boy's frankness was greeted with more laughter and banging of tables.

'Too right, mate! He knows a good thing.'

Captain Jones was disarmed. Even Tim Tovell allowed himself a smile. There was something endearing about the lad that reminded him of the family waiting at Jandowae.

'Perhaps he might join us, sir,' he said to Major Ellis.

'That's not for me to say,' replied the Officer Commanding. 'This dinner has been paid for by the men themselves. We officers are here as your guests. It's for the squadron to decide if the lad can join them.'

Tovell turned to the mess.

'What do you say, boys? Can this young digger sit down?'

More applause and shouting.

'Course, Tim! Move up there. Find the kid a place.'

'There's your answer,' said Les Ellis. 'But Tim, keep an eye on the boy. See him safe back to the Tommies. You're a father, and know about these things . . .'

'Certainly, sir.'

Les Ellis watched them walk across to the tables. He'd chosen the boy's guardian well. At forty, Tim was one of the oldest men in the squadron. He'd see the lad right. Every other airman seemed so much younger. George Jones, with six enemy planes shot down this year, was just twenty-two. And Major Ellis himself was only twenty-four.

The humour and the pathos of the moment caught him. He looked at his fellow officers, and said with a laugh that seemed to suddenly choke, 'Extraordinary little chap! I wonder who he is?'

The squadron discovered little of who the orphan boy really was.

Sitting on the railway platform at Fremantle, waiting for the train to take them into Perth, Tim's mind went back to all the questions that he and Ted, Major Ellis and the others had asked over the past six months. They were trying to piece Henri's story together. Some things the boy remembered only too painfully. But so much else remained obscure. His age, parents, birthplace . . . to all enquiries about his basic identity, the boy could give no answers.

'I'm sorry, monsieur, but I don't know. I was too young.'

Even his name was uncertain.

'What do they call you?' the airmen had asked, as Tim and his little mate sat down with Ted that Christmas Day.

'Honoré,' the boy replied, with a mouth full of salmon patties.

'Hungry?' They misheard him. 'Bet you are. Tuck in!'

'No! That's my name. Honoré!'

He said it again slowly, in his best French accent. *On-or-gggay*, with that rolling, guttural last syllable. It defeated the Australians with their nasal drawl. Even Tim and Ted had trouble with it, and they were Pommies!

'He probably means Henri. That's French for Henry.'

Ong-ree. It was easier to say than the other. So Henri it became, mostly pronounced Henry.

'Who cares about names,' an airman had grunted that day, as the plates of roast goose with stuffing and gravy arrived. 'The kid's got guts. He's a real young digger. One of us. Like he said.'

The nickname stuck. Digger. Young Digger.

When Christmas dinner was over . . . the plum pudding eaten, the toasts drunk, and the airmen were as stuffed as the ducks . . .

they went outside to have their photograph taken.

Captain Jones was called away briefly, and Tim stayed behind to pay off the German band (who had obeyed orders and finished with those vain British anthems, 'Rule Britannia!' and 'God Save the King'). But most of the others assembled in a pyramid group behind their officers: men looking replete and self-satisfied – a couple of them holding the national flag.

Henri, as their guest, was in the middle of them. The boy insisted on it.

'The Aussies!' he exclaimed. 'You'll do me!'

Afterwards, when day was drawing in and a deep chill settling on the landscape, they went back to the mess and stood by the wood stove, talking and laughing and drinking hot rum toddies. Even Henri tried to order himself a rum toddy – but Tim said he could have coffee instead.

'*Alors!* Mr Tim. The Tommies let me drink toddy.'

'You've already had two glasses of punch. That's enough.'

'Go on, Tim! It's Christmas!' said the men near by.

'You heard what I said.'

Henri sighed and muttered, but drank his coffee until Major Ellis said it was time to go. The officers were having their own party that night, at headquarters in a Cologne hotel.

'As for you,' Les Ellis turned to the boy, 'I hope you enjoyed your visit to us. But it's getting dark, and you should be cutting back to the Tommy squadrons.'

'I'd rather stay here with you Aussies.'

'Won't your friends miss you?'

'I've been with them long enough! It's better I come here now. Besides, you diggers are paid more than Tommy soldiers. You can afford to eat well *every* day.'

This provoked more laughter and shouts of 'Go on! Let him stay! The kid won't do no harm.'

'What do you think?' Major Ellis turned to Captain Jones. 'He's certainly making himself at home . . .'

'He's an amusing little fellow. It might even be good for morale if he comes to us for a bit. What do you say, Tim?'

'He'll be no trouble,' replied Tovell, putting a protective arm around the lad. 'I'll see to that.'

'Where will he sleep?' asked Ellis. 'I don't want him mixed up with rough company.'

'He can bunk down with me, sir,' Tim answered. 'I've a small hut to myself at present, and there's a spare bed.'

'Righto. That's settled, then.'

Major Ellis scribbled a note for the OC of No. 43 Squadron, to let him know what was happening.

'Don't want the Tommies to think we're *stealing* their mascot.'

After which he asked Tovell and Lieutenant Norman Johnson to go to the British lines – to explain things and, if everyone were happy, to bring back Henri's kit with them.

They walked across the aerodrome in the gathering darkness, the evening bells of Cologne Cathedral pealing faintly in the distance. The ground was heavy underfoot, and Henri found it hard to keep pace with the men, for he had a slight limp. But he chatted away, saying how happy he was to be going with the Aussies.

They found the duty officer in No. 43 Squadron's staff room, sipping gin and becoming ever more melancholy that he had to remain at his post on Christmas Night.

'Everyone else is enjoying themselves,' he said, reading the note from Major Ellis. 'And here is our new little mascot leaving to join you chaps. I'll be quite alone.'

'It *is* all right if the boy comes to us?' asked Norman Johnson.

'Oh, I dare say. We couldn't stop him. He's not exactly an *enlisted* airman, is he?'

The others smiled.

'Still, don't expect him to stay with you. He'll be up and off the moment something else strikes his fancy. You're very fickle in your affections, aren't you, Joe?' The duty officer stared at the boy with watery eyes. 'He was with 48th Squadron before he came to us, only a few days ago. Travelled up with them from Flanders. Then there was some trouble with the cook.'

'*Oui!*' exclaimed the boy. 'He called me a bloody nuisance.'

'Wasn't wrong, was he? Before the 48th, he was with 79th Squadron.'

'But *both* those squadrons are here at Bickendorf with 11th Wing,' remarked Norman Johnson.

'Yes, indeed. He has friends everywhere.'

'And before that?'

'Somebody said the artillery . . .'

'That's right,' said the little boy whom the Tommies called Joe. 'The Royal Field Artillery. I had a good friend there.'

'You see! And where's your good friend now?'

'He was killed, monsieur. Near Ypres. With his gun crew.'

'What?' mumbled the duty officer. A silence fell in the room, as uncomfortable as it was unexpected. 'I didn't know that. A lot of good men "bought it" out there . . .'

He poured himself another gin.

'Well, off you go if you must!' he snapped. 'Fetch the boy's things. Send him back when you get sick of him.'

Henri led the two airmen to his quarters, and quickly stuffed his few possessions into a haversack. Some Tommies asked where he was going. And when he told them, they laughed that these colonial diggers made slaves out of little boys.

'They'll smuggle you out to Australia, and starve you on scrag end of kangaroo.'

'Ha! I already work hard for nothing.'

'Come on, youngster.' Tovell took the boy's hand. 'It's time you had a sleep. Don't worry,' he told the men, 'we'll look after him. You'll still see him around.'

They returned across the aerodrome. Lieutenant Johnson left them at Tovell's hut, saying he'd see them in the morning.

The last man to share the room with Tovell had gone to hospital with Spanish influenza, then scourging the world in the aftermath of war. A pile of grey army blankets and a lumpy pillow sat on the spare iron bed. Tim quickly made it up. Henri undressed himself and pulled a torn nightshirt from his haversack.

'I'll find you something warmer tomorrow,' said Tovell. 'Will you be all right by yourself, young digger, if I go back to the mess? There's a chamber pot under the bed.'

'I'll be well cared for, Mr Tim.'

Henri unwrapped a small bundle, revealing a silver bust of the Emperor Napoleon, which he placed on the shelf above his bed.

'Where did you get that?' asked Tim with some surprise. 'It's worth a bob or two, I imagine.'

Henri's eyes twinkled.

'It's a *souvenir* from the war. The Emperor watches over me every night.'

He took out the French flag – a red, white and blue Tricolour – somewhat tattered like the boy himself, but treated with the same sense of respect. Henri spread it over his blankets and crawled into bed.

'Goodnight, Mr Tim. I will sleep well.'

And indeed, as Tovell turned out the light, Henri was already half asleep beneath his flag.

Tim took off his greatcoat, and laid it over the boy to keep him extra warm in the freezing December night. He closed the door and walked back to the mess. He lit his pipe. Smiled to himself. And nodded.

The seed of an idea had planted itself in his mind.

3: BICKENDORF

Young Digger quickly made himself at home among the Australians.

He stayed close by Tim to begin with. They rose early, Henri wrapping the silver bust of Napoleon and carefully folding his flag before going to the ablution block. Tim was among the first to break the morning ice in the wash basins, for he kept himself spruce and trim; though Henri had no joy when Tovell made him strip on that first day, and sponge himself in the bathtub.

'Oh no! Mr Tim! Please! It's freezing! You're killing me!'

'Nonsense boy! How long since you had a good wash?'

'The Tommies aren't as fond of cold water as you.'

'A bit of cold water did nobody any harm. That's one thing I learned in sunny Queensland.'

'But this is Bickendorf . . . in winter!'

Tim took pity on the shivering boy. He tossed over a towel and Henri began to rub himself dry.

'What's this scar above your right knee?' Tovell asked as Digger started dressing himself. 'When did you get hurt?'

It was a big scar, with the marks of multiple stitches, skilfully done. While the wound had healed well, it explained Henri's limp.

'It was the war, Tim,' the boy said simply, looking down. 'There were many hurts.'

'Yes, but this . . . ?

'I don't remember . . .'

'You'd remember something like *that!*'

He was passing Henri his shirt and jumper, both very worn. Tim looked at the boy – but Digger didn't look back. Instead he turned away, as if a cloud shadow passed over him. In his mind Henri could hear an enemy shell exploding, and suddenly his world was heaving with earth and steel fragments, and he was lying on the ground bleeding from his leg.

'It was that time near Ypres, two years ago,' he said softly, almost matter-of-factly. '*Les Boches* were shelling the battery, and I was hit by shrapnel. It hurt so much and I was crying, though I tried not to. My good friends sent me to a casualty clearing station and then to military hospital.'

The boy's face brightened again with the memory of hospital.

'I was there for a long time, Tim, while they stitched me up. The nurses were very good, and the food was *magnifique!*'

'You? A little kid in an army hospital . . . ?'

'Like any other soldier.'

'But I mean to say . . .'

'I was wounded *twice!* The second time, not so bad.'

'When was that?'

'Oh that . . .'

The dark clouds returned and gathered about the boy. His eyes grew distant, and he began to tremble just a little. He heard not only shells exploding, but the cries of dying men. The battery had received a direct hit. And he was stumbling over churned earth . . . looking into the face of an artillery officer, bloodied red as the poppies and ripped apart in the Flanders mud.

'. . . That was not long after I got out of hospital . . . the day my good friend and his gun crew "bought it". Me, it was just a little scratch . . . nothing to worry about . . .'

The boy's voice trailed away. With great effort he shut the door of memory on the scene: locking it safely, if not always securely, in that corner of his mind where such remembrances were hidden.

Henri finished dressing. Tovell found his heart going out to the little chap. Tim knew about war injuries. He'd copped a slight whiff of poison gas himself not long ago, crawling in a tunnel under a building which had been gas-shelled as the squadron advanced after the retreating German armies. It was nothing serious, but enough to affect his senses of taste and smell ever after. Then again, the boy wasn't much older than Tim's own children at home; yet already Digger had seen more suffering than Tovell prayed his family would ever know.

He held Henri's hand tightly – in case he slipped on the ice – as they walked back for breakfast.

With Tim's duties as mess sergeant, Digger soon got to know the squadron cooks, stewards and other important persons with ready access to food. Securing his lines of supply was always the first thing he did. It was basic strategy.

The orphan seemed forever hungry. He could be found at any time of day sneaking into the kitchen, pleading with the cook for a piece of cheese, a beef bone, or a slice of bread and jam.

'What's the matter with you, Young Digger?' asked a kitchen orderly, fetching the bread knife. 'Have you got hollow legs?'

'You're a very nice man, Bob,' the boy replied, licking plum jam from a spoon. 'The last Tommy cook *threw* the jam tin at me!'

'Why would he do that?'

'He said I'm a bloody nuisance. But I say, "*Non!* I'm bloody famished".'

In this, Henri imagined himself another starving war waif. But he wasn't – not like the German youngsters who constantly hung around the Bickendorf cookhouses begging for scraps. These children of a defeated nation knew what hunger really was.

At the end of 1918, Germany was on the verge of revolution. The government of Kaiser Wilhelm had already gone. The country was bankrupt, its people demoralised and desperate after the war. Things got worse when the Allies demanded Germany repay vast amounts of money and munitions, as reparations for having started the conflict. Ships of the German navy were to be impounded and sent to Scarpa Flow naval base in Scotland. And the British and Australian squadrons of 11th Wing RAF were at Bickendorf for the handover of much of the German air service.

Thus the children of Cologne, those despised 'little Huns', gathered in hungry groups outside the mess kitchens for scrap-ings from the victors' plates: going through the rubbish tins and squabbling over bits that the dogs had missed. Until the cooks got sick of them.

So it was, one afternoon, that Henri came around a corner of the barracks and saw Bob, the kitchen orderly, chasing away a dozen poor German kids.

'Go on, you lot! *Imshie!* Buzz off!'

Les Boches!

Henri's head span. He seemed to hear again the sound of a German shell bursting outside Ypres, and the screams of his dying friends. He screamed himself and ran at the youngsters, fists flailing and yelling at them to '*Imshie! Imshie!*' This was now *his* territory.

Most of the children fled. But one boy picked up a stone – and flung it at Henri, catching him full on the lip.

'*Froschfresser!*' he called. Before he, too, disappeared.

Digger roared with pain and anger, tasting the blood. His *third* war wound!

'What have they done to you, Young Digger?' cried Bob, as he came running up. The boy's face was all ripe and swollen. 'Struth! You look as if you're *still* in the wars.'

'I was buzzing them off and they threw a stone. Called me a frog-eater!'

'Rotten little beggars!' Bob shouted after them. 'It's the last time I give youse anything!' Then, turning to Henri, he added, 'We'd better get you some help.'

Tim arrived, drawn by the sounds of battle. Staunching the blood with a handkerchief, they took Digger to the medical orderly.

No teeth were broken, though the gash across his upper lip would always leave a small scar. Henri didn't cry when they dabbed the wound with iodine; but he didn't laugh much, either, when they tied a bandage from one side of his face to the other.

'I won't be able to eat, Tim!'

'It will teach you to pick fights with the young Germans.'

'I hate them!'

'No you don't.'

'They killed my good friend. They killed my mother . . .'

Maman.

Henri stopped. Another door in his mind suddenly opened. He could see a street and a ruined house . . . It was dark and burning . . . Tears started to his eyes, but he forced them away. His hand shook.

'Tell me about it, if you want to,' said Tovell gently, as the boy struggled with his phantoms.

'The guns were firing,' Henri murmured at last. 'The Germans were coming, Tim. I was outside in the street . . . when I saw my home hit by a shell and falling down, all smoke and rubble . . . and a woman lying in the garden . . .'

A woman so still and red.

'*Maman!*' Henri cried. And he slammed shut the door again.

'I know . . .' Tim bent down and held him tight, as he held his own son. 'I know it's hard. But it's not the children out there. They didn't fight the war. They're as hungry and lost as you are.'

'I still hate them. I'll kill them all!'

And next day, when he saw more young Germans outside the mess, among them the boy who'd thrown the stone, Henri slipped away and went to the guard room.

'Hello Digger,' said the duty sergeant, looking up from a letter just arrived in the mail from home. 'What do you want?'

'I want revenge on *les Boches*.'

'Don't we all,' replied the man. He had also lost many good friends in the war. 'Don't we all.'

The sergeant went back to his letter. Things were quiet at Bickendorf. The Armistice was holding. The Germans were beaten. And news from his wife waited for no one.

Henri seized the opportunity. He quietly picked up a loaded rifle leaning against the wall, opened the door, and carried the weapon outside. The Lee Enfield was almost as tall as he was, and heavy to carry. But Digger limped along with it, letting his anger grow. He'd make those Huns sorry! He'd show them!

'Hey!' A yell from the guard room door. 'Hey, you! Stop!'

A soldier had spotted Digger out the window, noticed his rifle was missing, and ran after him. It was a serious military offence. Allowing his weapon to be stolen by a little kid!

'Come back!'

Henri went faster. It was a good thing the rifle's safety catch was on. He turned to look at his pursuer – and ran straight into the arms of Lieutenant Johnson.

'What's all this?' asked Norman Johnson, holding the boy firmly, though he demanded to be freed. 'Who owns this weapon?'

'It's mine, sir,' panted the guardsman. 'Young Digger sneaked off with it. I chased him as soon as I saw, sir . . .'

'Very lax of you, Private,' said the officer severely. 'I should consider a charge. Go on! Off with you. Don't let it happen again.'

'Yes sir. Thank you, sir.' The man shouldered his rifle, saluted, and marched back to the guard house.

'As for you,' said Johnson, retaining Henri, 'what game do you think you're playing . . . stealing a rifle?'

'I'm going to shoot those boys.'

'And what then? I'd have to charge you with murder. You'd go before a court martial. Probably you'd be shot yourself. How would that make *me* feel? What about Tim?' he asked, as Tovell came hurrying up.

'What is it, sir? What happened?'

'A serious breach of discipline. Henri stole a rifle to shoot the young Germans.'

'They threw stones!' Digger was unrepentant. 'It's *my* place now, with the Aussies. Not *theirs!*'

'You won't be with us much longer if you do this sort of thing,' said Tim Tovell in his sternest voice. 'No weapons. No fighting. I told you: try and be friends with those children.'

'I don't want to be friends!'

The innocents of war – French children with British soldiers passing through a recaptured village, c. 1916. [AWM H08572]

Home to Australia – the troopship *Kaisar-i-Hind* at Fremantle, June 1919. The Tovell family believes the soldier marked with the cross is Tim Tovell. [Courtesy Nancy Elliot]

The men of No. 4 Squadron on Christmas Day, 1918. Major Ellis is in the front with his cane and Sam Browne belt; Henri is held above him; and Ted Tovell is fifth from the left in the back row. [AWM P02658.004]

A soupçon of petrol, a lighted match, and *pouf!* Digger with his rat-catcher's cart at Bickendorf aerodrome. [AWM P00826.151]

They flew as if born with wings – pilots of No.4 Squadron, AFC at Bickendorf, 1919. [AWM P00826.136]

Home at Jandowae – the backyard of Tovell's house with Tim standing at his workshop door. [Courtesy Nancy Elliot]

He shyly looked away from the camera. Tim with Gertie, Nancy and Timmy, just before the Tovell brothers left for war.

[Courtesy Nancy Elliot]

'I think,' said Lieutenant Johnson, 'that we should find Digger something else to do with his time.'

'I couldn't agree more,' replied Tim. 'But what . . . ?'

'Well . . .' Norman Johnson pondered. 'There is one thing . . . or rather, many things. Rats! The whole aerodrome is plagued with them. Rats in the hangars . . . rats on the airfield. The war against Germany is over, young man, so long as the Armistice holds. But the war against rats is *not*. What this squadron needs is a rat-catcher . . .'

To which Tim added, 'I wonder who it might be . . . ?'

'You mean *me!*' Henri cried. 'Oh, *messieurs*, I will be the best rat-catcher in the world. No more guns. No stones, I promise. Just a *soupçon* of petrol poured down each rat hole . . . a lighted match . . . and *pouf!* The rats are gone for ever.'

It was settled. Young Digger became Bickendorf's rat-catcher. Tim Tovell, the carpenter, made him a hand-cart, with two aeroplane wheels which brother Ted scrounged from the workshops. And there Henri set off around the aerodrome every morning, wearing a scarf and an old leather flying helmet: pushing his cart with a two-gallon tin of petrol . . . pouring a *soupçon* down the open rat holes . . . lighting a match . . .

Bang!

It was a dangerous and rather foolish thing to do, perhaps. But Henri was a wartime boy who had seen much worse – and it was immensely exciting.

He even acquired an assistant. Some of the German kids enviously offered to help, but Digger would have none of it.

'I don't want anyone else,' he said. 'This is *my* job.'

They left him alone, for his absence allowed them to beg undisturbed outside the cookhouses.

Yet a stray dog was also much attracted by Digger's activities, and joined him in the rat-catching expeditions. He was a rather inexperienced dog at first, and put his nose too close to the holes when the petrol exploded. But he was a quick learner, and after one or two singeings soon crouched well back as Henri made his preparations, ready to pounce on any rat that tried to escape.

The two became inseparable. Nobody knew much about the dog – a scraggy, half-starved thing – or where it had come from. Henri decided his name was 'Roy . . . a king among dogs', and that he'd wandered to Bickendorf from France.

'Why France?'

'Because I think he's a poodle, Tim. He understands French perfectly. Listen! *Viens ici, mon petit chien . . .*' And the dog would come up, tail wagging and tongue hanging out.

So Roy became Henri's dog. They hunted rats together. They sat together at meal times, Digger making sure Roy had his share of scraps that might have gone to the 'little Huns' outside. And at night, when Tovell went to his quarters, he found them asleep together: Young Digger curled beneath his French flag, and Roy snoring a contented dog's snore on top.

4: TIM

Christmas Week passed. As the calendar turned over into 1919, there came exciting news. Royalty would visit Bickendorf. Prince Albert, the second son of King George, was to come at New Year – followed a few days later by his brother, the Prince of Wales.

There was much bustle and hard work as men got ready. Prince Albert, especially, was interested in the flying qualities of the Sopwith Snipes, with which the Australians had been equipped not long before the Armistice. Major Ellis issued special orders: the eight planes in each of the squadron's three flights had to be in tip top condition – fabric freshly 'doped' and painted, guns and metalwork bright and shining – for the Prince's aerial display.

The mechanics were run off their feet all day. And at night, when they might have been enjoying a Charlie Chaplin picture show, they were scrubbing up *themselves!* Uniforms pressed; buttons gleaming; tan boots and leather all spit and polish; hair trimmed; beards shaved; and the tepid water in the ablution block was run almost dry.

The only specimen of less-than-perfect military turnout was Young Digger, with his patched clothes and broken shoes. The Tommies might have fed Henri and given him somewhere to sleep, but they left him to run about ragged.

'It is time,' said Tim Tovell, 'we did something about that.'

They'd already cut down a pair of pyjamas, so the boy could sleep warmly at night.

'Now we've got to get Digger a uniform for day wear,' Tim remarked. 'Trouble is, he's not exactly regulation army size. They'll have nothing to fit.'

'We'll have to make him a uniform ourselves,' replied Ted.

'Yes, but where will we get the cloth?'

'Leave it to me.' That night Ted arrived with a couple of khaki greatcoats 'borrowed' – with no little risk – from the quarter-master's store.

'How did you get them?' asked Tim.

'Better you don't ask me.'

The brothers looked at each other . . . and at Henri . . . and they all laughed.

Tim and Ted were very close. They'd worked together in England and in the Queensland bush, as builders and painters – with a sideline as district undertakers. They lived near each other at Jandowae. The brothers enlisted together in 1916; joined the

Australian Flying Corps together; embarked for training in England; arrived in France and been posted together as riggers to No. 4 Squadron. Now they conspired together to provide Young Digger with new clothes.

It was one thing to acquire greatcoats to be made into a uniform, another thing to have the job done properly. None of the airmen were tailors. They'd have to pay a civilian in Cologne – and once word got around, the squadron soon chipped in funds. Tim said it wouldn't cost much. The German people were so impoverished, he thought they'd make the uniform very cheaply!

Tim's duties gave him a few spare hours in the middle of the day. One afternoon, he cadged a lift into town with Captain George Jones, taking Henri with him. The coats were carefully wrapped in a parcel. Well, it would be silly to let the officer see them, and *ask* for trouble.

Officially, therefore, Captain Jones knew nothing. But as a squadron member, he knew the lot. He dropped them near the Alter Markt – the old market – not far from the gothic town hall.

'I'm told there's a decent tailor near by,' George Jones said, pointing down a cobbled street that led between tall, narrow houses to the river. 'See how you get on, and I'll return in an hour.'

Seated now in the train during the short half-hour trip between Fremantle and Perth, Digger and the airmen couldn't help but reflect on the vast difference between this prosperous homeland and the bleak, desolate Europe they'd left behind.

Here, the brief passages of countryside were peaceful and undisturbed. The houses, as they passed through the outer suburbs, were bright, new, and contented-looking. Kneeling at the window, Henri could see these Australians: well fed and busy, as they went about their lives . . .

There were children playing in a schoolyard. The butcher's boy delivering orders on his bicycle. Women in their gardens. Men on business. The high streets bustling with traffic. People with their shopping baskets going into stores stocked with everything you'd want to buy! Grocers and fruiterers. Bakers selling cakes and iced buns. Lolly shops. Milliners, mercers and drapers with bolts of coloured cloth on display.

But *there!* So much of Europe had been destroyed: the landscape a graveyard, and ruined buildings standing as skeletons against the grieving sky. Like Henri's house. So many people had been killed, lying with his good friend in the Flanders mud, and Maman among the flowers.

Digger breathed the words again on the train window, and wrote with his finger on the little patch of mist, *Mum*.

Even in Cologne, which had escaped destruction, there was hardship and deprivation. In the winter after the Armistice, people had nothing. No work. No food. No heating. They queued for hours to get a little bread, and fought over scraps of sausage. Their paper money was worthless. And there was nothing to buy.

So it was with the tailor shop near the Alter Markt, when Tim and Henri entered it carrying the greatcoats. It was barren, cold and wretched, like the tailor himself. Not long ago he'd been making uniforms for smart German officers. Now he found himself torn between contempt for this enemy soldier with a little boy, and a desperate need to get their good money to feed his own family.

The tailor spoke scant English. Henri had a few words of German, which he uttered with much scorn for the vanquished.

'*Mach schon!* Come on! . . . new clothes . . . for me . . . like him . . . *Mach schnell!* Quick quick!'

Tim mimed the part, gesturing to the boy, to his own uniform and the greatcoats. The tailor understood: and while he was measuring Henri, Tovell asked if the clothes would be ready by tomorrow for Prince Albert's visit?

The tailor rolled his eyes. '*Morgen?* Tomorrow? *Nein, mein Herr* . . . impossible . . . *Drei Tage* . . . three days at least.'

'Make it two, and I'll give you an extra English pound.'

Tim waved a banknote.

'Very well,' cried the tailor. 'But *zwei* . . . *two* more pounds.'

'*Eins!*' cried Henri. 'One pound – or we'll only pay you *half* the price of the clothes!'

The tailor could do nothing else but agree.

Captain Jones and his driver were waiting for them when they returned to the square.

'Everything fixed, Tim?'

'I think so sir, after a little haggling.'

'Good show. So, you're getting a uniform for Young Digger – what about his boots?'

'We hadn't thought that far . . .'

'I can't have a member of my flight on parade with his toes showing. There's a cobbler's shop along here . . .'

'We don't have enough money for boots, sir.'

'Well, it's a good thing I *do*,' said George Jones, who had known poverty himself, in childhood. 'Come on!'

The two men, with Digger between them, ducked down an alley opening into a courtyard with a bootmaker's shop.

It was the same tale as before. A poor, dingy place, with no boots to sell and no leather with which to make them. The only thing the cobbler had was a tanned sheepskin, which wasn't really strong enough for walking boots. Flying boots, yes . . .

'It will do,' said Captain Jones, 'until we get something else.'

So the cobbler measured Digger for his new pair of boots, watched by a group of German women who stood peering in the window and gossiping. They'd heard about this fierce young French boy who fought their own children out at Bickendorf, stole loaded rifles, and blew up rats with petrol. Here, he was treated like royalty, with new clothes, new boots, and driven about in a motor car! When good German families had nix.

Henri got his uniform in time for the visit by the Prince of Wales. He watched as Prince Edward inspected the Australian airmen. He craned his neck skywards as the pilots went through their stunts . . . rolls and dives, formation flying and loop-the-loops . . . showing royalty just what they and their machines were made of. These Snipes could climb to 10,000 feet in just nine minutes, flying at 120 miles an hour.

And afterwards, when the Prince had posed for his photograph with Major Ellis and the officers, and made a little speech to the men, Henri cheered and waved as he drove away. Prince Edward was just like one of them! And they all threw their hats in the air.

Or most of them did. Digger had no hat to throw. He had his uniform – his khaki tunic and breeches – and his sheepskin boots: but nothing, except an old leather flying helmet, for his head.

'Something else for us to rectify,' said Tim.

Sure enough, Ted soon produced a digger's hat, also 'borrowed' from the quartermaster. Tim spent the next few evenings cutting it up and sewing it into a small, peaked forage cap such as some airmen wore. Digger, required as a model, sat with the dog, Roy – stroking his wiry coat and sharing titbits of broken biscuit from Henri's pocket.

'Do you know the Prince we cheered will be our King one day?' asked Tim, for something to say.

'*Oui.* As his father today is King George,' replied Henri.

'I'll tell you something strange about that. My father once saved the life of King George's elder brother.'

'How is that so?'

'Many years ago my father was a gamekeeper at the royal estate of Sandringham, in Norfolk. He had to look after all the deer and game birds in the park. We lived there in a cottage: my mother and father, me and Ted, and our sisters, Louise, Florence and Elise.'

'Do they still live there?'

'No. Dad died when I was ten, and we had to move in with my uncle, a butcher at Princes Risborough in Buckinghamshire . . .'

'What was your father's name?'

'He was called Tim, too.'

'I don't remember Papa,' said Henri. 'At least . . .' as the door in this mind inched open, 'I don't know his name. But I can see a soldier in uniform, blue and red, kissing Maman as he leaves the house . . .'

The door closed again. Henri put his arm around the dog's neck and cuddled him.

'How old were you then?' asked Tim.

'I can't remember.'

'Did *you* have any brothers or sisters?'

'Yes! No! I was only little . . .!'

Panic began to rise in the boy as another dark door was flung open. He saw the shattered house again, the woman lying in the garden, and a figure . . . were there two figures? . . . silent beside her.

'Maman. And . . . I don't know!'

'It's all right . . .'

Tim reached out. The dog lifted his head and whimpered. Henri held him tight as the shadows retreated.

'I was telling you about my father at Sandringham,' said Tovell after a moment. 'The Royal Family always goes there for Christmas. One year, when it was very cold, my father heard people screaming in the park. He ran through the snow and saw that a little boy had fallen into a lake. He'd slipped on the ice by the edge, and tumbled into the freezing water.'

'What was his name?'

'He was the Duke of Clarence, the eldest son of the Prince who later became King Edward the Seventh.'

'Then what happened?'

'Quickly my father waded in. He grabbed the boy and hauled him safely back to shore. But the prince was turning blue with cold, and he could have frozen to death. So my father told one of the others to run for help. Then he went to a fold near by, where sheep were penned.'

'What did he do?'

'My father took out his gamekeeper's knife and killed one of the ewes. Cut her throat. He dragged the carcase back to the lake, and slit open the sheep's belly. He emptied the steaming intestines on the ground and pushed the young prince inside the ewe.'

'Why did he do *that?*' Henri was wide-eyed.

'Because the carcase was still hot. It's an old trick. The warmth of the dead sheep flowed into the child's own body. Little by little life returned . . . and when they took him back to the palace, it seemed the prince would live.'

'And did he?'

'For a number of years. But he died in his twenties, and his younger brother became King George – father of the two princes who visited us here at Bickendorf.'

'Is that true about the lake?'

'My father always said so.'

'Did they give him a medal?'

'No. But I have a picture of King George on the wall at home.'

Over the next few nights, as he sewed the cap, Tim told Henri more stories from his youth. Of his uncle, the butcher. Of another uncle – a Norfolk fisherman – and the rough, tough life of the sea. Of his sister, Elise, who was adopted by an Indian Army officer, and who they never saw again.

'They were hard times in England for poor families,' said Tim.

He told Digger how he'd always wanted to be a carpenter, because he was good with his hands and loved making things. In 1898, at the age of twenty, Tim saved enough money to become apprenticed to a local builder, Thomas Wright. He stayed for five years, learning the trade. Eventually, Tim struck out for himself, and his reputation as a craftsman grew. He worked for the gentry; made cabinets for the Victoria and Albert Museum; installed shop fittings for Harrods in London . . . all of which Tim wrote down in his work book with a fine, neat hand.

Ted, who was a painter and decorator, joined him in business. The two were part of the life of Princes Risborough. They belonged to the Friendly Society, the church choir, and the soccer club. Tim loved football – as he loved the church – all his life. When the brothers were training in England during the war, they played soccer for the AFC, and their team was never beaten.

'Played 16. Won 16,' Tim wrote on the photo he sent home.

'You've been beaten here at Bickendorf,' Henri said with some glee. 'I've seen you. The Aussies are no good at soccer.'

'Pretty good at rugby, though!' replied Ted vigorously. 'Our squadron's undefeated. And what about Australian Rules football?'

'What about it?' asked Digger. 'A strange jumping and kicking game. Very exciting . . . but nobody else knows how to play it!'

'That's why we had to field *both* teams ourselves – officers versus men,' said Ted.

'And either way,' added Tim, 'you can't say 4th Squadron was beaten!'

They laughed.

'Why did you go to Australia?' Henri wondered. 'What made you want to leave home?'

'Ill health,' Tim replied. 'I've had a bad chest all my life. Colds and flu every year. I thought about going to America – but the winters are as bad. So sunny Australia it was. Besides, I'd met a man . . . a Mr White from Queensland . . . who sponsored me.'

'And then there was Gertie,' reminded Ted.

'Who's Gertie?'

'My wife,' answered Tim. Lovely Gertrude Mary Ann Bass of

Longwick, not far from Princes Risborough, dark and slender, whom he'd married in October 1911 . . .

Tim fell silent, thinking of Gert as she was when he'd last seen her and the two children: young Nancy, now five-and-a-half, and his son, little Timmy, who was three.

'I always loved Gertie,' Tim said at last, 'though she's ten years younger than me. When we married, it was the happiest day of my life. Three months later, we sailed for Australia. We had a great send off . . . they gave us an album which my mother, and Mr Mander the vicar, and everyone signed, with a purse of money. Good thing, that. The voyage cost us six pounds each – travelling steerage, with separate cabins for men and women.'

'Not a lot of fun for young married couples!' remarked Ted. 'I know. My wife Emily and I made the same trip a year or so later.'

'We had our moments,' Tim blushed. 'But the storms and seasickness of the first week made that ship worse than a prison! It got better as we entered the tropics . . . the heat, lazing on deck, and concerts at night. We were rather sad, at the end of seven weeks, to land at Brisbane and be met by Mr White.'

'I've never been on the sea,' said Henri. 'I think I've seen it once . . . a long time ago . . .'

'Do you remember where *you* lived?' asked Ted.

'I think . . .' replied Henri, striving to find the keys that would open the locked doors of his mind once more. The dog, lying on the bed, beat his tail as if in encouragement. 'They said I was found near Lille, in France,' Henri went on. 'My good friend with the artillery said he picked me up from the roadside . . . There was a wrecked car, the Germans were advancing . . . people were running and our soldiers retreating . . .'

'*Where* near Lille?' pressed Tim. 'It's a big city. Do you know a name . . . ?'

Digger tried, but the doors wouldn't let him through.

'I'm sorry. I can't remember. I was just a little boy then . . .'

And turning to the man he suddenly laughed, 'But I would like to see your Gertie one day.'

'Hrmph. Perhaps. We'll see.'

The seed of the idea in Tim's mind had begun to germinate. Now it took root. The Tovell brothers looked at each other across the room, and the same thought passed between them, as it does with people who are very close.

'Maybe. Yes. It's something to think about.'

5: The Mascot

When Henri appeared in his uniform, complete with forage cap, the airmen greeted him with much applause in the mess.

'Look at him! He's a real young digger now!'

And they sat the boy on the bar where, with laughter and cheers, they gave him a glass of hot mulled wine. Henri drank it in one gulp, as he had seen the Aussies do, coming up coughing and with his eyes streaming. But that only caused more merriment, and more cries to give Digger another glass! Until Tim Tovell intervened . . .

The occasion was a party in mid-January, after a sports carnival to celebrate the second anniversary since No. 4 Squadron left Australia for the war. The squadron had been forming at Laverton near Point Cook, Victoria, in late 1916 – at the very time the Tovell brothers were enlisting in Queensland.

Lieutenant Johnson, who'd been at Gallipoli, was an original member of the squadron. So was the famous air ace, Captain Harry Cobby (DSO, DFC and two bars, credited with twenty-nine victories, the highest scoring pilot of the AFC). He'd since returned to the training squadrons in England. Yet the airmen still spoke of Cobby's daring in the air . . . diving from the clouds into German formations, the sun behind him and machine guns blazing . . . and of the time he led the squadron during a great raid on the airport near Lille, one of the French cities occupied by the enemy soon after the war began. They bombed and strafed, destroying over thirty planes. Cobby swooped so low that the force of exploding bombs threw his own Sopwith Camel fighter high in the air then dropped it – *crunch!* – until the wheels bounced along the runway. He was lucky not to have been hit by friendly fire.

Such exploits were well into the future when No. 4 Squadron sailed from Australia in January 1917. The airmen underwent extended training in England, before flying to northern France and the start of combat duty at the beginning of 1918. The party at Bickendorf in 1919 was thus a double celebration: two years since the squadron left home, and one year since it went into active service.

It was a great day for a sports carnival: cold but fine, as teams from each flight competed in foot races and obstacle races, long jump, tug-o-war and football kicking competitions. It was all part of that wider program of sport, entertainment and fellowship with which Major Ellis and his staff sought to occupy the airmen.

With the war over, their thoughts were turning ever more homewards. Keeping them busy and interested – with games, picture shows, concerts and generous leave – was good policy. Men were allowed to go into Cologne by tram after work, provided they were back for Lights Out. But fraternisation with civilians – at least in public – was forbidden. Even German personnel at the aerodrome weren't allowed near the barracks, offices or kitchens.

So on that Foundation Day sports meeting, the spectators were almost all from 11th Wing RAF. After the prizes had been presented by Brigadier-General Hogg, men crowded into the mess to drink to the winners (A Flight) and commiserate with the losers (Headquarters Flight). And there, Young Digger in his new outfit was plonked on the bar and given a glass of mulled wine. Which he emptied in one swig. Coughed. Spluttered. But with his eyes shining and cheeks burning, he shouted that he was ready for another.

'No you don't,' said Tim Tovell. 'One is quite enough for you.'

'Oh, come on spoil sport . . . don't nanny the boy . . . let him enjoy hisself . . .' from the mob.

'I said . . . he can have soda water instead . . .'

'Listen to Mr Tim!' cried Henri, the focus of such attention and amusement, 'He treats me worse than the Tommies!'

The dog, Roy, sitting on his haunches, barked agreement. But Tovell flushed and turned away. He was an upright, dignified man, who disliked being laughed at, even in fun – much less by a boy he cared about. But the others didn't take much notice of his discomfort. Another glass of mulled wine was passed up to Henri, who sat with it on the bar.

'I say!' called a voice from the crowd. 'We should make Young Digger our mascot.'

'What's that?' There was a stir of excitement.

'He's been the mascot of those Tommy squadrons. Why not us? He's got his digger's kit. All he needs is a Rising Sun badge, and that's easy fixed. Chuck us your jacket, young feller . . .'

Henri threw it across. With much joking and shouts of 'Yeah . . . why not . . . let the kid be our mascot!' the airman fixed his own lapel badge to Digger's new tunic.

The boy glowed with delight. Standing unsteadily on the bar he declared, '*Messieurs*, it will be an honour to be your mascot. I will bring you much luck. I always say, You Aussies will do me!'

Digger raised his wine in a toast to No. 4 Squadron, emptied the glass – and promptly threw up.

The men cheered as Henri toppled off the bar. They caught him and passed the little mascot, reeking of vomit, over their heads to the Tovell brothers at the back. The airmen called for more drinks. But Tim and Ted carried young Henri to bed. Roy trotted happily behind: for him, the boy could do no wrong.

When Digger woke next morning his head ached, his throat was dry, he felt ill and ashamed, and could remember little about the events of the previous night. Tovell was angry with him – and at himself – for having to clean up Henri's sick. Tim didn't *want* to remember. But everyone else did. When Digger came to breakfast, pale of face and saying (for the first time ever) that he wasn't hungry, he was greeted with cries of 'Give our mascot another hair of the dog!' Even the officers, themselves badly hung-over after a sumptuous Foundation Day dinner at the Kaiser Wilhelm hotel, were much taken with their squadron mascot.

'Jolly good idea. Fine thing for morale,' said Major Ellis.

'But a boy?' Captain Cooper, the Recording Officer, was uncertain. 'He's a likeable little fellow, but he's not a goat or a pony . . . not your usual military mascot. It's very odd . . .'

'I thought so too, at first,' remarked George Jones. 'But it's all in good fun, and we are helping the lad. He has no one else. He has nothing else. He's shown no sign of wanting to go back to the Tommy squadrons. Quite the reverse.'

'I agree,' said Les Ellis. 'But it is a point. We know nothing of Henri . . . who he is, or where he's come from. We don't even know how old he is. We should at least *try* to find the boy's identity, if he's to be the squadron mascot.'

Major Ellis took the matter up with Tim next time he was out at Bickendorf. Tovell told him what he'd learned from Henri's few anguished moments of remembrance: his mother dead in the garden . . . the wrecked car . . . found by the retreating artillery . . . his wound. But there were so many questions still unanswered. What happened after Henri's good friend was killed near Ypres? How did he come to be with the British airmen . . . ?

'It's lucky all three squadrons are at Bickendorf,' Ellis said. 'I'll make what enquiries I can from their officers. I hadn't much bothered until now, but if Henri is to be our mascot . . . And Tim, will you keep asking the boy?'

'Certainly, sir.'

'There's so much more we need to know. He was found near Lille, but it's a large place. Where are his relatives? Who were his parents? How old is he? We don't know his birthday.'

Digger remembered nothing of his birthday when they asked him. No door creaked even slightly ajar. Les Ellis thought he looked about seven. Tovell considered him closer to nine.

'He's been through the war,' he said. 'Henri's been hungry. He's seen much. Suffered much. It's not surprising he's small and thin, and has forgotten many things . . .'

'Let's have him checked by the experts,' said Les Ellis.

A panel of three air force doctors and two dentists gave Digger a thorough examination. His health was pretty good. But they – by majority vote – put his age at eleven!

So eleven he became. And when Major Ellis announced that Henri ('It's really Honoré,' the boy muttered) had been appointed mascot of No. 4 Squadron, he also advised Digger's birthday had been officially fixed for the day he came to them: 25 December.

Not a bad Christmas present, all round.

'I think,' said Henri, a day or two later, 'it's time I went for a joy ride in an Aussie aeroplane.'

'And why would that be?' asked Tim Tovell, frowning. He was no longer on mess duties, for his skills were needed back at the hangars, helping to get a snappy German Pfalz fighter ready for a test flight. 'Why is it time you had a joy ride?'

'Because I'm your mascot, of course.'

'I don't know about that . . . Did the Tommies take you up?'

'*Non*,' the boy replied with a shrug, 'but it was wartime then. There's nobody firing Archie at us now.' He carefully enunciated the term used by airmen for anti-aircraft fire. 'It will be quite safe.'

'I'm not sure the Major would like it. Things can still be dangerous up there.'

The skies above Bickendorf were crowded with aeroplanes: the Bristol Fighters, Sopwiths and De Havillands of the Allied squadrons . . . giant Handley-Page bombers . . . French scouting Spads . . . and the many German aircraft being handed over. The crisp, clear January days were perfect flying weather. Every pilot was eager to be in the air: and while Digger naturally wanted to go up with them, Tim was equally unsure.

'It can be risky,' he said. 'Accidents happen. Remember that chap in England whose safety belt broke while he was doing a loop.'

'Chance in a million,' said a mechanic working near by.

'And what if there's a collision with all those kites?'

'Hardly!'

'You say that, but it's like a flying circus up there . . . everyone showing off. Anything could go wrong . . .'

Henri gave Ted a nudge; and with a wink at the boy Ted told

his brother he thought it would be all right to take Digger for *one* flight.

'What about Major Ellis . . . ?'

'Why not ask Captain Jones first . . . or Lieutenant Johnson. They're Digger's friends.'

'*Exactement!*' said Young Digger.

So Tim, with some misgivings, went along with it. Norman Johnson thought it a splendid idea and offered to pilot the plane himself. After lunch next day, they all went down to the hangars where Henri was to go up in a German LVG two-seater aeroplane. The squadron had found the machine at Namur, in Belgium, during their journey to Cologne; confiscated it; and now used it to take visitors on sightseeing trips along the river Rhine.

Ted climbed into the observer's seat behind Lieutenant Johnson, and Henri was passed up to him. He sat the boy on his lap and strapped themselves in.

'You'd better sit still or you'll fall out, jumping about like a jack-in-the-box,' Ted warned.

Henri, however, wearing an airman's padded jacket, his flying helmet and a pair of goggles, was beside himself with excitement.

'It's the first time I've been in the air!' he exclaimed. 'The Tommies let me sit in the planes on the ground, but now I'm truly going to be a flying mascot!'

Digger fancied he could fly the plane himself. If only he had a 'joy stick' between his knees to make the LVG climb, and dive, and go through its whole repertoire of stunts.

'Look at *me*!' Henri cried, his arms outspread.

But Norman Johnson turned round and said, in a voice that wouldn't be denied, 'If you muck about in the air Young Digger, I'll drop you over the side like a little bomb – and you haven't got a parachute!'

None of them had parachutes during the war. The military didn't believe in them, except for balloon observers. Parachutes, it was felt, would only encourage pilots to vacate their machines too soon.

Digger sat back, very still and quiet in Ted's arms.

The ground crew spun the propeller. The LVG roared into life. Roy barked. Taking no notice of a mere dog, but belching petrol fumes into the faces of groundlings, the aeroplane kicked against the forces of gravity, taxied onto the runway, gathered speed, and within a few minutes was soaring into the skies above Bickendorf.

It was a fast and very responsive machine, but with Henri on board Norman Johnson took things easy. He flew at a few thousand feet above the silver ribband of the Rhine spanned by its bridges, giving Digger a bird's-eye view of the lovely city of Cologne . . . the Cathedral with its twin spires, the boulevards, buildings, parks and lakes . . . before heading west towards Belgium, flying low over the countryside through which they'd travelled at war's end.

The landscape here was largely untouched by the wreckage of war. It wasn't like Flanders. Fighting had stopped and the Armistice had been declared, before the red tide of battle reached Germany's borders. But still, Digger could see the camps and transports of the Army of Occupation spread below; towns and villages among the bare winter fields; soldiers and civilians going about their lives like ants far beneath him.

Henri turned to Ted. And he laughed for sheer delight.

It was an ecstatic little boy who clambered out some forty minutes later, when the machine had reluctantly returned to earth and come protesting to a halt where Tim was waiting.

Henri, his eyes alight when he took off his goggles, and his face flushed with the wind, reached out to be lifted down. And when Norman Johnson also climbed onto the ground, Digger wrapped his arms about the man and hugged him.

'You have made me the happiest person in the whole world.'

'You weren't airsick?' Tim enquired.

'After mulled wine, I will *never be sick again!*'

The Tovells, to their credit, both laughed.

Digger held their hands as he walked back to the hangars, Roy gambolling about them. Henri was overjoyed. He was a *proper* airman's mascot now!

'There is only one more thing I want to do,' the boy exclaimed. 'I want to see Tim's Gertie.'

The brothers looked at each other, and unspoken waves of communication and consent passed between them.

That night, when Tim sat down to write home to Gertie and the children, he came to a decision. Naturally he'd told them about Henri and how he was looking after the young war orphan. Now he added something else. Unless they could find Digger's family, which seemed unlikely, he was going to bring the boy home to Australia: to smuggle him, if necessary, back to Jandowae and rear him as his own . . . with Gertie as his new mother, with Nancy and little Timmy as the sister and brother that Henri no longer had.

'One more in the family will not matter,' Tim wrote.

He signed and dated the letter: Friday, 31 January 1919. Hoping – trusting – that his wife in Queensland would understand.

6: Home Thoughts

The snows came.

In early February Bickendorf was covered by a deep, white counterpane. The aeroplanes, like insects hibernating in winter, sat forlornly on the ground, unable to take wing until the weather cleared. Ice hung from the eaves, and the huts were freezing, because there was little fuel for the stoves.

The airmen were better off than the German people, however, who had almost nothing. Cologne had been spared physical destruction. But the privation caused by wartime economic blockade was terrible. Food was so scarce for civilians that Allied soldiers were not allowed to buy it in the shops, other than fruit and a few vegetables. Every day more and more children hung around the aerodrome kitchens. Even Digger began to beg for them, wheedling sausages and bread from the cooks. Henri was safe. He had his place with the airmen. He had his job catching rats. He could afford to be generous.

'That's all,' Bob the kitchen orderly would say, scraping the left-overs into a bucket. 'It's hard to get enough for ourselves.'

'You can spare this bit of pie,' Henri cheeked him, pinching a slice from the tray and running outside.

'Hey you, Digger! Bring that back.'

But he didn't. Over these past few weeks Henri had found that food was far better than a rifle to win the respect of the German children. Even the boy who'd thrown the stone now came pleading when Digger appeared with the scraps bucket. They'd do anything to avoid the extremes of hunger and disease.

For the Spanish influenza epidemic was claiming more victims, and not just civilians. Three men of No. 4 Squadron died in Germany, and many others went to hospital. Tim escaped, though he'd spent six weeks laid up in England with pleurisy in early 1918. It was his chest. No wonder his thoughts kept taking him home to Gertie and the summer heat at Jandowae, far from this bleak European midwinter.

There was one blazing moment, however! On a late January afternoon the headquarters office caught fire. Nobody knew how it started, but within minutes the building was burning fiercely. Luckily for the Australians, several airmen rushed into the room and saved the squadron's war diaries and service records, just before the roof collapsed in a roar of flames and crashing timber.

'It's like a bonfire on Bastille Day!' shouted Henri, watching with the airmen, his face hot and glowing, and the dog scratching beside him.

But suddenly it wasn't like July the fourteenth at all. Another door opened in his memory. And down a street Henri watched another fire, felt another heat, saw himself in another life running towards the ruin that had been his home, crying to the figures in the garden – so red against their white dresses – *Maman!*

Then there were other people and soldiers crowding the street. The Germans were coming! Everything was noise and turmoil, and Henri glimpsed himself in a motor car taking him away. Who was with him? An uncle . . . ? Henri couldn't remember, because a shell was bursting in flames and the car was crashing into a ditch. He heard more people shouting . . . and then the voice of his good friend, the artillery officer, saying quite close . . .

The man's dead, but the boy looks all right. Better pick him up and bring him along with us.

Henri struggled to shut the door upon the memory, and to stop the sounds and smells of war. He looked up. It was just a fire in an aerodrome building! It was only glass breaking and timber burning; and the voices were those of the Aussie airmen he knew, joking and saying it was as good as Empire Day . . .

Digger put his hand into the clasp of a tall man standing next to him. Who was it? Sergeant Wilson – Hec Wilson – of the armourers section, who'd been on the sports day committee . . .

'I'm warm as toast now, monsieur.'

It didn't last. More snow fell, and the lakes around Cologne froze over. It wasn't flying weather, but it was good for ice-skating. Several times Henri went with Lieutenant Johnson and the others to Stadtwald – a park in the suburbs – and skated on the rink reserved for the exclusive use of Allied troops. Afterwards, they went into town on the tram. Tim bought a bottle of the famous Eau-de-Cologne perfume with a postcard for Gert. On the back, Digger wrote his name – surname first, as some people do in France

Hamume, Honoré

Beneath it, Tim wrote a message to his son (with his own version of Digger's name):

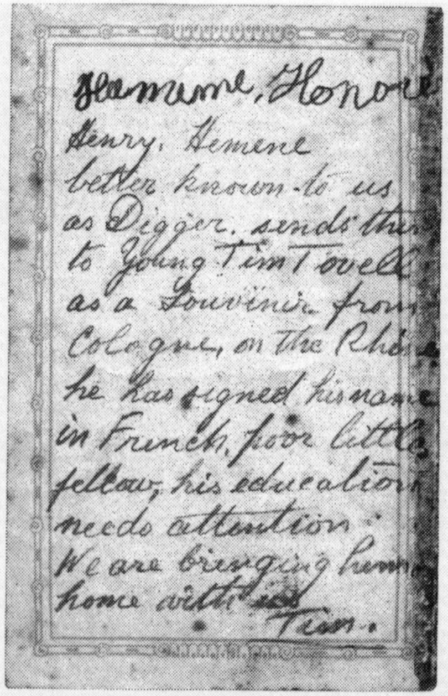
Hamume, Honoré
Henry Hemene
better known to us
as Digger, sends this
to Young Tim Tovell
as a Souvenir from
Cologne, on the Rhine
he has signed his name
in French, poor little
fellow, his education
needs attention.
We are bringing him
home with us
Tim.

Not long now, surely, before they'd be on the way back!

'What's it like at Jandowae?' Digger would ask at night, lying in bed, struggling to pronounce *Jan-dow-ee*, as his dog snuffled and the wind whistled through the cracks. 'Will I have to go to school?'

'Do you like school?' Tim asked across the darkened room.

'I don't know. I've never been to school . . . except once for two days, and then I ran away.'

'Oh? And where was that?'

'A house . . . somewhere . . .'

'Do you remember when . . . ?'

'I think . . . it was after my good friend was killed.' Henri stroked his dog under the ear – Roy's favourite spot. 'I had new friends then, with the Tommy pilots.'

'Ah. And what was your school like?'

'I can't remember! There was a house near the church . . . *les soeurs*, the nuns . . . and a garden with a high brick wall. One day the old gardener left the gate open . . .'

'And you ran away . . .?'

'. . . across the fields to the front, where I heard guns firing. I knew my friends would be there. But then I got lost, Tim . . .' Anxiety and then panic crept into Digger's voice, as it always did when he remembered. 'I was hiding in the ditches for days with nothing to eat except berries and turnips, and I was so cold and frightened . . .'

'Hush . . .' Tovell reached out a soothing hand in the darkness. 'You don't have to be afraid any more, son.'

The dog sensed Digger's distress. He lifted his head and whined, and the boy again held him tightly until the ghosts had gone. They were silent at last, and Henri asked another question about Queensland.

'Do you have snow at Jandowae?'

'It can get cold at nights,' Tovell grunted, 'and we have to light fires, because it's on the Darling Downs. That's about 200 miles west of Brisbane . . . But nothing like this!' He pulled the great-coat over himself.

'And are there lots of people, like Cologne or Lille?'

'Jandowae is tiny,' Tim laughed, 'like one of your villages.'

'Are the farms small, too, like France?'

'The sheep stations are huge. There's one place – Jimbour – with tens of thousands of acres . . .'

'*That* big!'

'It has a stone house on the rise, like a chateau, with stables and stores and a chapel . . . You can see way across the plains, to the bush over there on the hills . . .'

Tim could see it again. So very different to the neat, pocket-handkerchief English garden where he and Gert had grown up.

'Are they rich?'

'Yes. But it's not all like that. Mostly the houses are built of wood . . . weatherboards. There's a lot of timber in the bush. It's why we went to Jandowae. We'd only been in Australia a week when I heard that Mr Mulholland wanted a good carpenter to build a new hotel all out of spotted gum.'

'Spotted what?'

'Gum. It's a kind of wood we have in Australia.'

'Oh.'

'I'd come out to strike high and hard. So I applied for the job . . . got it . . . and started work. It took nine months to build . . . and when I finished all the fancy woodwork, and the hotel was opened, Gertie was the first person to go up the stairs inside.'

'She must be very special.'

'She is. To me.'

Tim lay there, thinking of her and the family, so far from himself and the Bickendorf snow. It seemed he could sense Gertie's presence next to him . . . smell her perfume, touch her long, dark hair, her skin so soft over high cheekbones. He could see her brown eyes smiling at him, yes even during those first weeks roughing it at Jandowae, when they'd had to sleep on mattresses stuffed with corn husks. Tim felt he had only to turn over in the narrow bed at Cologne, and there his wife would be . . .

The thought vanished. For here was Young Digger asking more questions about Mulholland's hotel.

'If it's all built of wood, won't the hotel burn down like the headquarters office? *That* was a good fire.'

'Not on your life. I built the pub very well. They'd have a job to burn that place down.'

'Do people burn down hotels in Australia?'

'Sometimes they mysteriously catch fire.'

'Do you have wars there? Guns and bombs?'

'No, son. We've been spared that, thank the Good Lord.'

They fell silent a moment, thinking of all they'd seen of war in Flanders. The devastation . . .

'What else did you build in Jandowae?' Henri asked at last.

'Let me see . . . there was a farmhouse for Herman Rennick . . . I helped to finish the Union Bank . . . lined a house for Pat White the butcher . . . did some extensions for Harry Mills. He's a wild one, that man! He rides his horse into a hotel bar and gives it beer to drink!'

'And then does he burn it down?'

'No. Not the hotel I built.'

'Did you build a house for Gertie?'

'Oh yes . . . A little, square, four-room weatherboard house to start with. Our first home, on our own bit of land. We could never have afforded that in England! But there we were, happy as a pair of turtle doves, and our first baby . . . Nancy . . . on the way . . .'

Except, Tim realised, his wife probably wasn't as happy as she pretended. Gert had grown up with the comfortable traditions of centuries at Princes Risborough, and was a schoolteacher before Tim married her. Then he'd taken her to raw Jandowae, miles from anywhere. Thirty miles just to the hospital at Dalby.

Gertie must often have been lonely and bored, yet she rarely complained. She started photography – though Tim usually looked shyly away when she took his picture. Nancy, and then Timmy were born. They added more rooms and a verandah to the house.

And they weren't completely alone. Sergeant Behm – Charley

Behm of the local police – and his family were friends. English people, Mr and Mrs Lee with their children, moved to a farm just out of town. There was the parish life of the weatherboard church. Ted and his new wife, Emily, emigrated to Jandowae. Tim sponsored them – but from the moment she arrived, Emily was unhappy in this new country, and wanted only to go Home to England.

Tim could never understand why. He and Ted went into business as builders and undertakers. Tim made the coffins; Ted varnished them; and Gert lined them with satin and lace (taking special care with the little ones for children). They had a handsome wagon and a pair of black horses. There were houses to build and paint. Tim took on a foreman, Bill Gooderham. They were making something of themselves with the opportunities this brash, brown land gave them. Home, the war had taught Tovell, was not a place. Not a country. Home was where the people who loved you were.

Young Digger, breathing softly in his sleep, had no place. No family to love him any more. They were all gone – destroyed in this terrible conflict. Now, Tim was determined to find a way to bring the little chap back with him: to give him another chance with his own family in the peaceful solitude of Jandowae.

Not that even Jandowae was untouched by war. Nowhere was!

Tim remembered the excitement when news came through in August 1914 that war had been declared. How the young bushmen rushed to join the newly formed Australian Imperial

Force! Yes, and the not-so-young. Their mother, Ann, had been visiting Tim and Ted in Jandowae at that very time. When war broke out, they took her by train all the way to Melbourne to catch a ship back to England. It was rather silly! The ship could have been sunk, yet the old lady insisted on going home! While in Melbourne, Tim tried to enlist himself, but was rejected because of his teeth and poor chest. In the first months of war, the army was accepting only the fittest men.

But this was to change. As the lists of dead and wounded rose, the gush of men volunteering to join them began to dry up. Recruiting campaigns started, with bands parading through town and country: but still the numbers of enlistments were not enough. In 1916, the government of Billy Hughes tried to introduce conscription.

Tim recalled only too well the bitter arguments from those who, as he and Ted saw it, shirked their duty to King and Empire. For conscription was defeated at a referendum held in October. Two weeks later, the government split. And two weeks after that, on 28 November, Tim and Ted took the train to Toowoomba to join up. This time the army didn't knock them back.

The brothers had almost two months leave before they had to report to the military depot in Brisbane. So they went back to Jandowae to celebrate Christmas, to settle the building business and to sell the weatherboard house. Tim thought Gert and the children would be better off going home to England and mother, with him away at the war and unable to look after them.

It was a mistake. Tim knew that now. Home was no longer his

dear, native land. For when Gert and the family moved to Brisbane to take ship for England, they weren't allowed to go. The authorities believed – rightly – that German submarines made the passage too dangerous for civilians. They had to return to Jandowae: for Gert and the children to move in with Mr and Mrs Lee on the farm; and for Emily – denied this one chance of going Home – to become more unhappy.

Gert, as always, put her best face upon it. To be sure, she had to go back to the monotonous bush. But there were friends and family to relieve her loneliness; and with them came the realisation that, for better or worse, *this* was now home.

Tim felt the surge of longing, warm within him. He burrowed deeper beneath the blankets and his greatcoat. Yes, Jandowae was his home too: and before long it would be Henri's home as well.

7: PACKING UP

Orders came through on 18 February. No. 4 Squadron was to cease flying. Aeroplanes and equipment were to be made ready for handover to other squadrons of the Royal Air Force. And the men were to start packing for the long journey back to Australia.

Their excitement was boundless. It was years since they'd seen the clear, sharp light of home. So long since they'd felt an Australian summer burn their faces, or smelt gum trees after rain. How they yearned to embrace their loved ones and tell them that, after all the trials and adventures of war, this was what made it worthwhile!

Though when families were to ask what war was *really* like, so many returning diggers would find it impossible to say. Impossible to tell of godless fear, and horror, and human frailty, and death.

Of bursting machine gun fire and anti-aircraft shells; vicious dog fights to the death high in the clouds, and the sight of a mate's aeroplane plunging helplessly ablaze towards the ground.

These things they could tell only to those who had been there – and sometimes just to the dark shadows of their dreams. Even Captain Jones still woke shrieking from his nightmares.

But terror wasn't something these airmen could publicly acknowledge. Everyone *knew* they were supposed to be fearless. So they crowded into the Bickendorf mess when orders for home came through, to celebrate with beer and merriment, and to remember the good times. Young Digger and his dog were there too. Of course.

'I just want to say to you fellows,' said Major Ellis above the hubbub, 'how proud we are of the job you've done here. In the past couple of months, 4th Squadron has handed over 150 enemy planes to the Allies – mostly in good flying order. It will be a long time before the Hun war machine threatens the peace again.'

'*Bravo!*' cried Henri from a corner of the bar, where certain young welders – despite Tovell's injunctions – were plying him with cherry brandy. 'Well spoken, *Majeur!*' And he let Roy lick his fingers, just to have a taste.

'Was that 150 planes?' asked one of the mechanics. 'We could add 'em to the squadron's list of enemy losses!'

There was much laughter. During its eleven months in France, No. 4 Squadron had shot down 161 confirmed German aircraft, with another seventy-one last seen spinning out of control and presumed wrecked. Its own losses were sixteen airmen killed in combat, eleven in accidents, and fourteen taken prisoner when forced down behind enemy lines. Among them was Lieutenant Len Taplin DFC, one of the squadron's more adventurous pilots, who'd destroyed eight enemy planes before he was captured. Gone, but not forgotten.

'Remember the time Len Taplin blew up his plane with his own bombs!' exclaimed one of the electricians.

'No, I don't,' said Les Ellis, for he'd only taken over as OC after the Armistice in November. 'Tell us about it . . . and barman, bring another round of drinks – on me!'

Henri, making sure Tim wasn't looking, pushed his glass forward for another cherry brandy, and listened with delight.

'Just as Taplin was taking off one morning,' the electrician said, 'his wheels hit a bad bit of dirt. The axle snapped, and as he was trying to land again, the undercarriage folded up. The impact pulled back his bomb release and his phosphorous bomb exploded. Lenny was thrown clear, and ran for his sweet life. But crikey! You should have seen the fireworks! The phosphorous was blazing! His high explosive bomb, machine gun bullets and flares all went off together . . . *Whoosh! Bang! Hold on to your hats, boys, and enjoy the show!* It was as if the Red Baron himself had suddenly risen from the dead!'

They all burst into laughter – though there was a margin of nervousness to it. Partly it was the recollection of the huge risks they'd taken during the war. And partly, too, the spectre of the German air ace, Manfred von Richthofen, the Red Baron, and his 'flying circus' of bright red fighters, still lurked in the clouds of memory, ready to swoop upon them – as he had done so often in life.

'They say he claimed eighty victims,' remarked Captain Jones. 'But I think that includes a lot of our chaps shot down with the help of others in the Baron's circus.'

'He was without mercy, that one!' Young Digger spoke from his perch by the bar. 'The Tommy pilots say he would wait high up in the sky, looking for stragglers . . . and then *voila!* Down he'd plunge like a hawk on its prey . . .'

'I wish I'd been near Amiens when they shot him down last April . . .'

'A mate of mine *was!*' piped up an engine fitter. 'On Morlancourt Ridge. Jeez! He said you should have *seen* that dog fight! Planes twisting and firing at each other . . . Suddenly a Tommy swooped out of the cloud, chased by a red triplane. Seems the Tommy's gun had jammed and he was trying to find somewhere to land in a hurry. Our Lewis gunners tried to get in a shot, but they couldn't because the planes were too close. Then . . . there was a chance! They opened fire at a hundred yards range. Pieces of wood flew off the German machine near the engine. He wobbled. Side-banked. Swerved in a half circle. Then hit the ground 400 yards away, smashed to bits. Our blokes ran over, of course, and from the mangled pilot's watch and papers they realised it was the Red Baron himself. Not a bad day's work, my mate reckoned – though he was to cop it himself, so I heard, in the August offensive . . .'

The fitter became silent, as men did when they suddenly

remembered friends who were no more. Captain Jones took up the last of the story.

'I know some of our 3rd Squadron fellows rescued Richthofen's body that evening, and gave him a decent burial. Trench war is barbarous, but there's still some honour in the air. I believe his successor as commander of the fighter group was someone called Hermann Goering. I wonder if we'll hear any more of *him?*'

'The Tommy pilots say it is all wrong for the diggers to claim they shot *le Baron*,' Henri interjected. 'They say he was shot down by Captain Brown – a *Canadien* – of the 209th Squadron, and it's just Aussie boasting to say he was not.'

The engine fitter roused himself angrily.

'Well, listen here you bloody little Froggie! You just tell your Tommy pals that my mate wasn't a liar. He was *there*, and only two machines came out of that mist . . . the Baron and the Camel he was after. The triplane was brought down by our gunners on the ground – and if you say any different I'll give you a belt under the ear!'

'All right! Settle down you chaps!'

Major Ellis intervened as tempers flared, the dog sprang to Henri's defence, and men threatened retribution on anyone who belted their little mascot.

'No one is going to hit anybody . . . and if they do, they'll spend the night in the guard room on a charge!'

'I'm not afraid of *him*,' Henri said to Tim as they walked back to the sleeping hut. 'When I'm a pilot, I'll show them how a *real* air ace should fly! Can I go for another joy ride before we go home?'

'No. Definitely not. You heard what the Major said. All flying is to stop.'

'But . . .'

'No buts. Get yourself into bed.'

Henri began undressing himself. But the clouds of tobacco smoke from the mess and the effects of the cherry brandy took their toll. He felt sick again.

Digger would never admit it, however. Saying he was going for a pee, he went outside with Roy and threw up by the lamp. The dog was interested to see that Henri's sick was pink in colour – and so was the boy's backside when Tim saw what had happened.

'I don't know!' Tovell cried. 'Whatever is my Gertie going to *do* with you?'

Digger cried too. He'd got his belting after all.

A few days later, when there was a break from sorting, labelling and packing the stores, Tim took Henri into Cologne to have his picture done. He'd sent Gert a photograph before, of course. It was the one taken with the whole squadron on Christmas Day. Now Tim decided on an old-fashioned silhouette: and there Henri stood against the light in his breeches and boots, his jacket, scarf and hat, while the artist drew his shadow in outline.

It was hard for the boy to stand still for an hour having his silhouette drawn. Afterwards, Tim had it mounted on a *Postkarte* and sent to Jandowae with the message: Our little French mascot, he is coming to Australia with us.

On the way back to Bickendorf, Digger asked again about an aeroplane ride.

'No. We took you up once, to say you've been. But no more.'

'Why not? I've been very good today . . .'

'Because Major Ellis wouldn't like it. Fifteen of our machines have already been handed over, and the rest fly out tomorrow.'

'Why don't you ask a Tommy squadron? The *Majeur* needn't know.'

'Because that would be sneaking, and I don't like sneaks.'

'It's not fair.'

'I don't want to hear any more about it,' said Tovell firmly.

So Henri said nothing more about it to Tim. But next day, while the squadron was watching their last nine planes take off for Belgium, he wandered across the aerodrome and spoke to his friends at No. 48 Squadron. They flew Bristol Fighters, which had an observer's seat behind the pilot.

'I was *your* mascot before I went to the Aussies,' Henri cajoled them. 'They took me up. It would be good if you also gave me a joy ride before I go, eh, *mes amis?* Such times we've had together . . .'

Later, when everyone else was busy handing over No. 4 Squadron's technical stores and equipment, Henri sneaked away and was taken up for another quick spin along the Rhine.

He came back glowing and breathless, boasting of the stunts he'd perform when he was a grown *aviateur.* When Tovell asked where he'd been, Digger replied frankly that he'd made his own arrangements to go flying, 'Because you, Mr Tim, would not.'

'You've *what* . . . ?' Tovell was furious. 'You've disobeyed me. I should put you over my knee and thrash you! I should leave you behind. You can stay here at Bickendorf, a little ragged waif . . . like we found you.'

'Oh no, Tim! Please! Thrash me now, but don't leave me here. Take me home to Gertie . . .'

Henri wept and stamped his feet. And when Ted came in to see what the noise was about, Digger clung to his legs imploring him to persuade his brother not to leave the squadron mascot behind.

'Who was it, eh? Who did you sneak to?' Tim demanded. 'Was it your Tommy friends . . . ? Was it one of us . . . ?'

'I can't tell you!' sobbed Henri. 'I'll be in such trouble . . .'

'You're in big enough trouble already!'

'Don't be too hard on him . . .' Ted intervened. 'There's no great harm done, and we're leaving Bickendorf in a day or two.'

'They're ruining the boy,' Tim said. 'They're spoiling him rotten one minute with liquor and too much attention . . . giving him everything he wants! And the next minute they're snarling at him . . . and calling him a "bloody little Froggie", and threatening to belt him under the ear . . .'

'Then don't take it out on the lad,' Ted advised. 'Take it up with the Major.'

Which Tim did, when Les Ellis came out for the squadron's last parade at Bickendorf.

'The thing is, sir,' said Tim, 'most of the fellows are young and thoughtless when it comes to Henri. They don't mean him any harm, but they don't consider the consequences of what they're doing . . .'

'What do you mean?' asked Major Ellis who was, after all, only twenty-four himself. 'What consequences?'

'All youngsters need someone to love them, and I know Digger hasn't had that lately. But they also need someone to correct them . . . to discipline them . . . someone to show them right from wrong. And with all this indulgence, he certainly hasn't had *that* either.'

'What do you suggest?'

'He needs someone to take control of him . . . to be responsible for him . . . without other people undoing all the good work.'

'And would you be that person, Tim? Until we can decide what is to be done with the boy . . .'

'I would, sir, willingly.'

'Then I give you such authority . . .'

Major Ellis took a sheet of paper bearing the orderly room stamp, and wrote the following instruction:

No. 2198 Air Mechanic Tovell T.W. is in charge of Henri Hemene and no person will interfere with his charge without my permission. A.W.L. Ellis, Major, Commanding 4th Sqn AFC 26/2/19.

'There you are, Tim. I expect this order to be obeyed by everybody – and I want you to report any breach of it to me.'

'Certainly, sir.'

Les Ellis stood up.

'We are responsible for the boy, as you say. I think we have to bring him with us . . . try to find his family if we can . . . and after that, we'll take things as they come.'

'It's my own view entirely, sir.'

'Good. I know you've been trying to learn what you can from the little fellow. I've got some more information from the Tommy squadrons. I suggest we compare notes later. A few of us are planning to visit Paris on the way back, but we'll all be at Le Havre to embark for England. Unless the squadron finds Henri's family during the journey, we'll make our final decisions there. In the meantime, you have your authority . . .'

Tovell saluted and left the room. He showed the order to Henri, who was brushing his dog, later that afternoon.

'What does it say?' asked the boy. 'What is this "in charge"?'

'It means that I am your superior officer. You'll do exactly as I tell you. And if you don't, I'll parade you before Major Ellis.'

'Will I be locked in the guard room?'

'No,' said Tim. 'The instrument of correction will be more suited to naughty boys.'

Roy pricked up his ears.

'What's that?'

'*This*.'

Tovell produced a broad, woven strap from his webbing, such as soldiers wear to carry their pannikins and water bottles.

'What's it for?'

'It's to tan your backside if you disobey me again.'

'Owww . . .'

'And to make sure you don't forget, it has a message.'

Tovell held up the strap. In large capital letters he'd inked the words THE DINKUM OIL.

'What does that mean?'

'It means I'm as good as my word, and the strap is oiled up and ready to be used.'

'Now . . . ?' The boy's voice trembling.

'No. Not now. But next time. Should you deserve it.'

Tovell put the strap away in his kit bag. But Young Digger didn't escape all punishment for his sneaked joy ride.

That evening, the squadron went into Cologne for a night of revelry. They were leaving in the morning; and after General Hogg had complimented them at the last parade on their dash and energy, they were determined to prove him right by celebrating their departure in the most energetic manner possible.

Henri, however, had to stay behind at Bickendorf, sobbing at the unfairness of life. The little war orphan was unwanted and alone in the world – all except for his dog Roy, and 2nd Air Mechanic Tovell packing his things for home and Gertie, and THE DINKUM OIL winking at him from a corner of Tim's kit.

British airmen gather to farewell the Australians from Bickendorf, 27 February 1919. [AWM P00826.086]

The desolation of war – No.4 Squadron airmen stopped outside a ruined town in Flanders, March 1919. [AWM P00826.263]

Denied a few days' pleasure in Paris, Major Ellis and his officers are in the Crossley touring car which broke down. [AWM P00826.107]

The horror of a gas attack: dead Russian soldiers on the Eastern Front. Such photographs were available in France, where Tim Tovell probably got this one for his collection. [AWM P03638.001]

[AWM H13589]

Three photographs from Hurdcott showing how Digger was smuggled out of Europe: Digger and Tim with the sack marked *Oats 100 lbs*, Digger inside the oat sack, and Tim with sack and raincoat over his shoulder.

[AWM A03056]

[AWM H13591]

Nancy and Timmy at Jandowae, photographed by Gertie not long before Timmy died.
[Courtesy Nancy Elliot]

Digger learning how to box at Hurdcott with Ted (right) as his second. [AWM P00867.004]

8: FLANDERS FIELDS

The convoy carrying the airmen on the first stage of their journey back to Australia left Cologne on 27 February.

The 183 officers and men, plus one excited young mascot, were up early, getting ready for the week-long drive through Belgian Flanders and northern France, to the port of Le Havre. From there, they'd get a boat for England – and eventually a troopship for the voyage home. Home! To everything and everyone that cherished word conveyed. Men went about their routines that damp Thursday morning with a spring in their step that not even the headaches from last night's revelry could diminish.

'Oh Tim, I'm so happy to be going,' Young Digger exclaimed. 'I can't eat a *thing* for breakfast.'

'And then you'll complain you're starving,' said Tovell. 'We've a long day ahead. A bowl of porridge will stick to your ribs.'

'I don't want my ribs sticking.'

'Shall I give it to the dog . . .?'

The threat was enough. Henri spooned the thick oatmeal porridge into his mouth with much slurping.

'And will Roy be travelling with us in the lorry?' Digger asked, putting the bowl on the floor for the dog to lick clean.

'No . . . well, I've got to tell you about that.' Tovell searched for the right words as the boy's face fell.

'But Tim . . . what will happen to him?'

'He'll be all right. Roy's needed here.'

'Who needs him more than me?' The old fears of loss and panic began to rise in the boy.

'The other squadrons . . . your Tommy friends – they're staying on. Who's going to catch rats for them without Roy?'

'Let those German boys . . .'

'Yes, but Roy will have to show them how to do it. He's a soldier's dog. His duty is at Bickendorf.'

'Oh . . . what am *I* going to do?' Digger wanted to cry – but wouldn't.

'Tell you what . . . suppose Roy stays here to keep an eye on those young Germans . . . and when we get home I promise I'll get you another dog, just like Roy . . .'

Thus reassured – though still with some reluctance and a few parting tears – that was agreed. Digger got his haversack from the hut; and after he'd passed it to the men in the lorry, he tied an old rope around Roy's neck and led him across to some mechanics from No. 43 Squadron near by.

'Well, Joe,' they said, calling Henri by the name the Tommies gave him, 'are you all ready for the trip?'

'I am happy . . . but my dog is sad. I have to leave him behind. Will you look after Roy for me, *mes amis?* He is a king among rat-catchers. He'll serve you well.'

'Course we will, young Joe. Don't you worry about him.'

'And if any of those Germans throw stones, tell him to bite them hard!'

Digger burrowed his face in Roy's coat, so the airmen wouldn't see him cry.

'As for you,' he said to Roy with a large, brave sniff, 'conduct yourself as a true French poodle should. *Vive la France!*'

Roy licked the boy on his face. Henri thrust the rope into the hands of his friends, and ran back to the waiting lorries, not daring to look behind.

Many British airmen from the seven remaining squadrons of 11th Wing were waiting to farewell the Australians. They joked and chatted together, shaking hands and pledging the friendship of comrades-in-arms. They'd shared many of the same aerodromes during the last dreadful year of the war. They'd fought, suffered and played together. Now they were to part: but memories of their time on the Western Front would seal a bond between them for the rest of their lives.

The road transports were cranked up. The Australians clambered aboard, and the canvas covers were laced down. Major Ellis and his senior officers climbed into the Crossley touring car, in which they planned to visit Paris for a few days. Men waved and cheered. Horns blew. Gears meshed. And slowly the convoy of trucks left Bickendorf aerodrome and turned onto the road that would lead them, after many weary miles, back home.

Now, with so many of those miles behind them, Tim and Ted and Young Digger found themselves on the platform at Perth railway station. The train from Fremantle had just pulled in with much hissing of steam; and they stood there, looking momentarily lost as crowds of passengers eddied around them. Which way to go?

'When in doubt, follow the mob,' said Ted.

Which they did: joining the queues at the barriers; presenting their tickets; and a few minutes later they were walking down Wellington Street, blinking in the sunshine and trying to get their bearings. After so many weeks on a troopship, the city seemed as unfamiliar as life at sea had been when first they boarded the *Kaisar-i-Hind*.

Perth was like London, if smaller. Such a bustle! So many people on the footpath! The traffic noise! And signs of the war were still everywhere: recruitment notices on hoardings, and fading posters urging Western Australians to give generously to the patriotic funds for our boys overseas. Soldiers in uniform mingling with passing civilians. Yes, and so many of those boys who'd returned wounded from Gallipoli and Flanders were selling newspapers or hawking trinkets and scarlet paper poppies from wooden trays.

Such a cost. Though Perth had not been bombed as London had been. And unlike London, where shops were still half-shuttered because of shortages, the emporiums of Perth were overflowing with goods to sell.

'So much! So many things to buy!' cried Digger, stopping at every window. 'I always said, you Aussies have everything!'

'Not everything,' said Tim. 'We don't have your new clothes. And we don't have a plan to get you back aboard ship. Come on!'

They went into several department stores and bought Henri some new underwear, a couple of cotton shirts, socks and a pair of shiny black shoes – rather different to his tan army boots.

'Do we have enough money to buy Gertie a present?' Digger asked, dawdling outside a goldsmith's shop and looking at the sparkling jewellery. 'I'd like to get something for my new mum.'

Trying out the word again.

'Not this time, son. It's a nice thought, but we must watch our pennies. We've still to buy your new pants and a jacket.'

They walked on . . . through to Murray Street and Hay Street. They were about to go into a place that sold suits for boys, when Henri stopped outside a teashop, his face glued to the window.

'Oh Tim!' he drooled, gazing at a large sponge cake, dripping with cream and pink icing and strawberries. 'Look at that!'

And nothing would make him consider any more clothes, until Tim agreed they had enough money to buy a slice of cake and a pot of tea before going on. They turned down an arcade to the teashop, when suddenly they were confronted by a blind ex-serviceman, missing an arm and a leg, sitting on a little stool and begging with a tin.

He was only a young man, clean shaven and not poorly

dressed. His medals were shining. He had someone to care for him. But his sightless eyes and the lines drawn on his thin face spoke more eloquently of pain than any words could convey.

'Could you spare something? I have a wife and kiddie . . .'

The airmen and their little mascot stopped. They fumbled in their pockets, looking for something to say. All three were shocked. The horrors of war, which they thought had been left behind those thousands of miles away, were all at once before them again in the busy, comfortable streets of home. Suddenly they were reliving all the anguish they'd seen in Flanders, and especially at a cemetery near Mons not long after they started the journey home.

'Where were you wounded, soldier?' asked Ted, putting some coins in the returned man's tin.

'Near Ypres. 1917. Hellfire corner.'

'We're with the Flying Corps,' said Tim. 'The boy we have with us has come from Flanders.'

'*Oui, monsieur.* That is so.'

'Ah. Then you will know what hellfire is.'

Shaken and strangely anxious, they went into the teashop. But the strawberry cake seemed stale now, and their tea was tasteless.

The streets of Cologne were quiet when the convoy set out that February morning: a substantial procession of nineteen trucks, the Crossley, a motor bike with side car, and a cookhouse trailer.

Few citizens were about, and they were glad to see the backs of these *englische Soldaten*. Look what they'd drunkenly done to the statue of the Kaiser last night! Draped him with lavatory paper, crowned his head with a chamber pot and daubed vile messages on the base. Turn away from their transports, and thank God the first of them are going!

There was little other traffic, and the lorries were soon on the open road, heading towards the Belgian border. It was flat, monotonous country and, to pass the time, men started to sing 'Mademoiselle from Armentières' and 'It's a Long Way to Tipperary', to which some wag had put new and saucy words:

It's the wrong way to tickle Marie,
It's the wrong way to kiss!
Don't you know that over here, lad,
They like it best like this!
Hooray for la Française!
Farewell, Angleterre,
We didn't know the way to tickle Marie,
But we learned how, over there!

Tim Tovell didn't approve of those words. He wanted only to kiss his Gert. But Henri started to laugh and clap. And when someone said he was too young to know what the words meant, the boy replied that the Tommies had taught him a ruder verse than that, and would they like him to sing it? Tim told him to be quiet.

They stopped at the market town of Aachen for lunch. And

there was much cheering when a little later they crossed the border into Belgium: brave little Belgium, which had been invaded by the Kaiser's armies along this very route in August 1914. It was the reason the British Empire became involved in the Great War.

They weren't long out of Aachen when the touring car broke down. Major Ellis, Captain Jones and other officers saw their chance of a few days' pleasure in Paris fade away. They had to chase the convoy down the road in a taxi, and the officers – feeling distinctly unhappy – were obliged to sit in the trucks with the men.

They wound through woodland, and villages clinging to hill-sides, as the road dropped towards the river. On one descent a trailer uncoupled itself, slewed in a ditch, and had to be towed into the town of Verviers by a following transport.

Here, the travellers knew they were in another country. The old buildings had stepped Flemish fronts and mansard roofs. Everyone spoke French and, unlike the citizens of Cologne, they greeted the airmen with smiles and undoubted warmth. They saw these Allied soldiers as their liberators – even the little boy calling to them from the lorries in their native tongue! The airmen spent the night in an RAF camp, and set off through drizzle next day to drive along a pretty river valley to Liège for lunch.

'But look, *mes amis*, at what the guns can do,' said Henri, as they neared the city's outskirts. 'Such ruins!'

And indeed they began to see first evidence of the vast

destruction caused by the war. Shattered buildings and the blasted earth. For while the German armies had occupied Liège soon after the invasion, it had taken them another ten days of heavy bombardment to reduce the ring of forts surrounding the city.

As the airmen went further into Belgium, the road passed through ever more rubble and wreckage – even as they drove beside the river Meuse to the village of Andenne for their second night's sleep, and on again next day to Namur. Barges were working again on the river; but although life was starting to return to normal, the winter landscape still seemed frozen in the aftershock of conflict. So many millions of soldiers and civilians had died in those four terrible years. So many had lost everything.

The little town of Namur was well known to the airmen. They'd been based near there for a couple of weeks after the Armistice, before going to Cologne. At Namur they'd commandeered the LVG aeroplane in which Henri went for his first joy ride. Here, too, Major Ellis had taken over command. As they passed through the town, men fondly pointed out familiar places and, even more fondly, the pretty girls they'd known.

Henri was of an age where he had no time for girls, pretty or unpretty. But he'd spent almost a month near Nivelles with No. 48 Squadron, before travelling with them to Bickendorf.

'Look *messieurs!*' he cried, when they stopped for a late lunch. A lorry had broken down and had to be towed to Nivelles for repairs. 'There's the restaurant where I made myself sick with *café-crème!* And there's the bar where the Tommies got drunk on strong beer and fought the *gendarmes*. It was such a *mêlée* . . .'

'I don't think we want to hear any more about your fighting,' said Tim.

'*I* wasn't fighting!' replied Henri with spirit. 'It was *they* who were fighting. I was just watching.'

'Well, I'm sure you'd never find *this* squadron brawling with policemen in bars.'

'Oh no, father Tim! Never ever!' shouted one of the mechanics in tones of mock solemnity. And they all rocked with laughter.

'Still, you shouldn't rattle on so much,' Tovell replied.

In all honesty, however, Tim was just as interested in Digger's chatter, hoping to glean some scrap of information about his past. But while such scenes prompted Henri's recent memories – a puppy he had found and lost, a fresh chocolate éclair – nothing stirred him to speak of more distant experience.

'When did you first come to 48th Squadron . . .? Do you know when you met the men from the 79th . . .?'

His answer, as always, was the same.

'I think . . . no, I'm sorry, I can't remember . . .'

It was mid-afternoon when they left for Mons. The country was becoming more industrialised, more peopled with factories and coalmines as they descended to the rich, low-lying plains of Flanders, over which armies had fought for centuries.

Most of the men were billeted outside Mons, although lucky ones like Young Digger got quarters in town. Henri stayed with a Belgian family – a barber and his wife, who lived above their shop. It was the first time he'd slept in a proper bedroom or lived with French-speaking people since that time last year, when he'd been put in the home run by *les soeurs*. Even then, he'd escaped when the gardener left a gate open.

There was no thought of running away this time, however. Tim and Ted promised to call for Digger in the morning, and take him sightseeing. The next day was Sunday; and as troops on demobilisation had orders not to travel on the Sabbath, the squadron was to spend a rest day in Mons.

Henri lay in bed, listening to the chimes of the great belfry on its summit above the town, and the answering calls of the church bells. He rose early, put on his freshly pressed uniform, and went with Madame to the Church of Sainte-Waudru. It was the first time, too, that Henri had been inside a church since he could remember – he hadn't been long enough at the orphanage to go to Mass.

He liked the service. But best of all was a golden chariot in the church and in which, every year, the shrine of Sainte-Waudru was paraded around the town.

'And do you know what,' Henri babbled with excitement, when he and the Tovell brothers went walking. 'After the procession they have a festival, where Saint George and his friends kill the dragon. Oh! I should like to see that. Madame says if you can catch one of the dragon's hairs, it's a lucky charm . . .'

'Are they good to you, the barber and his wife?' asked Tim.

'*Oui!* They talk all the time of the brave Allies,' Henri said. 'And I think Madame means *me*, too, for she brushed my uniform and cleaned the buttons last night.'

They went to the belfry and climbed the stairs to the top, gazing across the broad, flat lands around Mons, where British troops had tried to halt the advancing German armies in August 1914. They hadn't been able to stop the onslaught, however, and Mons was occupied. The British and French were forced into a retreat, which didn't end until the Germans reached the River Marne near Paris and, after a great battle, themselves retreated to northern France. There, the armies dug themselves into trenches that stretched from Flanders to Switzerland. Millions of men became involved in a relentless, bloody war of attrition that lasted another four years.

But it was at Mons that the Great War had drawn the first British blood. For Tim and Ted Tovell – as for all the Empire's soldiers – the events of August 1914 became part of their very consciousness. And they were glad, that Sunday, to have time to see the battlefields where their fellow countrymen had died.

'Madame told me all about that fight,' Henri went on, as they left the belfry and walked to the town square. 'She told me about the angels of Mons . . .'

'She knows that story, does she?'

'Oh yes! The British soldiers were in danger of being surrounded. But in the night, the angels came down from heaven with bows and arrows, and stopped the Germans from advancing. So the Tommies were able to retreat from Mons, and were saved . . .'

The boy fell silent. Henri turned away and his eyes took on that far-away look the brothers knew so well. It always meant some door had opened deep in the child's memory, and the shadows of the past were abroad.

'Do you want to tell me about it?' asked Tim.

Digger shook his head. And Tovell, who loved him, knew better than to press.

'Let's go for a ride,' he said.

Lorries were parked outside the Town Hall. Ted persuaded one of the drivers to take them to the village of Saint-Symphorien, a mile or two down the road. There was an aerodrome used by the RAF, and also a military cemetery they wanted to visit.

The graveyard was not then the lovely garden it would become. The fields were still strewn with the debris of war. But the cemetery was already well known. Not only was the British Empire's first blood of the Great War spilled at Mons: so was some of the last. At Saint-Symphorien were buried two soldiers – an Englishman and a Canadian – killed as the town was liberated on the very last day, 11 November 1918.

Major Ellis and some of his staff were there when Henri and the Tovell brothers arrived. He greeted them warmly, and they spent a few minutes walking among the graves, reading the names painted on the wooden crosses – German as well as Allied soldiers, for at Saint-Symphorien men had no difference in death.

When suddenly Tim sensed some profound change in Young Digger. The boy had said very little during the last half hour; but now, as he held his hand, Tovell felt Digger's whole body begin to tighten. He looked down, and saw tears pouring from Henri's eyes. A dreadful sob shook him.

'What is it?' Tim stooped and held him. 'Tell me, son . . .'

'Oh Tim! Tim!' And he began to cry as only a child can. 'The angels saved the Tommies, but they didn't save my papa . . .'

'Your papa . . . ?'

'I remember . . . a knock at the door . . . a messenger . . . and Maman crying. It was the words . . . *at Mons* . . . and my papa, a soldier of France, killed in the retreat . . . lying we don't know where.'

'There . . . there now . . .'

Tovell comforted the boy, rocking him back and forth in his arms as Henri wept, his heart breaking. 'The angels didn't help Papa . . . they didn't save Maman . . .'

The airmen, standing by, were more affected than they dared acknowledge. As soldiers they'd risked their own lives every day. They'd taken up the weapons of war, and knew the consequences for themselves and their enemies. They'd seen towns and countryside wrecked by their bombs and shells, and witnessed streams of anonymous civilian refugees, among them thousands of children.

But they had not been as close as this before to all it had meant for the innocent on the ground. Their own families and children were safe at home, half a world away. But here was Young Digger, whom they *knew*, crying unbearably before them as if he carried the sorrows of humanity.

'The angels didn't save Papa . . . nor my maman . . .'

'Hush . . . hush . . .' whispered Tim Tovell, hugging the boy to his chest. 'Your father and mother are *with* the angels now . . .'

And there was not a soldier hearing them who did not

wonder, in his most secret heart, if he had not – all unknowing and in the line of duty – brought the same grief to some other family . . .

'I think,' said Major Ellis at last, 'we must do all we can for this young son of France.'

To which everyone present murmured his assent. *This* seemed their duty now.

9: HENRI

That night, a group of airmen sat down to dinner in Mons, to discuss just what they could do for Henri.

Major Ellis was there, with Captain George Jones and Lieutenant Norman Johnson, Sergeant Hec Wilson, Tim and Ted Tovell. Digger himself was absent. Having seen his distress at the cemetery, the men thought it best if Henri spent the evening at home with the barber's family, while they met privately, away from prying eyes and ears, in the upstairs room of a little restaurant off the Grand Place.

The bars and cafés around the great square were crowded with troops stationed at post-war Mons. In the military atmosphere of 1919, the distinctions of rank were keenly observed. People would have been very surprised to see an OC and his officers eating at a public restaurant with a sergeant and a couple of air mechanics.

So in this small, private room, warmed by a coal fire and with delicious smells wafting up from below, the men ordered drinks – sharp Flemish beer and good red wine. They called for the menu, and got down to business.

'Let's start with what we know about the boy,' Major Ellis began. 'We've all made our enquiries with the Tommy squadrons. There are many gaps and confusions in Henri's story . . . and a lot we may never find out, for much has been lost in the war. But from everything the Tommies have told us, it's fairly clear he was first picked up near Lille, along the road to Armentières, late in August 1914.'

'It's been *assumed* he came from Lille,' said George Jones. 'The fellows from 48th Squadron went there last November, but they found no trace of Henri's family.'

'Somebody said they heard his father managed a brewery, before he joined the French Army when war broke out,' Norman Johnson remarked.

'And as we learnt today, the father was killed soon afterwards, possibly near Mons,' added Major Ellis. 'It would seem Henri's mother died not long after that, in the German advance.'

'Digger remembers it only too vividly,' said Tim. 'He was in the street, when he saw his house hit by shellfire . . . with his mother and two others – perhaps a brother and sister – lying dead in the garden.'

'But he can't remember *where* this was?'

'No, sir. Not a name occurs to him.'

'I've heard Seclin mentioned,' said Hec Wilson.

'Where's that?' asked Ted.

'A town south of Lille,' Captain Jones replied. 'It has a 'drome. Perhaps someone heard of Digger there, and associated the two.'

Bowls of hot onion soup arrived, with cheese and bread croutons. As the airmen ate, they pondered the many unknowns of Henri's story.

'Was 48th Squadron able to turn up *anything* from their enquiries at Lille?' wondered Norman Johnson at last.

'Nothing.' Les Ellis was definite. 'Not a scrap of paper. Not a relation. Really, the boy could have come from anywhere along the line of retreat. Don't forget, he was found near a wrecked car.'

'That's right,' said Tim. 'Henri remembers the car being hit and overturning in a ditch. Somebody had rescued him from outside his house. He thinks perhaps it was an uncle, but he can't remember a name. Digger knows only that his friend from the artillery found him . . . said his uncle was dead . . . and took the child along with his unit.'

'Do we know that it was the British artillery?' Johnson asked. 'Some say it was a French howitzer battery.'

'It seems pretty certain it *was* the Royal Field Artillery,' Ellis observed. 'That's what the 79th and 48th Squadrons told me, and Henri lived with them for some months. An officer – I don't know his name – found the boy and took him along with the battery. He fed him . . . bunked him down . . . looked after him for a couple of years . . . He taught Digger to speak English . . . to read and write . . .'

'He was a lucky young blighter in one respect,' said Hcc Wilson. 'So many refugee kids were left to fend for themselves, unwanted by anyone.'

'Lucky in one way,' remarked Norman Johnson. 'But look where he ended up! In the Ypres salient.'

The room fell silent as they remembered the horror that name conjured in their minds. Ypres. Where the trenches bulged out from the Allied front to encompass the town known as 'Wipers' to almost every English-speaking soldier who fought and suffered in the mud.

'It was hell on earth for those poor devils,' said George Jones. 'I flew over the battlefields after the Armistice. I've never seen such devastation. Scarcely a tree or building was left standing. They say you can sit on a horse at Wipers and look across the ruins from one side of the town to the other.'

In the silence again, they remembered comrades lost near Ypres: at Polygon Wood, Tyne Cot, Messines and, above all, at the slaughter of Passchendaele . . . More than one million Allied and German dead over four dreadful years.

Soldiers who'd given their lives by the thousands to advance a yard or two. Who'd been killed going over the trenches, charging enemy barbed wire and machine guns. Who'd stumbled, in the endless rain, off duckboards laid across the morass of mud, and drowned in shell holes filled with water. Who'd been blown to pieces by artillery shells that fell like hailstones. Or died in the silent, suffocating mist of a gas attack . . .

Hellfire corner, indeed.

How was it possible Young Digger had survived all that for something like two years?

'The artillery was fairly well back from the front line,' said Les Ellis. 'He'd have had some shelter. And he'd have gone into Poperinghe from time to time.'

Many soldiers had marvelled at the high old life in that transit and supply town known as 'Pop', only seven miles behind Ypres. Yes, and of another place called Talbot House – 'Toc H' in signalman's lingo – run by a clergyman called 'Tubby' Clayton, where men could sit at peace in the loft chapel, or read a book in the garden, or eat a simple meal, free of all rank and distinction, for a few blessed hours away from the guns.

They were reminded of food, for a rich Flemish stew cooked with beer and onions arrived on the table for the hungry airmen.

'There were certainly many tent hospitals and casualty clearing stations in the fields outside Poperinghe,' Captain Jones remembered. 'It's possible Henri was sent there when his own luck ran out sometime in mid-1916, and he was wounded in the knee by a shrapnel burst.'

'Quite likely,' said Les Ellis. 'It would explain how he returned so quickly to the battery when he got out of hospital.'

'I've never been able to understand how Digger managed that!' Tim remarked. It still amazed him. 'He was in hospital for two months or so. The doctors did a first-class job stitching his knee, and he speaks of the nurses with real affection. But I mean . . . a little boy in a *military* hospital! How did he get away with it?'

The others chuckled.

'Those artillery men must have been Regular Army,' Sergeant Wilson observed. 'There wouldn't be a trick they didn't know.'

'And then look what happens!' said Les Ellis. 'Henri's back with the battery for only a few days, when one of the guns gets a direct hit. Most of the crew is killed, including the officer who befriended him . . .'

'The boy saw him lying in the mud.' Tim recalled the anguish in Henri's voice. 'He's seen more violent death than I hope my little chap at home will ever know . . .'

'And not only is the officer killed,' Major Ellis took up the tale, 'but Henri is himself injured again. Not badly, it seems . . . but enough to decide the artillery to send Digger well behind the lines.'

'Do you know where they sent him?' asked Ted. 'We've been unable to get anything much from Digger about what happened after his friend was killed.'

'He's blanked so much from his mind,' Tim added.

'And so much is blank on the record,' said Ellis. 'There are about eighteen months, until the middle of last year, when we know very little of Henri's movements.'

'Do we have *anything* to go on?' asked Norman Johnson.

'From what 79th Squadron told me, it appears he was handed over to a balloon section of the RAF.'

'Makes sense,' remarked George Jones.

The others nodded. There were many observation balloons in northern France, right along the front. The artillery worked closely with them, for balloon observers reported enemy positions and the success of your own fire back to the gunners by wireless telephone.

'Henri *may* have gone to other units,' Les Ellis said, as a delicious fruit tart arrived for dessert. 'We just don't know. But apparently a balloon section is where he ended up.'

'And then . . .?' asked Tim.

'He went from the balloon section to 79th Squadron. They were stationed close together. That's the connection. That's where he first came into the care of the Tommy flying squadrons.'

'Ah! So *that's* it!' Ted breathed.

'Yes. From May to October last year, No. 79 Squadron was based at a 'drome just outside Sainte Marie Cappel, a nice little village not far from the border . . .'

'Do we know *why* Digger went to the 79th?' Tim asked.

'Who can say,' Les Ellis replied. 'You know what he's like. He takes a fancy and moves in . . . Christmas dinner brought him to us. Then he uses all his charm to win your affections.'

'Yes. I know.'

'Was he with 79th Squadron long?' enquired Ted.

'A few months, I believe. Eventually, he was handed over to some nuns who run a small house in Sainte Marie Cappel for poor children and orphans displaced by the war.'

'The school!' cried Tim.

'What?' exclaimed Les Ellis.

'He told Ted and me about this. He remembers a house run by *les soeurs*. It's the only time in his life he's been to school – and even then he didn't stay long. He sneaked off through an open side gate.'

'That certainly fits in with 79th Squadron's story. They said he ran away . . .'

'I don't know whether Henri was trying to make his way back to their aerodrome,' Tim went on. 'But he got lost, and was very frightened living out in the open. He hasn't said who found him . . .'

'A Chinese Labour Company, would you believe.'

'Well, I'll be blowed!'

The Major might as well have said Digger had been rescued by the Man in the Moon, though on reflection it wasn't so strange. Over a quarter of a million labourers – including Chinese, Indians and Africans – were employed during the war to move ammunition and stores, repair roads, bridges and railway tracks, work in the quarries and, elsewhere, to free Allied soldiers for the main job of fighting.

'It appears Digger was found in a very distressed state by this Chinese Labour Company,' Major Ellis said. 'The officers took him in, fed him, and he went along with them for several days until he found himself in very familiar country near Poperinghe . . .'

'Then what did he do?' Ted wondered.

'Almost at once he's off again,' Les Ellis responded. 'The Tommies said an Army Service Corps transport arrived at the depot to pick up rations for the front. Henri watched them, slipped into the back of a wagon when nobody was looking . . . and hid under a tarpaulin.'

'Why would he want to go back to the fighting?' asked Norman Johnson. 'You'd think he'd have had enough of it.'

'Perhaps he wanted to find his friends from the artillery,' Hec Wilson volunteered.

'God knows! In any event, he nearly got there,' Major Ellis replied. 'He was discovered, just behind the lines!'

'The Service Corps sent him back, of course . . . ?'

'Next day. They questioned him, and eventually returned him to the aerodrome at Sainte Marie Cappel.'

'Back where he'd started!'

'Yes. But not quite with the same unit. Both the 79th and 48th Squadrons were sharing the 'drome for a few weeks last October. In the third week, the 79th was moved to Rekkem in Belgium, near the border. There was a lot of heavy action around there, because the Germans were falling back . . .'

'We remember it only too well,' said Captain Jones. 'It was some of the fiercest fighting we experienced . . .'

'You won your DFC then,' reminded Lieutenent Johnson.

'Yes. And my flight lost five pilots . . . Percy Sims, one of the bravest men I ever knew, shot down . . . Arthur Palliser . . . he was due to go home on leave. He said to me that last morning, "If I break my finger on the hangar door, I won't be able to fly today and I'll leave for Australia tomorrow." But he didn't break his finger – and he didn't return from that flight, remember . . . ?'

Everyone remembered . . . so many brave, dear friends lost in battle. And not for the first time, that evening, the room fell silent.

'So Digger stayed behind at Sainte Marie Cappel with 48th Squadron,' Major Ellis said at last, stirring his coffee and sipping a liqueur. 'But they were only there another week before No. 48 also moved to Rekkem at the end of October . . .'

'. . . taking Digger with them,' Tim supposed.

'Exactly. And the rest we know. The boy travelled with 48th Squadron as it moved forward with the 79th . . . to Nivelles, and then to Cologne. Where Henri had a row with the cook and moved to 43rd Squadron for a few days . . . until he came to us at Christmas.'

'It was during the move from Rekkem to Nivelles, I take it, that the 48th asked at Lille about the boy,' remarked Norman Johnson.

'The route's not far out of their way, and the road's much better for their transports. No. 48 asked many questions but found nothing. Mind you, Lille was occupied by the Germans for four years. It was only liberated and handed back to the French last October. Public records would have been a mess . . .'

'They probably still are,' said George Jones. 'The question is . . . now that we know this much about Henri, what do we do next?'

'We leave for Lille in the morning,' Major Ellis answered. 'We'll ask again. Something may have turned up since November.'

'It's not very likely,' Jones observed.

'Perhaps. But the Armistice had just been signed. Things would have been very confused at Lille. We *must* ask . . .'

'Oh, I agree, but I don't think there's much hope of finding anything. The authorities will have more to worry about than yet another war orphan . . .'

'And if we *don't* find anyone who knows about Digger?' Tim asked. 'What happens then?'

'If there's a family waiting for him near Lille, we'll take him to them,' Les Ellis said. 'Otherwise, I suggest Henri travels with us to Le Havre – where we'll make a decision before embarking for England. Perhaps we'll find another orphanage . . . a decent place run by the nuns, to take him in.'

'An *orphanage!*' Tim exclaimed. 'Excuse me, sir, but the little fellow wants to come with us to Australia. He's got his heart set on it, and I haven't the will to deny him. I've told my wife . . .'

'Back to Australia!' Ellis sounded surprised. 'That would be very irregular. I can't see the French agreeing to that. Dear me, no.'

'He's our mascot!' Ted reminded them.

'We can't just dump Henri in an orphanage to take his chances,' said Hec Wilson. 'It wouldn't be right.'

'I don't know what else we can do,' Major Ellis replied. 'I mean . . . officially . . . I couldn't consent to anything improper . . .'

'There's more than one way round a difficulty,' Tim said.

His soldier's voice cut like a blade through a knot, and the officers noisily cleared their throats. Military experience suggested there were some things it was better they didn't know. Not officially.

'We don't have to decide anything yet,' said Captain Jones.

'Quite so.'

Major Ellis folded his napkin and stood up, bringing the meal to a close. It had been a successful evening – even if, in hindsight, it would appear any enquiries about a boy with the surname 'Hemene' or 'Heememe' would probably be useless. Few families around Lille, Armentières or anywhere else in Flanders were likely to have such a name. 'Herman', now – or 'Hermann' – *that* was familiar everywhere. Yet it would seem that the boy's misspellings on the cards Tim had sent from Cologne had put them all off the scent.

But these Australians couldn't know that. So they said goodnight and went their separate ways: the officers to a military club for a nightcap, and the other ranks to the bars around the Grand Place, in search of their own entertainment and an early lift back to camp.

Tomorrow was to be an important day. For Young Digger. For everyone.

10: Padre Gault

True to his word, Tim came to the barber's house after breakfast to collect Henri for the day's journey. The boy was already waiting. Indeed, he was becoming impatient as the barber's wife fussed and held him to her breast.

'Ah! Le pauvre petit garçon . . .'

She'd lost her only son in the war, and was hoping this 'poor little boy' would stay and become her own. But Henri would have none of it. He was off with *les Australiens*, and he struggled against her embrace.

'We must try to find his own family, madame, when we get to Lille,' Tim explained.

'I know, monsieur. But if you cannot, we would dearly love to have him back . . .'

She kissed the boy until he felt the wet on her cheeks, and he pulled away crying '*Non!*' He couldn't stay! So, putting a little packet of *bonbons* in Henri's pocket, the good lady sighed and stood at her door, watching them walk to the square where the lorries waited.

The distance between Mons and Lille was only forty miles, but the roads were in a dreadful state with shell and bomb craters, and littered with wreckage. It took the convoy hours to reach the pilot's depot at Ronchin, outside Lille.

Major Ellis and his senior officers, however, had taken a lighter vehicle and, crossing into France, reached the city early. They saw the civil and military authorities, and visited orphanages, searching for any clue about Digger's real identity or of a family waiting for him. Yet, as Captain Jones had warned, their enquiries were fruitless. There was no record of anybody looking for the boy.

'You will understand *messieurs*,' the officials said, 'but everything is in disarray. The German occupiers destroyed so much . . . There are thousands of families homeless and fatherless . . . How can we help you find *one* orphan's family among so many . . . ?'

How could they, indeed? So Major Ellis thanked them, left his name and forwarding address with the Australian Flying Corps in case something turned up, and said *adieu*. When he spoke to the airmen at Ronchin late that day, there was no question that Digger would continue with them to Le Havre.

The boy, of course, was overjoyed. Major Ellis was trying to reunite him with his surviving family – with any aunts or uncles he may have. But Henri couldn't remember them. They'd be strangers from another life. Maman and Papa were dead. So were any brothers and sisters. Henri knew that. Now he had to find a new maman – and that could only be Tim's Gertie and the family at Jandowae. The question, in fact, was this: how best could he get there?

It was something of a squeeze when the convoy set off again next morning – and something of a discomfort, too, for Tim Tovell.

The lorry in which he'd been travelling the previous day had hit a shell hole and a rear wheel fell off. The vehicle was so damaged it had to be left behind, with its men and equipment transferred to other trucks. Tim had been thrown heavily in the accident and his back injured. Like the whiff of gas he'd had at the end of the war, he refused to report it to the doctors, however. Henri was unhurt – although the jolt didn't help his knee wound. But he put on a sheepskin jerkin against the cold, as they left Lille to drive through northern France.

The landscape was familiar to the airmen. They'd flown over it constantly in wartime. Now they saw from the ground the effects of their bombardments: the ruins that had once been people's homes; the broken backs of bridges and railways; the wounded land. Yet in these early days of March, spring was already beginning to spread a green mantle of healing over it, and soon the poppies would be in bloom. They drove through Fournes to La Bassée and Béthune, where they stopped for lunch. Tim and Young Digger were photographed beside a road sign – painted over an undertaker's hoarding – showing where they'd come from.

At day's end they reached the aerodrome at Estrée Blanche, not far from Serny where the Tovell brothers had joined the squadron in October 1918. Here, the returning airmen stayed for two days, handing over their remaining equipment to the RAF.

It was bitterly cold in the metal Nissen huts. The men played a bit of sport, drank more than a bit of warming grog, and, when the handover was done, spent time seeing old friends, revisiting old haunts, and recounting old tales from the war.

'You'd have thought we mechanics would be safe at our aerodromes, well back from the front,' Tim said to Digger. They were out walking to keep themselves warm and to exercise sore muscles. 'But we had our share of risk too. Did I tell you of the time I came under direct fire?'

'*Non!*' Like all boys, Digger loved stories of death and danger – so long as they happened to somebody else. 'When was that?'

'Towards the end. We were just outside Lille, very close to the action because our lads were chasing the Huns back to Germany.'

'*Bravo!*'

'Well, one of our planes got hit and came down in no-man's-land. The pilot scrambled out, but his machine had its tail stuck in the air. Fritz was using it as an artillery range-finder. So we were ordered to go and dismantle it.'

'What happened?'

'We crept out, and I climbed up to push the tail down. But a German machine gunner saw us and opened up! The other blokes took off . . . but I was stuck on the plane. Lucky for me the machine gun was fixed at chest height, and I was higher up. But the bullets started cutting through the fuselage, and slowly the tail began dropping lower and lower . . . with me still hanging on to it.'

'And then what . . . ?'

'Just when I was about to be a target for Fritz, his machine gun ran out of bullets, and he had to stop firing to change the belt. I leaped off . . . threw a match into a pool of leaking petrol to set the plane alight . . . and ran for my life . . .'

'Is that true . . . ?'

'Would I lie to you?'

Digger thrust a gloved hand into Tovell's, and tried to keep pace with the man.

'You are always a nice person, Tim,' he said. 'Now I know you're a brave one, too.'

The airmen left the following morning for the final stages of the journey to Le Havre. Major Ellis kept hoping some message about Henri's family might come from Lille. But nothing did. So the convoy set off again, driving through Abbeville in Picardy to Neufchatel, where they spent the night in a former prisoner-of-war camp. They had a jollier time of it than the German POWs had enjoyed, with plenty of good French wine to drink; and it was with sore heads that the men climbed aboard the lorries next morning for the last day's run.

They drove across glorious country, until they reached the coast and Le Havre. That afternoon, No. 4 Squadron marched into the Base Depot of the Australian Imperial Force at Rouelles, only a few miles from the ships that would carry them back to England.

The depot was located in a lovely valley. Tents and Nissen huts, stores and recreation halls climbed up green slopes to the officers' quarters, among the beech woods on the hilltop. The camp had a pleasant, rural atmosphere, so different to the desolation which soldiers, returning from distant battlefields, had known.

They often walked about Rouelles to peaceful farms and villages, and looked across the River Seine to the ancient seaport of Honfleur. On fine Sunday afternoons the depot chaplains would hold woodland services for the men, with singsongs and 'stunts', such as prizes for the funniest poem about military policemen, or a sentence on 'The Most Beautiful Place I Know': *The Orderly Room on Pay Day. Reason, understood (signed) Hardup.*

One chaplain, Padre James Gault from Melbourne, had a great gift for getting close to the soldiers. It was his deep human sympathy – the fun days he organised – and his ability to dress moral advice in the garb of good humour. When men had leave to go into Le Havre, with its bars and brothels, the Padre would talk to them as they got their passes. He'd tell the story of a Tommy captain who was sent a pair of socks knitted by his fiancée, and promised never to wear them in any place she wouldn't approve.

'You're going into Le Havre on leave today boys,' Padre Gault would say. 'So WATCH YOUR SOCKS!'

There were no leave passes for the airmen of No. 4 Squadron that Sunday. The day after they arrived at Rouelles was fully occupied getting ready for the journey home. They lined up outside the medical huts for their health examinations. Digger went too. Naturally. He was one of them. And he got his certificate:

Henri Hemene aged 11½ years, 4th Squadron AFC.
Henri Hemene is free from vermin and disease.
(Signed) Raymond A Ward, Captain 9/3/19.

After that it was a haircut. Then off to the bath house for a long soak and a scrub, as if trying to cleanse themselves of every last bit of wartime dirt deeply ingrained in their skins. They were fairly successful, for the bath water was grey with grime and had to be changed often. Though, in years to come, the soldiers would find it was not so easy to wash away their memories.

Finally to the quartermaster's store, where men were issued with new kit: fresh uniforms, underwear and shirts, clean socks and puttees. New boots, too – but mostly they were resisted.

'Aw, Sarge, I've marched across half of Europe in these old boots. It'll take weeks of sore feet to get the new ones right.'

'Just do as you're told soldier, and stop complaining.'

There were no new clothes for Henri, however. The quartermaster didn't keep stores to fit a young digger aged eleven-and-a-half, whether or not he was free from vermin and disease.

But the boy was happy with a cut-down vest and some socks that had shrunk several sizes in the wash. And it was with some exhilaration that he stepped out, later that afternoon, for a walk around camp with Tim. He'd made it this far, on the way back to Australia!

Excitement quickly turned to apprehension. The first person they met, as they climbed towards the woodland, was Major Ellis.

'Ah, Tovell,' he said, returning the salute, 'I've been wanting to have a word with you.'

'About Henri, sir?'

'Yes. I'm afraid no news at all has come down the line from Lille about his family. Not a peep.'

'What would you like me to do, sir?'

'We move tomorrow afternoon to the drafting depot, closer to the wharves, ready to embark on Tuesday. We'll give it until then, but . . . er . . .' (the Major glanced at Henri and spoke to Tim in a low voice) '. . . in the meantime, I think you should enquire about a home . . . an orphanage where the boy could be placed.'

'But sir! I've promised . . .'

'I know, I know. Officially, you understand, I can propose no other course. If the boy's family doesn't turn up, the French authorities will agree to nothing else.'

'But . . .'

'We'll speak again, Tovell.'

'Sir!'

The officer went on his way. Digger could see at once from Tim's face that something was seriously amiss.

'Tim! What is it? What's gone wrong?'

'There's been no trace of your family. And now they say I have to find an orphanage to take you, when we go back on Tuesday . . .'

'But I don't want to go to *les soeurs!* I want to go with you!'

The tears gushed forth and drowned Henri's words. Tovell put a consoling arm around him, as they walked up the hill.

'It's all right, son. Don't upset yourself. I'll think of something.'

They kept walking until they were among the trees, still bare against the cold sky. There'd be another frost tonight. But the fallen leaves were soft underfoot, and the undergrowth was green with bracken. It was a restful, gentle place; and it wasn't surprising, when the path opened into a little glade, that they found Padre Gault. He often went there, to renew his spiritual energies.

'Hello!' he called in friendly greeting. 'Come and join me. I'm James Gault . . . Chaplain Gault . . .'

Tovell introduced himself and Henri.

'Ah! I've heard of *you!* The little mascot with 4th Squadron. You're quite a topic of conversation around the depot. I'm very interested to meet you.'

The Padre shook hands and, sitting on a log, invited the boy to tell his story. Which, with some hesitation, he did – Tovell filling in the many blank spots where Digger's memory failed him.

They told the story as quickly as they could . . . from the very beginning until that moment in the wood above Rouelles. But even so, it was a good half hour before they finished and Padre Gault, clapping his hands, said it was the most remarkable tale he'd heard for a long time.

'Upon my soul,' he exclaimed, 'I find it hard to believe! A little boy . . . to have survived four years among the horrors of Flanders. The Good Lord must have been watching over you. And then to have brought you safely here . . .'

The Padre seemed to offer a little prayer of thanksgiving, for he said nothing for a few moments. Tovell lit his pipe, and the fragrant tobacco smoke mingled in the silence with the woodland scents. Until the chaplain uttered the thought that, in one way or another, was occupying them all:

'I suppose the question now is . . . what happens next?'

'Major Ellis has been trying to find Digger's family . . .'

'And if he can't?'

Tim took a deep puff on his pipe and slowly exhaled the smoke, before replying very deliberately:

'If we can't locate anyone. . . and that seems probable now . . . I'm going to take Henri home to Australia with me. He'll grow up with my family in Queensland.'

Padre Gault looked up, rather sharp.

'That's taking a big risk, soldier. And a foolish one. The French authorities won't let you take the boy out of the country. If you're caught, it will mean at least two years in jail with hard labour!'

'The risk is mine to take, sir . . .'

'Yes, but smuggling a child . . .'

'I had an uncle who was a fisherman on the Norfolk coast. I got my sea legs as a boy, Padre, and I'm not afraid of storms. You leave the smuggling to me.'

'I wonder if you've thought of the consequences for the boy . . .'

'What consequences would they be?'

'You'd be taking him from his own people, his own language and ways of doing things, to somewhere completely foreign . . .'

'I've lived with the Tommies for long enough, monsieur,' said Digger, piping up in his own defence. 'I speak English . . . I wear a digger's uniform . . . yes, and I've eaten boiled mutton and cabbages!'

'But your family . . .'

'I have no other family now, except with the Aussies . . . and Tim's Gertie, and Nancy, and little Timmy . . .'

The Padre turned back to Tovell.

'But it's almost as if you're *stealing* him . . .'

'He's a very willing victim, Padre.'

'I must say, Air Mechanic, I find this extraordinary. There are many fine places in Le Havre that would care for him . . . I could arrange it. They're well-run institutions, set up especially to look after the thousands of war orphans. The sisters would give him a first-class Christian education and upbringing . . .'

'No!' cried Henri. 'Not *les soeurs* . . . !' And he clung to Tovell.

'He doesn't want to go back to them, Padre.' Tim soothed the child. 'He wants to come home with me. And, unless we find his family by Tuesday, I'm going to take him.'

'But what do you think you're doing, man?'

'I think I'm giving him a chance in life, sir. A better chance with my family than ever he'll have in an institution here . . . one, as you say, among thousands . . .'

'I dare say you may be right . . .'

'I *know* I'm right.'

Padre Gault sighed.

'Then all I can do is urge you to think it over carefully. Weigh the good you may do for the boy, with the risks you will certainly run if you try to smuggle him out of the country in your kit bag, as it were. You're a praying man, I take it?'

'I am sir. Always have been.'

'Then pray to the Good Lord for guidance . . . and we'll speak again before you leave.'

The conversation with Padre Gault did nothing to ease Young Digger's apprehension.

To be so near his dearest wish! And now to see it slipping away! He'd travelled so far with his soldiers. In only a few short days they'd sail for England. Yet here were both Major Ellis and the Padre saying Henri should be left behind . . . should be placed in an orphanage like Sainte Marie Cappel. Shut behind high brick walls and locked gates! And when at last he *could* run away, his friends would be gone across the sea to Australia, and he'd never see them again.

Digger's leg wound began to hurt again as they went back

down the hill to the tents. He held out his hand.

'Oh Tim,' Henri said in a small, thin voice. 'I'm so afraid.'

'There's no need to be frightened, son. I'll see you safe. There was something the Padre said . . .'

'*Oui!* He wants to send me away!'

'No. That won't happen, Henri. I promise you.'

'But he said . . .'

Tim stopped and, squatting down, he held the boy by the arms and looked him clearly in the eye.

'It was something else, Digger . . . something he hinted. It's given me the makings of a plan. A pretty good plan, I think. But it will need both of us – and all our secrecy – to carry it out.'

11: A Sack of Oats

Tim put his plan into operation next morning. He talked it over with Ted – strictly hush-hush – and both agreed it could work.

'It's the kit bag. The Padre said ". . . if you try to smuggle the boy out of the country in your kit bag . . ." Well, it's worth a go.'

But when they tried it out, they discovered Digger couldn't fit inside a canvas kit bag. He was a small boy – but not small enough.

'We've got to find something else.'

They found it in one of the store sheds, when no one was about, among a pile of empty horsefeed sacks.

'What about this?' Tim asked, holding up a hessian bag marked *OATS 100 lbs.*

'Let's see.'

The oat sack was much bigger than the kit bag, giving Henri

plenty of room to squat down inside. Tim slung it over his shoulder. His back still hurt after the accident. But he grimaced, stuck his pipe between his teeth, and turned to Ted.

'What do you think?'

Ted studied them.

'There's a problem,' he observed. 'The outline is a give-away. The sack looks exactly as if you're carrying a little kid inside it.'

Tim put it down and Digger crawled out, brushing himself and complaining that, 'It's not nice in there. The dust gets up my nose, and the hessian hurts my knees.'

'Yes, that's another problem. The oat bran could make you sneeze at the wrong time. I'll give the sack a good shake and put in a blanket to kneel on. But what can we do about the way you look?'

'We can't change Digger,' said Ted. 'Perhaps we can alter his shape . . .'

They cast around until Tim found a shallow wooden box – like a grocery box – in a corner of the shed. He looked at it with a carpenter's eye.

'I could use that,' he said, as an idea came to him. 'Take out the two ends . . . strap the back and sides around Digger, and put him in the sack . . . From the outside, it would look as if I'm just carrying a box.'

'Makes sense,' said Ted.

'I'll need a saw and hammer . . .'

'Leave that to me. I can borrow them from the workshop. Better you don't ask too many questions.'

When everyone else was having lunch, Tim cut down the box, strapped it around Digger's back with THE DINKUM OIL, put him in the sack, and looked at himself in a mirror.

It wasn't too bad. The profile looked just like a square box – not like a boy at all. They even padded a couple of jam tins for Henri to kneel in, so that his knees wouldn't give the game away, and put a folded blanket at the bottom of the sack.

The final effect was pretty convincing. Here was an ordinary airman returning with a few souvenirs from the war: a box inside an old oat sack with his kit, some food tins, and his waterproof raincoat slung over the top to protect it from damp.

'It will do me!' said Ted.

'And me as well,' replied his brother.

Late that afternoon the airmen went by lorry to the drafting depot, not far from the wharves. Tim carried the sack with the box inside, so that men would know he had such an article and not ask awkward questions at the docks.

Digger travelled with them openly. There was no suggestion that, come tomorrow, he might be *inside* the sack. Ted carried two kit bags – his own and Tim's – into which Henri's few things had been stuffed. The flag and the Emperor Napoleon, however, were left behind. Digger was leaving France for good!

The following day, Tuesday 11 March, was embarkation day. After lunch, Padre Gault went around saying goodbye to those leaving for home.

'I hope I'll soon be joining you,' he remarked with a smile and a handshake. 'Good luck, and God go with you.'

But when he saw Tim and Henri, the clergyman became more serious. 'Have you thought about our conversation?' he asked.

'I have, sir.'

'Will you give the boy to me? I'll make sure he's placed in a good home. I'll send the address, that you may write to him.'

'It's very kind of you Padre,' Tim replied evenly, 'but the only home I'm going to take him to is in Queensland.'

'You intend to persist?'

'I do.'

'Knowing the risks for yourself?'

'You asked me if I was a praying man, Padre. I am – and I have. Now I must trust to the Good Lord to see us through.'

'Then . . . I will pray for you as well,' said the minister. 'I don't want to know what you have in mind. But it may also require human intervention if things go wrong. Here . . .'

Padre Gault took out a business card printed with his name and address, and scribbled a note in French.

'What is it?' asked Digger, his voice breaking with anxiety. 'What does it say?'

'It's a message for the *gendarmes*,' Padre Gault said. Handing it to Henri he explained kindly, 'I want you to keep the card. When the officers find you, as they probably will, give it to them. It says they're to bring you back to me, and I'll make sure you're cared for.'

'Tim, what will happen to me . . . ?' cried Henri, close to tears.

'Nothing awful is going to happen, son.'

And turning to Padre Gault, Tovell added in a voice that was also heavy with emotion, 'It's very decent of you Padre, and we thank you, Digger and me. Let's hope your card won't be needed.'

'Let's hope so indeed,' replied James Gault.

At four o'clock, Major Ellis asked to see Tim. Alone.

'It's about Henri,' said Les Ellis, as if it could possibly be about anything else.

'Yes sir?'

'As we all expected, nothing has come from Lille. The boy would seem to be quite alone in the world.'

'I believe that to be true, sir.'

'We're faced with the moment of decision, Tovell. Have you made arrangements to hand Digger to the French authorities?'

For the second time that afternoon, Tim found himself looking a superior steadily in the eye, and having to deny his request.

'Major Ellis, I have to tell you that I don't wish to hand the boy to anyone but my wife in Australia.'

There was a sharp intake of breath on the other side of the table. Then a short laugh.

'Don't be a fool, Tovell.'

They faced each other calmly for a moment.

'Do you intend to try to stop me, sir?'

'No, I won't stop you, Tovell. But I can't give you my official consent. If you're caught, I know nothing. You understand that?'

'Perfectly, sir.'

Les Ellis paused.

'We leave for the ship in an hour. Carry on the good work.'

The airmen climbed into the lorries for the short run to the docks, after five o'clock parade. Digger waited in the tent, strapped in his box and hidden in the oat sack, until Tim came to pick him up.

'It's not very comfortable in here,' the boy sniffled.

Tim said he could stay behind if he wished – and the sniffling stopped. Tovell tied the top of the sack, whispering, 'Hang on, Digger. It won't be for too long. Keep quiet, and say your prayers like a good boy. Our big adventure has started.'

Hoisting the oat sack over his shoulder with both hands, Tim left the tent. He passed Ted on the way, and they exchanged nods.

All's well.

Tim handed the sack up to a mate, and clambered into the last truck.

'Struth, Tim! Your kit's heavy enough. What's in it?'

'A war souvenir. For the wife.'

'Ah. And where's the young feller? I thought Digger went everywhere with you?'

'I had to make other arrangements,' replied Tim, stowing the sack under the bench. 'We couldn't find his family, and the Major said I should look for an orphanage . . .'

'Aw . . . that's hard on you, Tim. He was a nice little cove . . .'

'Yes.' Tim protected the sack as best he could behind his legs. 'It hasn't been easy . . .'

They moved up to make more space as Ted arrived carrying both kit bags.

'Here, Tim! You nearly left this behind. Gert wouldn't be too pleased.'

He tossed up the kit bags, and climbed aboard. The trucks were cranked up. With a jerk and a shove, they rumbled out of the drafting depot and headed for the docks.

It was just after half past five when the airmen lined up on Le Havre wharf, where the troopship *Lorina* was waiting. Customs officials and a few *gendarmes* stood by in the gathering twilight, looking for a small boy who, rumour had it, might try to sneak past. They watched carefully – but saw no sign of any *petit garçon* – as No. 4 Squadron proceeded on board.

Tim drew a deep breath. Uttering a little prayer, he shouldered the sack, and shuffled in the moving ranks to the ship's side. Ted fell in closely behind him, carrying their kit bags and crowding his brother to stop anyone seeing the oat sack too clearly.

Slowly, Tim said to himself, *past the watching eyes of the* gendarmes. *Eyes fixed on the man ahead as you move by the customs officers. Give thanks that it's nearly sunset. Breathe softly – steadily – and keep an even pace. Give your name and number to the embarkation officer.*

'No. 2198, 2nd Air Mechanic Tovell T.W. Sir!'

'Go aboard.' Ticking his name on the list.

First foot on the gangway. Step up. Now the other foot. The sack is heavy and my back hurts. Don't let me think about it, Lord. One foot after the other . . . up the gangway and don't trip . . . Now step onto the deck. There. Easy does it. Move away from the ship's side. Don't let them see me from the wharf. Put the sack down, covered with my raincoat . . . So far so good, thank you Lord . . .

On board the *Lorina*, Tim sighed with relief, the sack at his feet and Ted beside him.

'What now?'

'I'll look for a hiding place,' Tim murmured. 'You keep watch.'

He joined the men thronging the ship for the overnight voyage to Southampton. The decks were crowded, and so were the saloons. It took a lot of searching before he found a vacant locker-room below, like a small hold, with a couple of benches. He nipped back to tell Ted and, carrying their valuable cargo, the brothers descended the companion stairway.

Once inside the locker, Tim lowered the sack and whispered as he pushed it under the bench, 'Are you all right, Digger? Not long now!'

But the only answer he got was a small, muffled grunt.

The ship's siren hooted. Bells rang, and orders were shouted to 'Lower away!' The gangway was cleared. Hawsers cast. And at six o'clock the *Lorina* began to edge away from the wharf.

Softly past the watching quays of Le Havre. Slipping through the breakwater and into the rolling sea. The decks were crowded with soldiers, silently watching the sun sink. But as the coast of France grew dim they cheered and sang 'Take Me Back To Dear Old Blighty!' They were on their way. The war-ravaged soil of Europe was behind them, where so many friends lay beneath blood-red poppies. But they were safe. They were going home. And so was a small, cramped orphan boy hidden in an oat sack, stowed in a little hold below.

The brothers waited until the *Lorina* was well at sea before they let Digger out of the bag.

'Ho, Tim!' Henri cried, as he emerged, 'that was such a good adventure!'

'It's not over yet! We've got to get you off at the other end.'

'But was I good? Did I do well? I was as quiet as a mouse!'

'You were first class,' said Ted, guarding the door.

'You've still got to stay hidden,' Tim warned. 'We can't risk anyone spotting you.'

'I don't want to hide any more. My legs hurt. I want to run around.'

'It can't be helped. Someone might come in. You'll have to lie under the bench . . . stretch yourself out . . . and I'll cover you with our greatcoats.'

The coats made a sort of bed, into which Henri crawled, still protesting a little. But he gave way, as Tim promised there was more good adventure to come.

'It's such fun! I nearly burst out laughing in the lorry when they asked where I was. I wanted to call out, "Here I am! Digger's under the seat!"'

'Well, don't spoil things now with too much talk. If they find you, they can still send you back to France and the orphanage.'

'And put us in jail,' added Ted.

'So close your eyes and go to sleep.'

'Very well. I will try. Goodnight, Tim. *Bonne nuit*, Ted. I won't let them put you in jail . . .'

Rocked by the waves and the motion of the ship, Henri drifted into sleep. The men stayed awake, however, keeping watch. Ted eventually went up for something to eat, returning with sandwiches for Tim and an orange, which he kept for Digger.

The hours passed. The ship settled down and, soothed by the rhythm of the sea, the brothers also fell asleep. A deeper sleep than they supposed. For suddenly Tim awoke with a frightened start. He'd been dreaming of Gert at home in Jandowae . . . of Nancy and little Timmy. Something awful had happened and he didn't know what it was . . . waking up like this in fear, sweat running down his face.

Digger!

'Tim . . . Tim . . .'

A low voice calling him from under the bench.

So that was it.

'What do you want, son?'

'I've got to have a pee, Tim.'

'Now? Can't you wait?'

'No. Truly . . .'

'Oh, Lord . . .'

Tovell found an empty jam tin, and passed it down.

'You'd better use this. Quickly.'

When he'd finished, Digger handed the brimming receptacle back to Tim, buttoned himself up, and announced that he was going back to bed. Tim, in his role of night nurse, went on deck to dispose of the contents. Leaning over the rail, Tovell could see the shore lights of England. The *Lorina* had already entered Southampton Water, and was lying at anchor until morning.

Tim pulled out his pipe and had a puff, nodding to a mate who'd also come on deck.

'It's a pity about Young Digger,' said the airman. 'Your having to leave him behind like that . . .'

'Yes. I didn't want to . . .'

'We'll all miss him. I can't see why Major Ellis wouldn't let you bring him . . .'

'It was the French. They wouldn't allow it.'

'Ah . . . them Froggies! Forget 'em!'

'I won't forget Henri.'

'None of us will. Pity about him, all the same . . .'

Tovell went below. And there he sat out the night, dozing fitfully and still troubled by his dark dream.

When daylight came, they were woken by the anchor being raised and the *Lorina*'s engines stirring into life. They were moving to the wharf and the next part of the adventure!

Quickly the brothers stowed their gear, covering Henri with a greatcoat until the last moment when he'd get into the sack.

'It will be quite a wait before we can get you out again,' Tim warned. 'You'll have to be a very brave boy.'

'I'm hungry . . .'

'I've got an orange, and we'll get you something from the breakfast table.'

But they'd overslept, and all Ted could find was a couple of bread rolls. He only just got back when they felt the ship bump against the wharf. Orders were shouted, and the decks clanged with men getting ready to disembark. There was no time for eating!

'Quick, Digger! In you get! Before we're missed.'

'But I'm still hungry.'

'Later!'

The boy was strapped in his box, popped into the sack, and the performance of the previous afternoon was repeated. Out of the hold, Tim with the oat sack covered by a raincoat over his shoulder, Ted carrying the kit bags . . .

Up the companion stairs. Ease the burden on the deck. Wait patiently, as men file down the gangway and onto Southampton wharf. Pick up the sack and keep looking at the man in front, hoping Ted is close behind. You've seen us this far, Lord, see us safely through the rest . . . Up to the gangway, one foot after another . . . down . . . down . . . name and serial number . . . until you step onto the soil of Mother England. Don't stop or look around. Keep moving past the officers . . . Sergeant Wilson shouting orders . . . Where are we going . . .? To the railway siding on the wharf . . . not far, but the bag is heavy and my back's hurting again. Don't think about it, soldier. Nearly there. Thank you Lord, and breathe easy . . .

Orders were to stack their kit bags, and await the train that was to take them to Hurdcott Camp, a couple of hours away at Fovant, in Wiltshire. Tim placed the sack on the outside of the pile, and stood guard. Poor Digger! He'd be ravenous and sore.

Tovell heard Digger whimper a little. When nobody was looking – and with Ted acting as a screen – Tim slipped a bread roll inside the sack.

'Quiet as a mouse, Digger,' he whispered. 'Not long now . . .'

But it was longer than anyone expected. Men were starting to grumble. Typical bloody army! And they were asking where the toilets were.

'You'll just have to hold onto yourselves, boys,' said Sergeant Wilson.

But Digger couldn't: and with some alarm the Tovell brothers noticed a little rivulet of pee trickling from the oat sack and across the railway siding.

'Are you all right there, Private?'

'Yes, Sergeant. I . . . er . . . I dropped my water-bottle.'

'You want to be more careful next time.'

'Yes, Sarge. Sorry Sarge.'

The men went ashore at eight o'clock, but the train for Hurdcott didn't arrive until eleven. Three hours! Digger had been in the sack for twice as long as yesterday. Tovell was becoming worried when at last he entered the railway carriage, and placed the sack on the floor between his knees.

'You must have something very precious in there, Tim, for your missus,' said an airman sitting opposite.

'I have.'

'You've been looking after that sack like a baby.'

'Mmm . . .'

The train blew its whistle, belched steam, and began to pull away. Along the wharf siding and into the main railway line it puffed. Beyond the dockside warehouses and smoking factory chimneys. Over the bridge. Hurrying past shops and offices, and into the suburbs of Southampton . . .

Not yet. Wait until we're clear of the city . . .

'You'll find it strange to be without Digger at your heels.'

The conversation resumed in the train.

'I'll manage.'

'Funny little kid . . . we got used to having him around.'

'So did I.'

The houses were thinning out. Not long and they'd be in the countryside.

'An orphanage, they reckon. Our mascot! Poor little feller. I wonder what he's doing now?'

There was an explosion from the sack.

'What's that?'

'I didn't hear anything . . .'

'Course you did! There it is again.'

As the sack began to wriggle and bounce and emit shrieks of laughter.

'What have you got in there . . . ?'

Tim looked out the window, where the fields and hedgerows were beginning to bud and send out the first green shoots of spring. Of new life. A new beginning.

Now.

'Just this . . .' he said.

Reaching down, Tim lifted up the sack marked *OATS 100 lbs.* He put it on the seat and untied the top.

As he pulled back the hessian, Henri's face appeared like the sun, crying, 'Here I am, *messieurs!* Here is your mascot, all the time!'

And the shouts of delight and recognition by the Australian airmen could be heard from one end of the train to the other.

12: HURDCOTT

Henri gloried in his triumph. As the airmen leapt in astonishment, the boy's face was lit with what Tim ever after remembered as 'the wonderful smile that always adorned it'.

'*Mes amis!*' Digger cried. 'Wasn't that a good trick? Are the Aussies surprised . . . ?'

Indeed they were.

'Fritz never surprised us so much!' the men exclaimed. And they crowded round, laughing and clapping the Tovell brothers on the back, and tousling the lad's brown hair.

'I wouldn'ta believed you could get away with it! Not for a million quid!'

Their shouts drew others, and soon the corridor was thronging with soldiers, all jostling and crowing the extraordinary news that their mascot had been smuggled out of France.

'In an old sack, like Santa Claus! He opened it – and out popped the kid! You coulda knocked me down with a feather!'

Lieutenant Johnson came, and so did Sergeant Wilson. But, for all his smiles, Digger was distressed. As Tim unstrapped the box, lifted him out of the sack and stood him up, Henri almost collapsed.

'How long has he been in there?' asked Norman Johnson.

'Since before eight o'clock, sir, as the ship was berthing.'

'That's over three and a half hours! The poor little fellow will have terrible cramps. Make room there!' Lieutenant Johnson took charge. 'Lay him on the seat, Tim . . . there . . . and gently massage his legs and arms. Feeling better, Henri?'

'I'm a bit sore.'

'I dare say you are . . .' as they rubbed his aching limbs to get the blood circulating.

Ted passed his water-bottle, and gradually the lad's colour returned. But the crowd pushed in, and Johnson had Hec Wilson keep order while he went to fetch a medical officer.

The man examined Henri, but said there was nothing wrong that time and massage wouldn't cure. Oh, and a little food, too.

'When did you last eat, son?'

'I've had nothing since four o'clock yesterday, except an orange and a bun, and I'm starving, monsieur!'

'Who's got some tucker?'

The airmen produced more chocolate bars than could possibly be good for him. But they did the trick, and at last Digger felt strong enough to get his legs used to walking again.

The news of Henri's adventure spread through the train, and there was quite a commotion when they reached Fovant. Men tumbled onto the platform, anxious to glimpse him. Even Major Ellis and the officers joined in the good humour.

'We're looking at a child prodigy!' Les Ellis declared. 'I thought he was in France. But look here, gentlemen, it seems our young mascot has gained his wings already and flown with us – showing all the courage that saved his countrymen at Verdun in 1916!'

The high spirits were kept up through lunch; and when the squadron set off to march through the rolling Wiltshire countryside, it was like a triumphal procession. The land looked young and verdant in the spring sunshine. Just outside Fovant the airmen saw their Rising Sun badge, carved into the white chalk downs by Australian troops during the war. And as they neared their own camp, there on the hillside was a large map of Australia.

'Look, Tim! That's where we're going!' cried Digger.

'Yes, son. That's home.'

And the whole parade broke into cheers.

Henri walked as far as his legs would carry him. Tim carried him on his back the rest of the way. The mascot insisted on getting down and going the last little bit, however, side by side with the men in his uniform, as the squadron marched into No. 4 Command Depot, Hurdcott Camp.

The big military training base near Fovant, on the edge of the Salisbury Plain, had been built during the war. Untold thousands of the Empire's soldiers had passed through its training ranges and parade grounds, its lecture halls, barracks, hospital, cinema and YMCA recreation huts, on their way to the front.

So many of them never returned, of course, to see Hurdcott as it was in those first delicious months of peace, when men were getting ready to go home. In early 1919, its most warlike activities were rival football and hockey matches, boxing tournaments, tugs-o-war, and pillow fights between soldiers sitting on a greasy pole.

Into this congenial company marched the men of No. 4 Squadron. Once settled in, the first thing they did was to photograph Henri and Tim, showing how the smuggling had been done: Digger standing next to Tim with the oat bag; Henri crouching inside the sack; Tim with the sack and raincoat over his shoulder, slouch hat jaunty on his head and pipe clenched between his teeth. Just as the men had seen him on the *Lorina*.

The second thing the squadron did was to open a fund to buy Digger a proper uniform – one made by a military tailor in London. Donations came from the airmen, from the officers and sergeants, and even from the girls in the canteen. In the first week, the fund collected seventeen pounds, thirteen shillings – a good sum for those days! The figures were written down in Tim's notebook, starting from the day they left France. The first entries, however, were in a hand other than Tim's . . .

For suddenly Timothy Tovell had other, more dreadful and pressing business of his own to deal with.

Shortly after the squadron arrived at Hurdcott, mail arrived from Australia. It had been chasing them all across Europe, and it was an eager mob of men who collected their letters, newspapers and parcels from loved ones so far away.

With Digger off making friends with the canteen girls, the Tovell brothers received the Jandowae post and began walking back to barracks. They turned the envelopes over, savouring the moment when they'd open them and exchange all the news from home.

Until Tim came to a letter, postmarked early February. It seemed to freeze in his hand. And then to burn. Something about Gert's writing alarmed him. At once the fears for his family, which Tim had sensed in his dark dream, came flooding back. And overwhelmed him. And turned into terrible certainties.

He handed the letter to Ted.

'You read this. I already know what's in it.'

They walked on until they found a quiet place, and Ted opened the letter. It was true. Tim's nightmare had been realised.

On Friday, 31 January – the very day he'd written to say he was bringing Henri home – his own son, young Timmy, had died of infantile paralysis. Polio. He was only three-and-a-half years old.

One more in the family will not matter, Tim had written. Well, there wouldn't be one more now. There'd be the same number of places at table. But one of them would be different . . .

'I'm going to take Digger home with us,' Tim vowed very softly. 'I don't care how . . .' And then, as his heart went out to his wife, he cried, 'If only I'd been there . . . if only I'd been with her . . .'

Tovell's grief broke down his barriers of reserve. With his brother to comfort him, he wept aloud. And the tragedy of Timmy's death entered the family memory.

January had been hot and sultry at Jandowae, as always, with sudden storms breaking across the black soil plains, turning the roads into quagmires. For Gert, such humid weather always brought wishful thoughts of gentle England. Her friends, Mr and Mrs Lee, had sold their farm. Gert and the children moved back into town, which in summer swarmed with flies and nasty, biting insects.

Besides, the wet brought illness, so that 1919 became known as the plague year. The Spanish influenza epidemic arrived. Gert stayed up, night after night, making pots of beef tea for the sick. Even so, adults and children still died, as other diseases appeared: measles, scarlet fever, meningitis . . .

And then young Timmy fell ill. It seemed just another fever at first, with a headache and running temperature. But he soon got much worse. Soon he could hardly breathe, and he became delirious crying, 'Mummy . . . ! Mummy . . . !'

Mrs Behm, the police sergeant's wife, came to visit. One look at the child and she said, 'Your kiddie's very sick, Mrs Tovell. You've got to get him to a doctor, real quick.'

'There *is* no doctor at Jandowae! The nearest one's at Dalby . . .'

'That's right. And the next train's not due till tomorrow.'

'What will I *do?*' cried Gert in her anguish.

'There's only one thing,' said Mrs Behm. 'My husband, Charley, will get a constable to harness the buggy and drive you.'

'But it's thirty miles!'

'Quicker than waiting for the train. It could be too late.'

Shortly afterwards a young policeman drove to the house, the buggy hood pulled up against the drizzling rain. Gert was waiting, with Timmy wrapped in a blanket. Young Nancy was by her side, weeping at having to stay with Mrs Behm and her family.

'I want to come, too, Mummy . . .'

'Hush, dear.' Striving to stay calm. 'We have to go a long way for the doctor to make Timmy better . . .'

Gert climbed in and, holding the sick boy in her arms, they set off down the boggy road that led through town and across the Jimbour Plain to Dalby.

'Can't we go any faster!' pleaded Gert, as the child whimpered.

'I daren't, missus,' said the young constable. 'I can't tire the horse too much, or risk overturning in the mud.'

It was a long way, jolting through the scrubby bush and onto the open plain. The light rain stung their faces, and their clothes were spattered with slush thrown up by the horse's hooves. For two hours they drove, Gertie rocking her son and singing to him as the little boy began to pant and struggle.

'Oh, hurry! Hurry!'

'I'll do the best I can for you.'

The horse strained and heaved through the mud, his flanks sweating and nostrils streaming, until the big homestead of Jimbour came into view, and they drove in the gate.

'We need a fresh horse. They'll help us here.'

Quickly the rouseabouts put another horse between the shafts.

'I'll return him on the way back,' the constable called as they left, the buggy rollicking down the hill past the outbuildings.

'Gee up there!'

Flicking his whip. And, with renewed urgency, they turned back onto the road for Dalby.

For mile after agonising mile they went, Gertie trying to control her panic.

Hush-a-bye, hush-a-bye . . .

But unable to, as she saw Timmy undeniably getting worse. He began to choke, his head shaking and foam dribbling from his mouth.

Oh God, oh God, oh merciful God!

Gertie wrapped the boy tighter, weeping and rocking and calling on the Almighty. But Timmy seemed to collapse utterly, twitching, and gurgling for air. And, to her horror, Gertie saw his skin – so fair and young – begin to darken: his lips turned blue, and the grey pallor of death was already around his eyes.

'Oh! Please! Can't we go any faster!'

For the outlying houses of Dalby were taking shape through the afternoon drizzle.

The whip cracked and the horse flew.

Quickly, quickly, past the shops and the church and the stock and station agents. Turn up the street to the hospital, where there'll be *someone* to save him. It's not too late . . .

Except, Gertie realised when they stopped, it *was* too late. She looked at her boy, wrapped in the bundle at her breast. His face was dark. And still. She knew his soul had already flown somewhere out there on the vast plain.

Suffer the children to come unto me . . . But why Timmy, God?

'I'm sorry, Mrs Tovell,' said the doctor when they'd carried Timmy inside. 'This form of infantile paralysis is uncommon. But when it occurs, there's little we can do.'

She didn't go back in the buggy, but returned next day with the undertaker by motor, her son in his coffin lined with lace. And there, at Jandowae, Gertie buried him in the cemetery. Emily was with her. Charley Behm and his family. Friends from everywhere. Young Nancy's life became even more precious.

But for Gertrude Tovell, the grief within was a gulf that seemed unbridgeable. Only one person could help her cross it, and he was on the other side of the world.

Oh Tim, my darling, when are you coming home to us . . . ?

After his first outpouring of despair over the letter, Tim returned to the barracks with Ted and, when the time came, told Henri what had happened.

'Oh, Tim,' said the boy, throwing his arms around him. 'I'm so sorry. I know what it is like . . . And I was looking so forward to seeing your Timmy . . .'

'God has His reasons,' answered Tovell, trying to make sense of things. 'We don't always know what they are. I can only think that, when God took Timmy, He sent you for us to look after instead . . .'

That evening, Tim sat down to write to his wife: to share her grief, to reassure her of his love, and to offer what comfort he could. And a little while later he sent some words they both had known in England, which he thought would suit their son's headstone:

WHO PLUCKED THIS FLOWER?

THE MASTER.

THE GARDENER HELD HIS PEACE.

Tim also wrote verse in his notebook, trying to express sorrow for his son and commitment to the orphan who'd come into his care. Most of the airmen were barely half his age. However sympathetic, they could know nothing of a father's mourning! They'd seen death often enough in the war. If anything, it had taught them that life must go on. Every moment was valuable. But Tim wanted only to go home – at once – and nowhere else. He had no other interest.

His brother urged differently.

'We can't get back any quicker,' Ted reminded him. 'I know what you're going through . . . but we've got Henri to think of now. He won't replace Timmy in your heart – no one could – but he'll help to fill the gap. We've got two weeks leave, Tim. Why don't you come to London with us, and get Digger his new uniform?'

'You go. I'll stay here.'

'Henri won't do anything without you.'

'Ah . . .'

'It will help to take you out of yourself. And we *must* visit the family . . . our mother . . . Gertie's people . . . They'll want to see you . . .'

'Please, Tim!' cried Digger. 'There's so much to show me!'

So, with a heavy spirit, he agreed. They collected the money from Henri's fund and took it with them when the squadron left next Monday morning, 17 March, for the train that would carry them to London . . .

Now, in June, for the Tovell brothers and Digger sitting in a Perth teashop, such griefs seemed at once far away – and ever-present. So much had occurred since Mons and Hurdcott, it felt like another life. But the blind, disabled soldier outside with his begging tin had reawakened their pain. It might have happened yesterday.

And yet, as they sat remembering over stewed tea and stale strawberry cake, there came also the knowledge that they were on their way to the one person who would comfort them, and be comforted. Gertie. A new Maman, with a new son, so soon after losing her own.

'Mum.'

Henri tried the sound of it – to feel the word in his mouth again. It wasn't much more than a whisper. But it was enough to stir Tim from his reverie, and bring his thoughts back to business.

'We'd better get moving,' he said at last. 'There's a lot to be done. We've got to get Digger some new civvy pants and a jacket . . .'

'And we've got to think of a plan to get him back on board the *Kaisar-i-Hind*,' added Ted. 'We can't risk any more scares.'

A waitress brought the bill. While they were counting out change, Ted looked up and saw a boy staring in the window at the same pink cake which had so attracted Henri.

'I say,' he remarked. 'Isn't that young Jack Ryan . . . the son of the Queensland Premier, who came out with us on the ship . . . ?'

The others lifted their heads.

'Looks like it,' said Tim.

As if to confirm his words, Tom and Lily Ryan came past the window. After a few short, no-nonsense words with the boy, they hurried him away.

'Funny,' remarked Tim. 'You could have mistaken him for Young Digger, out there in the street.'

'No one could make that mistake!' Henri was indignant. 'I'm older than Jack Ryan. And I wear a uniform, not a serge suit.'

'You're much the same height,' Tim said. 'Much the same build. Put you in the same clothes, and you might almost . . .'

'. . . have the makings of an idea!' Ted finished the sentence.

The brothers looked at each other.

'What do you think?'

Pondering.

'It's possible . . . with a bit of luck . . .'

'What idea?' cried Henri. 'What are we going to do?'

'Another adventure, Digger. What are you like at play-acting?'

'I can play anything you want, *mes amis.*'

And he could, too. It was how the war orphan had survived.

With a laugh and another tip to the ex-serviceman sitting outside with his tin, the brothers and Henri left the teashop and walked down Hay Street to the stores. Their steps were light, for they had a renewed sense of purpose. Somewhere they would find a grey serge suit and a cap that would fit Young Digger – just like the one Jack Ryan wore.

The afternoon sun warmed them, and their thoughts went winging back. They were reminded again of London, and the time they'd bought Digger his miniature uniform . . .

Despite his heartache and misgivings after Timmy's death, Tim actually enjoyed the two weeks with Ted and Henri in London. It was wonderful – all except for the day Tim spent at Princes Risborough. There, Tim and his mother sat above the butcher's shop. He grieved with Gert's family, finding comfort in their tears. Tim found solace, too, in St Mary's church, where he and Gert had married, and he said a prayer for their son.

In London, though, Tim's laughter returned as he and Ted showed Henri the pleasures of the metropolis, now that the lights of peace were being turned on again. They saw Buckingham Palace and went to Westminster Abbey. They explored the Tower of London, where the Yeomen complimented Digger on his uniform.

'Messieurs!' cried Henri, in his most Frenchified manner. 'This is nothing. This is made from greatcoats. Wait till you see me next. I'll be wearing a *proper* Aussie uniform!'

Almost the first thing they did was go to the Australian military tailor Captain Jones had recommended in Horseferry Road, and have Henri measured. They ordered a tunic, two pairs of breeches and slacks, gloves, a slouch hat, leather leggings, puttees, and regulation tan leather boots. No more sheepskin for Young Digger Tovell! He was one of Tim's family now. There was also enough money to buy him some new underclothes and a 'British Warm' overcoat.

'Oh Tim! I'll be as smart as the Prince of Wales!' Digger sighed.

No prince of the blood could have looked prouder when Henri paraded himself in his new finery: a perfect miniature specimen of an Australian soldier. On his left arm he wore the AFC colour patch. On his right sleeve were the inverted chevrons worn by soldiers who had served from 1914. And he had a gold wound stripe, to show that this Young Digger had done valiant service.

When all was ready, Digger had his photograph taken wearing his new uniform. Tim, still grieving for his own son, sent it home to Gertie as a postcard. And on the back he wrote a little about this newest family member:

> 'Here is Digger as he appears in England, it cost the Squadron £15 for his outfit and he looks some boy. He is an intelligent little fellow and can tell many tales of the hardships of war. I

am in charge of him and have to act as Father. What a record for a child so young. He says his age is eleven, but he is so small and looks about nine. He has been on service since September 1914. The Royal Artillery rescued him in the retreat from Mons, and he has been with all sorts of troops since, but says The Aussies will do him for a quiet life.'

Quiet? On Friday, 28 March, Queen Marie of Romania visited the YMCA hostel in the Aldwych Theatre, where Digger and the Tovells were staying. As Her Majesty entered, Henri was honoured to step forward and present her with a bouquet of flowers. After which he saluted, as Tim recalled, 'like a real veteran.'

Queen Marie was much impressed, and asked about the little soldier. Tim briefly explained.

'What a wonderful story,' murmured the Queen. 'I wish I had time to stay to hear the whole of it.'

As Tim afterwards told Gertie, 'I think she meant it.'

So that when they boarded the train for Fovant, Henri was fizzing with elation and a rather dangerous sense of self-importance.

'Look at me!' he boasted to his fellow passengers. 'I'm the most famous mascot in the world! I've been presented to a queen!'

'It's time you came down to earth, young fellow,' said Tim Tovell. 'Time you lost some of that pride.'

But his admonition went unheeded. For when Major Ellis saw Digger in his new uniform at Hurdcott, he promoted him to Acting Corporal.

That evening, the little Corporal strutted up to Tim and announced that, as he (Henri) was the NCO now, he'd shortly be issuing orders to *him!*

Tim Tovell, however, with Major Ellis's written authority from Cologne still safely in his pocket, and THE DINKUM OIL still nestling in his kit bag, had rather different ideas.

13: The Dinkum Oil

Digger's high opinion of himself kept inflating like a barrage balloon after No. 4 Squadron returned to Hurdcott.

Following his presentation to Queen Marie, a few newspaper paragraphs appeared about the little mascot – which Acting Corporal Henri naturally showed to everyone.

'Look at this! It's all about *me!* I said I was famous!'

'And so you are, Young Digger,' said his friend Lieutenant Johnson. 'I'll never forget you.'

Norman Johnson was leaving the squadron. So were several other officers, taking advantage of retraining schemes to help servicemen settle back to civilian life. All of them smiled with fond remembrance when they saw Digger's name.

But Tim found such publicity a worry: not just for its effect on the boy, but for what it might mean for their future plans.

'It's the last thing we want,' he said to his brother. 'This show's not over yet. We've got to get Digger aboard ship for Australia.'

'We can't use the sack again,' observed Ted. 'The customs police will be wise to that.'

'Exactly! And the more there's talk about the boy, the more they'll be looking out for any other trick.'

They tried to stop Digger's boasting, but it seemed a waste of time. Henri's conceit was in full flight. While it was bound to end with a crash, for the moment he refused to listen.

'You're always telling me what to do, Mr Tim! But *I* was the one smuggled in the oat sack. Not *you!*'

Hurdcott Camp was much larger than Bickendorf, and it was impossible for Tovell to constantly supervise the boy. Henri was always off somewhere: charming the canteen girls who gave him sweets and chocolates, or flattering the soldiers, who fed his vanity!

So it was, one afternoon, that Digger was discovered at the two-up school which flourished in a field opposite the camp. He stood in the 'ring', surrounded by dozens of shouting soldiers.

'Place your bets!' as the 'spinner' got ready to toss two pennies, betting on himself that he'd throw a pair of heads.

'Tails! Pair a tails!' cried the mob, betting against him on the side.

'Hey, Digger!' yelled an airman to the mascot, all flushed and heady himself. 'What will it be? Heads or tails?'

'Heads this time, monsieur!' shouted Henri.

There was much laughter as the last bets were placed.

'He's tinny, this young coot. Gets it right almost every time!'

The ring fell silent.

'Come in spinner!' called the 'boxer' in charge of the game.

All eyes watched as the spinner placed the pennies on a small piece of board they called the 'kip'. He tossed them in the air, the copper coins (with the King's head all polished up) glinting in the sunlight. They fell to the ground.

'Heads a tail!' as all eyes followed. 'No throw! Toss 'em again!'

Once more the pennies dazzled as they spun and fell to earth.

'He's headed 'em! Pair a heads!'

'I told ya! The kid's tinny! Here, youngster . . . !'

As the crowd roared approval, a gold sovereign was tossed across. Digger caught it, and put it in his pocket.

'This is a good game, *mes amis!* Play it again!'

When suddenly Tim Tovell appeared.

'Digger! Come away from here. This instant!'

But the boy pretended neither to see nor hear him.

Tovell had been in the barracks writing home, when an airman approached.

'Tim, it's not right the way that boy of yours is carrying on.'

'What do you mean?'

'Do you know that Digger is over at the swy school?'

'What!'

'It's disgraceful, Tim. You should keep better control of him.'

Tovell put his letter aside, and went to find Digger in the middle of the two-up game.

'Digger! Come away from here. This instant!'

But the boy ignored him.

'Digger! I've told you . . .'

'Leave the kid alone!' The burly man, to whom Henri had brought much good luck, intervened. 'He's doing all right . . .'

'I'm responsible for the boy. This is no place for him.'

'You're not his nanny. Buzz off yourself.'

'Yeah!' came a chorus of swy players. 'Go on! Scram!'

'It's not right!'

'You want to make something of it . . . ?' The man clenched his fist.

The mood became threatening. Tim saw Henri shrink into the mob, hiding himself among coats and legs. It was no place, either, for empty heroics.

Tovell turned on his heel, and went to the orderly office to see Major Ellis.

'What's the problem?' asked his OC.

'It's Digger, sir. He's grown altogether too big for his new khaki britches. He's giving cheek and taking no notice of anything I say . . .'

'You have the authority I gave you in Cologne.'

'Yes, sir. And everyone disregards it, including the boy himself. He's over at the two-up school now, and refuses to leave.'

'You've been there? You've asked him?'

'Yes, Major Ellis, I have.'

'And he ignored you?'

'Correct, sir. The atmosphere became ugly. Rather than make more trouble, I thought it best to come to you, as you asked.'

'Quite right. We can't have this. I'll not have my authority flouted, nor yours.' Ellis then called to the duty NCO. 'Sergeant!'

'Sir?'

'I want you to take a squad of four men to the two-up school. You know where that is?'

'I believe I've heard of it, sir.'

'Bring young Henri back with you. He's to remain in his quarters overnight. The boy will see me here in the morning, to be dealt with.'

'Sir!'

So the guard was despatched across the road, with bayonets fixed. There was no trouble this time. No lip from the gamblers. No hesitation in producing Young Digger, who was led off under armed escort to spend the night confined to barracks, awaiting court martial and his Squadron Commander's displeasure.

'Oh Tim, what is to happen to me?' All white and trembling.

'You'll discover that tomorrow.'

They spent a miserable night. Next morning, Digger ate his breakfast like a condemned man; and at ten o'clock went with Tim and Ted to see Major Ellis. Henri was wearing his new uniform, though just before he entered the room his hat was removed, as was customary for soldiers facing a charge.

Major Ellis and Captain Jones were sitting behind the table, stern of face, as Henri stood to attention before them.

'We're here on very grave business,' Major Ellis said. 'Disobedience is a serious matter for a soldier.'

'But I'm not . . .' came a tiny voice from the prisoner.

'Be quiet, Henri. You'll have your chance to speak later. It's 2nd Air Mechanic Tovell's turn now.'

Briefly, Tim told of Digger's increasing rudeness, ending in his refusal to leave the two-up game.

'Is this true?' asked the OC.

Silence from the dock.

'What do you have to say for yourself, Henri?'

'Nothing.'

Very soft.

'What's that?'

'Nothing.'

'Ahem.' Major Ellis cleared his throat. 'I won't permit any insubordination in 4th Squadron of the Australian Flying Corps. Since the young man has nothing to say – not even sorry – I think we'll have to send him back to France.'

'Oh no, *Majeur!* Please, I beg you . . .' Henri suddenly found his voice. 'Please, Captain Jones . . . Tim! I'm sorry. Truly . . . But don't send me back to France!' He burst into tears. 'Not back . . .'

Major Ellis watched him cry for a few moments, then turned to George Jones.

'Well, Captain, it seems he is sorry after all, for refusing orders from the man in charge of him. What do you think . . . should we give him another chance?'

'Oh, yes! Please, monsieur . . . I'll never do it again!'

Captain Jones thoughtfully stroked his chin, remembering from his own boyhood the gravity shown by adults at such moments.

'Hmmm . . . Perhaps we should give him *one* more chance.'

'Thank you . . .'

'So be it.' Major Ellis was brisk in his decision. 'You won't be sent back. But you'll have to be punished, and your guardian will do it.' Leaning forward he added, 'You'll also lose your stripes and no longer be an Acting Corporal . . . You understand, Henri? This squadron wants a mascot to be proud of – not one who makes us ashamed.'

Thus Digger was led away to the barracks hut. Where Tim produced THE DINKUM OIL from his kit bag and, taking down the boy's britches, laid him across his knee.

'How many strokes am I to give him?' he asked the crowd who'd gathered to watch.

'Six,' they replied. 'And not one stripe more.'

Henri began to howl as THE DINKUM OIL laid its first welt on his backside.

'It hurts!'

'It's meant to.'

Some of the audience began to get upset as well – and they counted each stroke until all six had been delivered and Henri, pulling up his pants, ran to his bed bawling his eyes out.

'It hurt me as much as it hurt you,' Tovell said.

'No it didn't!'

But in truth, Tim knew if he'd gone past those six whacks, the airmen might have taken THE DINKUM OIL to him! As it was, he felt miserable, having to beat the boy for whom he cared so deeply – however much he believed it was for Digger's own good. And it was comforting when an airman came along with an offer of help.

'It's not fair, Tim. Digger gets into trouble at the swy school, but the poor little feller has nothing else to do. There are no other kiddies to play with. He's got no toys . . .'

'I know that. How do you think *I* feel?'

'Well . . . they've made up our back pay, and what with the school winnings we blokes clubbed together and . . . Here's some money for you to buy a few toys . . . Anything you think is good for him like . . .'

With Digger's two-up tips, extra money in the squadron fund, and cash given by the hut, Tim had almost twelve pounds when he applied to the camp commandant's office for a leave pass.

'What's this?' enquired the duty sergeant. 'Requesting leave to go into Salisbury to buy *toys?* I've come across some tall stories in my time, but this beats them all! What do you make of it, sir?'

He passed the application across to the leave officer, who read it with a closed expression. Then he looked up and saw Tovell.

'Just a moment,' he said. 'Are you the chap looking after the little French boy at Hurdcott?'

'Yes, sir.'

'I've heard of you from some of your Australian officers. Extraordinary story! Yes, I think we can grant you leave in the circumstances. How much do you want?'

'Until midnight, sir.'

'All right. Issue the pass, will you Sergeant.' And before turning back to his paperwork and the next tall story, the officer smiled thinly and said, 'Good luck, soldier.'

Tim caught the lunchtime train into Salisbury with Digger – a more amenable little boy after his taste of THE DINKUM OIL, but still greatly excited at buying whatever toys he wanted. Henri couldn't remember having any of his own . . .

They had such an afternoon! After the tears of yesterday, it was all treats and sunshine. They visited every toyshop twice, before Henri decided on a set of lead soldiers, an airgun and a box of pellets, a wind-up tin cannon, and some toy trucks.

'We've enough money left for one more thing.' Tim said. 'What will it be?'

'Oh, that's really hard . . . let me think . . .'

They sat eating iced buns, as Henri made up his mind. He decided on a mouth organ. ('Because then I can play music for Gertie,' though the ears of many an airman came to regret it.)

A soldier told Tim the last train returned to Fovant at half past eight. There was plenty of time to buy the mouth organ, stroll along the river, visit the lovely cathedral, and eat sherbet in a warm corner of the close. After which they carried their parcels to the railway station to catch the last train back to camp.

Trouble was, the last train had already gone. There wouldn't be another till morning.

'The soldier was wrong!' exclaimed Digger, 'and we've got to be back at Hurdcott by midnight! What will we do, Tim?'

'We'll have to walk.'

'But it's eight miles!'

'Yes. And the quicker we start, the sooner we'll get there.'

They set off: through the old town and over the bridge, until they were in the open countryside just as night was falling, heading down the road to Wilton and Fovant.

'It's cold and dark,' Henri complained.

'The walk will warm you up, and it's a clear evening . . .'

They kept walking. One mile became two. And then it became three. The moon rose, spilling its silver light across the landscape, and a night bird could be heard calling in the distance.

'Tim . . .'

'What is it?'

'My leg's hurting again.'

'Ah. The old wound. Can you still walk on it?'

'For a little bit.'

'Good boy. See how far you can go. I'll carry the parcels . . .'

They went a little further, until they came to an intersection with a high stone wall in front of them.

'That's the park of Wilton House,' Tim remarked. 'We're close to halfway home already.'

They rested a few minutes. But when they moved off, Tim saw that Digger was limping badly. He couldn't go on like that. Tim would have to carry him. He let Henri climb onto his shoulders. With Digger perched on high with the toys, Tovell continued the weary trudge back to camp.

I feel like Saint Christopher carrying the Christ Child, he thought to himself.

And indeed, as he passed by the great gate of Wilton House and through the sleeping town, Tim's back injury began to hurt him. Digger became heavier – like the Child bearing the sins of world, in Saint Christopher's dream.

Tovell didn't know about the sins of the world. But as he plodded the last painful miles, and turned into Hurdcott just before midnight, he could feel every one of the stripes he'd given Digger with THE DINKUM OIL, over and over again.

The toys were a huge success. With everybody. Digger set up his army of lead soldiers on a table and, with the airmen taking opposing sides, re-fought many battles from the Great War. The Somme. Passchendaele. And Captain Jones, who'd been at Gallipoli, showed Digger how the Anzacs scaled the ridges (which he made out of clay), and held on against the Turks for eight gallant months in 1915.

The toy artillery on the barracks floor defended Ypres again.

'Boom!' cried Henri, as a cannon tumbled over. 'See! That's when my good friend and his crew were killed. I know. I was there!'

And when it wasn't all pretend, they went to the rifle range where the airmen showed him how to use his airgun properly.

Never did a boy have so many willing experts to advise him in weaponry . . . or in self-defence, when they tied on Henri's first pair of boxing gloves and he began lessons in the noble art, with Ted as his 'second'.

The only game Digger didn't play was back at the two-up school. However painful THE DINKUM OIL, he'd learnt that lesson. And, strange as it seemed to others, the fact that Tim had chastised Henri only strengthened the bond between them. The two went everywhere together, once again.

None of the airmen doubted that Henri would come home to Australia with them. As the time for their departure grew closer, the only matter to be resolved was how exactly it might be managed.

Then came word that the men would definitely sail on the *Kaisar-i-Hind*, leaving Southampton in early May. There was much excitement – even more so when the squadron was told there'd be seven days pre-embarkation leave, starting on 23 April.

Digger asked Tim about the arrangements. Would they stay at the Aldwych again? Did any more queens want bouquets presented?

'I don't know, son. We'll have to ask.'

But Ted arrived with a message that Major Ellis wanted to see all three of them in his office. At once.

'Tim! He's not going to have me thrashed again?'

'It depends. Have you been naughty? Have you been over to the swy game?'

'No! I promise. I've been as good as anything!'

They found Major Ellis trying to look very strict. And when he asked Henri if he'd been behaving himself, the boy burst out, '*Oui!* I've been an angel. Ask Tim!'

'Is this true?'

'Not *quite* an angel, sir, but good enough.'

'Hmmm. So I've heard. However . . .' and Les Ellis paused for effect, 'I have to advise that there'll be no pre-embarkation leave for *you*, Young Digger. Or any of you. Not immediately.'

'No leave? Oh, monsieur, please, we're going to London!'

'Yes. You'll be going to London. But not on leave.' Major Ellis grinned broadly. 'You see, I've picked a squad of twenty-five men and two sergeants to march with other Australian troops in the Anzac Day parade on April 25th. And since I've heard such excellent reports of you lately, I thought it only right our mascot and his two guardians should march with 4th Squadron.'

'Oh *Majeur!* Thank you!'

'And your stripes have been restored, Henri. You're an Acting Corporal again.'

The boy almost climbed over the desk and hugged his OC.

'Major Ellis, it will be an honour,' said all three together.

'Well, you've a lot of work to do. The Anzac Day salutes will be taken by the King and the the Prince of Wales. I want every man and his equipment to bring the greatest possible credit to 4th Squadron. Understand?'

'Yes, sir!'

'And afterwards you can take your leave. We return to Hurdcott on May Day.'

So it took place. But the airmen of No. 4 Squadron brought more attention to themselves than anyone expected.

After lunch on Anzac Day, the marching troops assembled, as immaculately turned out as Henri's toy soldiers. The London streets were thronged with people waving flags and cheering. The bands began to play. The men shouldered their weapons with bayonets gleaming. And off they moved, among them Young Digger Tovell stepping out like a Field Marshal, carrying a swagger stick, with the Mons ribbon on his breast and his heart ready to burst.

Many Australian airmen not in the march were already enjoying leave in London. They'd spent the morning boozily celebrating Anzac Day in the pubs, when word got around that interested pilots could borrow planes from nearby aerodromes and fly over the city during the parade. Many did so – among them the air ace Captain Harry Cobby, who'd flown with No. 4 Squadron in France.

By half past two, there were nearly sixty aeroplanes in the sky, rolling and looping all over the place like a swarm of drunken bees, jostling to be the first to pass the Prince of Wales taking the salute near Australia House in The Strand.

When suddenly, Cobby dived low in his Sopwith Camel and began flying along The Strand itself, just above the heads of the startled crowd. He was followed by another pilot in a Sopwith Pup. And once down they had to stay down, because overhead wires prevented them from zooming up again until they'd flown three quarters of a mile through the streets to Trafalgar Square.

'It was probably the most foolish thing I have ever done,' Cobby admitted later. It was lucky the Pup was behind him. Had it been in front, the faster Camel would have soon run him down. 'I would not have been able to avoid him, and with the roads packed like sardines with onlookers, the casualties would have been terrible.'

Acting Corporal Henri, watching these aerobatics with amazement, didn't think them the least bit foolish.

'Oh Tim, what a day!' he whispered, as he snuggled down to sleep at the Aldwych.

They'd marched past the Prince of Wales. They'd gone by Buckingham Palace and saluted King George himself. They'd had their studio photographs taken, these warriors so bold and proud. And afterwards they'd eaten such a *grand* dinner. Tomorrow they were going to Princes Risborough to say goodbye, for the last time, to Tim and Ted's old mother.

'What a day!' murmured the boy again. 'And what an *aviateur* is that Captain Cobby. I'm going to be a pilot with the Aussies, just like him, when I get home and grow to be a man.'

14: Sporting Goods

It was raining when the airmen marched out of Hurdcott on the morning of 6 May, bound for the train to Southampton and the ship that would take them home.

Cold. And wet. But, as Major Ellis noted in No. 4 Squadron's war diary, it would take more than that to dampen their spirits! At this journey's end they'd be under Australian skies, and feel an Australian sun on their skin. Thus they had that same sense of elation as when they'd marched in, two months before, bearing their mascot in triumph.

Perhaps not *quite* the same. This time Digger wasn't with them. Nor were the Tovell brothers. Tim and Ted were travelling with the baggage handlers. As for Henri, it was wiser not to ask!

These arrangements had been decided only the previous day.

Time was getting on, but the brothers hadn't been able to come up with any feasible plan to smuggle Digger on board the *Kaisar-i-Hind*. There was a problem with every suggestion.

'We can't put him in a kit bag. He's too big,' said Tim.

'Could we hide him under a greatcoat and carry him aboard?' pondered Ted.

'Too risky.'

'I keep thinking of the sack. It's our best idea – and it works!'

'And the customs men know all about it.'

'We have to think of *something* before tomorrow . . .'

At this uncertain point, Major Ellis asked to see Tim. Again, alone.

'It's about the boy,' Les Ellis began, as he had at Le Havre.

'Yes, sir?'

'As you know, we leave in the morning for the ship.'

'At ten o'clock. Yes.'

'I'm wondering, Tovell, if anything has changed in your intentions towards Henri . . .?'

'No, Major Ellis. I'm of the same mind.'

'Ah. Well, I must tell you that the port authorities have been told to keep a particular eye open for stowaways.'

'We thought that might be the case, sir.'

'Quite right, of course. There's been a lot of chatter in the press, and I couldn't allow any breach of the emigration laws.'

'Indeed not, sir!'

'So the question arises . . . er . . . have you made any arrangements yet about Henri?'

'No, Major Ellis, we haven't. The situation has presented us with considerable difficulties . . .'

'Yes. I can imagine.'

There was a pause as the two men looked steadily at each other. Then Ellis relaxed, walked around his desk and sat on the edge with folded arms, as Tim waited for the next move.

'See here, Tovell, we've a few difficulties of our own with the transport tomorrow. There's a lot of extra baggage to pack . . . sports material, shipboard entertainment and so on . . . The Equipment Officer, Lieutenant Ellison, needs more men to help.'

'Yes, I can understand there'd be much work to do.'

'So I'm detailing you and your brother to assist.'

'Certainly, sir.'

As a smile began to creep across Tim's face.

'In fact, you'd better cut along and report to him now. He'll show you what's there.'

'Thank you, sir.'

Les Ellis rose from the desk, and returned the salute. But as Tim was leaving, he spoke again.

'You remember I told you at Le Havre that, should the authorities discover anything amiss, I can have no knowledge of it whatsoever. That is still the position, you realise?'

'Major Ellis, nothing has changed. I understand perfectly.'

The chances of Henri getting safely aboard the *Kaisar-i-Hind* had been widely discussed and many wagers placed – and not just at the swy school. In the officers' mess, the previous evening, Major Ellis and his senior staff were going over arrangements for the trip, when the subject of the squadron's mascot arose.

'It's amazing he's managed to get this far,' observed Lieutenant Jo Ellison, the Equipment Officer. 'But I don't think he'll get any further. English customs officers are much sharper than French *gendarmes* . . .'

'Oh? The men got Henri *off* the ship at Southampton,' reminded Captain George Jones. 'Why couldn't they get him back on again?'

'There'll be military police everywhere,' said Jo Ellison. 'There's a big farewell ceremony planned. Generals Glasgow and Gellibrand – and the Surgeon-General – are sailing with us . . . as well as the Premier of Queensland and his family.'

'I imagine the authorities will be more concerned to keep them happy than worry about us,' remarked Major Ellis.

'I wouldn't pin much hope on that, sir,' replied Lieutenant Ellison. 'The police have heard about Henri and will know what to look for.'

'Tovell wouldn't try the sack again! He's not foolish.'

'What, then?'

'Who can tell,' said Captain Jones. 'But I know one thing: Tovell is an inventive man. He cares for the little fellow deeply . . . even more, since the death of his own son.'

'True,' agreed Jo Ellison. 'It's been very sad for him and his brother. But I don't think they'll outwit the authorities this time. I'd be prepared to stake money on it.'

'Really?' responded Les Ellis. 'If you're serious, I'd wager a few pounds that they *will*.'

'I'd accept that,' said a sporting Jo Ellison.

'I'd go a fiver . . .' offered George Jones.

Other officers joined them. Eventually, a twenty-five pound stake was riding on whether the men would successfully smuggle Henri aboard the *Kaisar-i-Hind*. It was agreed the bet would be won if he reached a cabin without being detected. And when asked what would happen if Digger were found afterwards, Major Ellis gallantly replied, 'It depends where it occurs. But, gentlemen, if our mascot is discovered as a stowaway at sea, I'll happily meet any additional expenses.'

That was settled. But just as they were leaving, Major Ellis called to his Equipment Officer. 'One more thing, Lieutenant. We've a lot of extra luggage to take with us, and I know you're short-handed. I propose the Tovell brothers should assist you . . .'

There was a round of laughter.

'Thank you, sir,' said Jo Ellison. 'I'd welcome it.'

So, next afternoon, Tim and Ted reported to him and were shown into a back storeroom. There were many last-minute things to be packed and labelled. Sporting gear. Theatrical costumes. Books and magazines. Indoor games.

'We'll be wanting most of this on the voyage,' Ellison said. 'It will be loaded last. You might make yourselves useful here . . .'

He left them alone. The brothers looked around until they spied some large wicker baskets, used by wartime concert parties. Inside one basket they found several pierrot costumes –

white, baggy clown suits, with frills and pompoms.

'This might do,' said Tim. 'We could hide Digger under the fancy dress. There's room for him to stretch . . . plenty of air . . . the lid opens easily . . .'

'And the basket won't be put in the hold.'

'Exactly.'

They spent the rest of the afternoon sorting and labelling, and getting the basket ready: putting in more costumes for padding, and packing boxing gloves and football jumpers on top. On the handle they tied a label, WANTED FOR VOYAGE, though they couldn't say *where* it would be wanted. Or by whom.

But as they were leaving the stores, Captain Jones passed and said casually that any additional cargo could be sent to his cabin.

'Yes, sir. Thank you, sir.' What a brick he was!

After breakfast next morning, Tim told Henri what he planned. He'd wisely not said anything earlier, in case the boy gave the game way. And Digger was enthusiastic about the idea.

'In a basket? With dress-up clothes and sporting goods? Oh! That will be good fun.'

'You'll have to keep very quiet again. There's more room than the sack, but you'll be in the basket for much longer.'

'You can trust *me!*'

'I know you'll do your best, son.'

Lieutenant Ellison was already supervising the loading when they arrived at the stores. Everyone was so busy that nobody took much notice as they entered the back room. Quickly the basket was opened. The loose clothing was removed and, in a happy thought, Tim tossed one of the costumes to Henri to wear over his uniform.

'It will help to disguise you.'

The boy slipped into the pierrot suit and, gurgling with delight, was lifted into the basket. Ted dropped in fruit and a water-bottle – and a large jar for emergencies! Tim threw in the oat sack.

'You never know . . . it might come in useful again.'

Shouts came from Lieutenant Ellison outside.

'We're ready for the last of the gear. Bring it out!'

'At once, sir!'

Henri was covered with the costumes and sports gear. The lid was closed. Tim wrote CAPTAIN JONES on the label in crayon, whispering as he did so, 'Good boy. This is our next big adventure!'

The remaining boxes and baskets were carried out and loaded into the waiting lorries. Digger's was last of all.

'Strike, Tim! This is heavy enough,' said one of the handlers. 'What have you got in here?'

'Sporting goods. For the ship. Captain Jones wants us all to be kept active and amused.'

'Does he, now? Well, I plan to spend the whole six weeks snoozing in the sun on the afterdeck.'

The Tovell brothers travelled with the lorry, past the other airmen lining up on the parade ground in the rain, jolting out of Hurdcott and down the mile or so to Fovant railway station. The basket of sporting goods was carefully put to one side. Only after all the other equipment had been stored was it carried into the luggage van.

They followed the same procedure when the train reached Southampton dock some hours later. The basket was stowed in the van until everything else had been unloaded and taken aboard ship.

There was much work for the baggage handlers. No. 2 and No. 3 Squadrons had also travelled from Hurdcott. Men from the four training squadrons were sailing in the *Kaisar-i-Hind* as well, together with some top brass and fifty-seven civilians – including Premier and Mrs Ryan, with their two children.

And were they being farewelled in style! Crowds had gathered on the wharf, despite the weather. Flags were flying. A military band was playing. A dais had been erected, where the Lord Mayor would make a speech. The AIF commander, General Birdwood, was already saying goodbye to these Australians, some of whom he'd known at Anzac, and whose spirit he so greatly admired.

The men who had just arrived from Fovant, however, were still getting aboard. Sorting kit bags. Lining up. Shuffling along to the embarkation officers. Having their names ticked off the boat roll. Parading past the military police and customs officers, with eyes averted, for who could tell what manner of contraband was hidden in their kit? Until, at last, they mounted the gangway.

The authorities weren't interested in the odd bottle of whisky or war souvenir. But the matter of a French boy, who'd been smuggled past their very noses by these airmen, was something else again. They were inspecting the gear being unloaded from the luggage van, with more than usual thoroughness.

'Next!' called the official, as a cabin trunk came out.

'What's in here?'

'Captain Wright's clothing, sir.'

'Give us a look.'

Captain Wright's spare uniforms, civvies, shirts and underwear were exhibited.

'Pack it up again.'

'What a flamin' waste o' time this is, mate.'

'What did you say, soldier?'

'I said we won't get away before Christmastime at this rate.'

'Next!'

A wooden crate was unloaded.

'What's this?'

'I dunno. It says "Equipment Various".'

'Open it up.'

'Bloody hell . . .'

The crate was opened, and the police and customs officials rummaged through a pile of dirty ammunition pouches, webbing, sweaty football shorts and grubby second-hand boots.

'All right. Do it up. Next!'

So it went on through the afternoon. Until Tim Tovell, with Ted watching the sporting goods, took a turn on the wharf to stretch his legs. Where he was approached by Captain Jones . . .

'Ah, Tim. How's it going?'

'It's a slow business, sir.'

'They'll have to get a move on! The Lord Mayor's about to arrive for the speeches, and we leave after that.'

'Yes. I expect the last of the loading will have to hurry up.'

'One hopes so. I'm going aboard myself now,' Jones went on. 'Keep an eye out for me. As soon as I know my cabin number, I'll come on deck and let you know where I want my goods delivered.'

'Certainly, Captain Jones. That's very considerate of you, sir. It will make our task a little easier.'

'Mine, too.'

Ten minutes later, Captain Jones appeared at the stern of the *Kaisar-i-Hind*. Exchanging a brief wave of recognition with Tovell below, he dropped a small bag, weighted with a key, onto the wharf. Inside, was a piece of paper bearing the number '21'.

Tim picked it up, put it in his pocket and returned to the luggage van, where he wrote CABIN 21 on Captain Jones's label.

'Are you all right, Digger?' he murmured.

'*Oui*. But it's very smelly in here,' came a muffled voice.

'It's not for much longer, son.'

Outside, there was a heightened sense of activity. A procession of motor cars, carrying the Lord Mayor and distinguished passengers, drew up at the dais. The band played 'Rule Britannia' and 'God Save The King.' The *Kaisar-i-Hind* blew welcoming blasts on its siren. The misty rain kept falling. And as the Lord Mayor in his robes began speechifying at one end of the ship, the work of completing her loading sped up at the other.

'Next! Hurry along. What's in here?'

'Hockey sticks and soccer nets. Want a game?'

'Don't be cheeky, soldier. Get it aboard. Next! What's this?'

'Major Ellis's personal effects. Do you want to see his toothbrushes?'

'Don't be insolent. Next!'

They were getting towards the last. Tim and Ted picked up the basket.

Carefully carry it out of the van and pass it down. Speak politely to the customs officer.

'What's in here?'

'Sporting goods, sir.'

'What kind of sporting goods?'

'Boxing gloves and football jumpers, I believe. Fancy dress costumes. For Captain Jones. He's organising the social activities on board. Shall I open the basket for your inspection, sir?'

'Get along with you! Blooming theatricals!'

Keep breathing calmly. Carry the basket with Ted across to the cargo sling. Is Captain Jones watching? Yes. Give a signal . . . they'll think it's for the crane driver . . . Good. Take it up smoothly . . . don't hurry yourselves boys, and please, Lord, don't let them drop it . . . Up . . . up . . . nearly there . . . and over the rail. Put it down . . . steady . . . Now, George Jones, where are you . . .? Good man . . . walk across to the goods . . . point out the basket . . . tell the crew to take it to your cabin . . . that's right . . . thank you, Lord, and see us safely to the end.

Tim watched as the men on board carried the basket away. After which he nodded to Ted, and they went to Lieutenant Ellison.

'The last of our squadron's luggage has just gone aboard, sir.'

'All safe and sound?' Ellison asked.

'So far as we can tell, sir. We were wondering . . .'

'. . . if you should make sure everything is stowed away properly? Good idea. Get your kit and go aboard . . .'

'Our pleasure, sir.'

'I'm certain it was.'

The Lord Mayor was finishing his speech as the brothers stepped aboard the *Kaisar-i-Hind*. They wasted no time watching the show, but asked the way to cabin 21. Knocked at the door. And when George Jones answered, they entered and saw the basket in the middle of the room.

Tim handed Captain Jones his key.

'Thank you. I must have dropped it.'

'It's a good thing I picked it up for you, sir.'

George Jones locked the door.

'The goods have arrived. We'd better find out if they're still in one piece.'

The basket lid was opened. The contents were strewn on the floor. And reaching down, Tim pulled out the young pierrot.

'Oh! Tim!' Digger cried. 'Wasn't that fun? And when you asked if they wanted to inspect the basket, I nearly shouted *Non!*'

'It's as well you didn't. They'd *really* have been interested!'

'You'll still have to keep quiet, young fellow,' said Captain Jones. 'We've not left port yet. I have to go and make my farewells. Get changed. Have a stretch. And then, Tim, can you get Henri safely down to the troop deck?'

'I believe so, sir.'

Reaching back into the basket, Tovell pulled out the oat sack. 'I thought it might come in useful again,' he said.

So for a second time Henri was slung over Tim's shoulder in the smuggling sack and carried below. For a second time he heard airmen saying, 'It's bad luck, Tim, you had to leave Digger behind.'

'We did our best, Ted and me.'

'What will become of the kid now?'

'Who can say?'

The sack was lowered to the floor as Tim said, 'Better come and make a screen around me, you fellows.'

For a second time the sack was untied, and Henri heard gasps of astonishment as he emerged among them crying, 'I'm not left behind after all, *mes amis*. Digger is here, all the time!'

There wasn't the same noisy celebration as before, however. As men started to exclaim 'Strike me pink!' and cheer, Tim silenced them.

'Hush! We're not in the clear till the ship's at sea. We've got to hide the boy, before anyone finds him.'

There were few places to secrete Digger on the open troop deck. The men hadn't yet collected their hammocks, and the mess areas were busy with ship stewards who couldn't yet be trusted. Nor was there much time. Outside, they heard applause as the farewell ended. Soon the bigwigs would be aboard, and there'd be officers everywhere. They had to find a hiding place at once.

'There's only one thing,' said Ted. 'Get back into the sack. We'll stack the kit bags around it . . . just as we did on the railway siding that first day at Southampton.'

It was a good idea, and quickly done. Shudders along the ship's hull told them the *Kaisar-i-Hind* was getting ready to depart, as tug boats came alongside. The engines gathered steam. The crowd cheered. The band started playing. And with Ted offering to watch the kit bags, airmen thronged onto the deck to see the ship leave.

The rain had stopped, but clouds were hanging low and a late afternoon mist was rolling in from the sea. On the dais, General Birdwood was saluting, and the Lord Mayor was raising his cocked hat. The last of the passengers came up the gangway.

'There's a Long, Long Trail Awinding', played the band, and 'Keep The Home Fires Burning'. People started to sing and weep and hug each other, their emotions finding expression only in the most basic human actions and the simple words of a popular wartime song.

The ship heaved against the wharf. The siren blew. The gangway was removed, and the ropes holding the *Kaisar-i-Hind* were cast off. Her engines throbbed. Tug boats pulled, as the ship inched into the harbour. The Lord Mayor, waving his hat, led three cheers. People at the rail and on the dockside were shouting and waving.

Now the band played 'Australia Will Be There' as the ship moved further into Southampton Water, and 'God Save The

King' again. The notes carried ever more faintly across the waves, until, at length, they faded altogether.

They were going at last! Dusk fell, and soon the city lights disappeared as the fog grew thicker. Indeed, the *Kaisar-i-Hind* was only at sea for an hour before it dropped anchor in The Solent, to wait for morning and a clear passage.

In the saloons and cabins on the upper decks, officers, wives and distinguished passengers began to organise their social calendars for the voyage, as batmen and maidservants laid out their dress clothes for dinner. All except in the cabin occupied by Major Ellis, where his senior officers had gathered to share a laugh. To toast success. And to settle certain outstanding matters of sporting business.

While below on the troopdecks, soldiers drew their hammocks and recovered treasured possessions from their kit bags. Not the least of which was a small, exuberant orphan boy, barely able to control himself for excitement.

'We did it, Tim! You and me and Ted! We're here together. And now we're *truly* going home to Jandowae!'

15: THE *KAISAR-I-HIND*

The *Kaisar-i-Hind* weighed anchor just after six o'clock in the morning. The sun came out. It was a glorious day. The sea was calm. And after a hearty breakfast of porridge, steak and onions, bread, jam and coffee, airmen tumbled onto the decks to find their sea legs, to unpack some of the sports gear – quoits and medicine balls – or to find a sheltered spot to sunbathe.

Or most of them did. Down on No. 4 Squadron's troop deck, Henri wasn't amused when Tim told him he'd have to stay below for the time being – perhaps for the whole voyage.

'Why?' Digger complained. 'I've been shut in a basket for hours. I had to hide among kit bags. I couldn't sleep properly in the hammock, and nearly fell out twice . . .'

'You'll get used to it.'

'Why can't I go on deck to play?'

'Because you're not supposed to be here. If the captain sees you, he'll put you ashore as a stowaway.'

'Captain Jones knows I'm here.'

'Yes, but he isn't the ship's captain.'

'Why can't the *Majeur* tell the captain of the *Kaisar-i-Hind?* Then everything will be all right.'

'It's not that easy, son. Other people might not be as understanding as Major Ellis. There could be trouble if the big brass find you. That's why you've got to stay out of their way . . .'

'But what will I do all day?'

'You've got the toys we bought, and your mouth organ . . .'

'The Aussies say I drive them mad with my music.'

'Tell them to plug their ears if they don't like it!'

So Henri stayed below. He explored the troop decks, making friends with the other squadrons and the crewmen who kept the ship running. But he slipped quickly out of the way if he saw any of the ship's officers. And when Lieutenant-Colonel Watt, OC Troops, made his regular inspections, Acting Corporal Hemene was always absent.

Weekly prizes were awarded for the best-kept troop deck. No. 4 Squadron, on mess deck 5A, won twice. They took their duties seriously. Even the ship's Troop Officer, Mr Sparkes, reported on 'the scrupulously clean mess utensils' and 'the polish attained on the cutlery' which 'must have entailed a considerable amount of conscientious labour every day.' He didn't know the half of it!

There was always somebody keeping a weather eye open: somebody to mutter a word of warning to Henri if the ship's master,

Captain Palmer, or the First Mate, Mr Smith, were approaching. Somebody to take the blame if the Adjutant complained about 'that infernal mouth organ', or to say he was 'especially hungry', if anyone were to ask why seventeen meals were served to the sixteen men seated at a particular table on deck 5A.

Not that anyone *did* ask. As the days passed, the ship's stewards quietly became as much in the know as the airmen. Henri was able to eat his dinner undisturbed – 'not mutton and rice pudding *again!*' – though ready to hide under the table at a moment's notice. He wasn't even troubled by seasickness. As the *Kaisar-i-Hind* crossed the Bay of Biscay and steamed down the coast of Portugal to Gibraltar, the ocean was as calm as a fish pond.

The sun shone almost every day, and the troopship quickly took on the atmosphere of a holiday liner. The only military activity was half an hour of 'physical jerks' each morning. The rest was all fun and games. Teams were formed for the wheel-barrow, potato-sack and three-legged races. A boxing tournament was organised. Training began for gymnastics displays and tug-o-war contests. Tennis and cricket teams were chosen to play against the sports club at Port Said, where the ship would stop before entering the Suez Canal.

At night there were indoor games, concerts and dancing to the string orchestra and the officers' jazz band. Best of all was No. 3 Squadron's cinema. Men crowded onto the poop deck to watch Charlie Chaplin and the beautiful Lillian Gish. Even Young Digger was allowed to creep up under cover of darkness, with his guardians, to watch the silent pictures.

One thing that didn't please was Lieutenant-Colonel Watt's announcement on the first day of the voyage that, by strict orders of the Australian Government, the *Kaisar-i-Hind* would be a 'dry' ship.

Captain Palmer was all in favour of it. He'd skippered many boozy Australian diggers during the war, and now was quite happy to have them cold sober. But everywhere else, news that the canteens wouldn't serve alcohol was badly received. The officers publicly grimaced, but privately hoped they'd packed enough liquor in their cabin luggage. Below, complaints were long and loud.

'Gawd! What sort of nanny brigade is this? We volunteered to risk life and limb for 'em in the war! And now we're on the way home, they say a man can't have a beer! It makes ya mad!'

Yet there is no calamity that doesn't advantage someone.

As they steamed through the Mediterranean heat, there was a great demand for soft drinks. This gave Henri a splendid money-making opportunity. There was a refund of twopence on empty lemonade and soda bottles. He'd go round the troop decks with the oat sack collecting empties, which Tim cashed at the canteen. When a steward presented Digger with a bottle-opener, he even started earning tips: opening bottles for the men and saying, in his best Tommy voice, 'And jolly good luck to *you*, sir!'

In the ten days after leaving Southampton, the accounts in Tim's notebook showed that Henri had earned over two pounds, nine shillings from his bottle round below decks.

He was so engaged on the afternoon of 16 May. The *Kaisar-i-Hind* had anchored off Port Said just before lunch, and feelings on board were running high. The airmen had to parade at their boat stations as they entered harbour, saluting the warship HMS *Hannibal* and the French naval flagship. They were to be in port for two days, taking on coal, water and more passengers, when word came through that all shore leave was prohibited.

Due to what the Base Commandant, Lieutenant-Colonel Elgood, called 'discreditable behaviour' by drunken troops aboard previous transports, no soldiers in transit were allowed to disembark. Even the cricket and tennis matches against the Port Said sports club were cancelled. The nanny brigade was out in full force. And it was no comfort when Elgood later sent a cable to the *Kaisar-i-Hind*, congratulating the men upon their bearing and discipline. He didn't know how hot tempers were – or how busy Acting Corporal Hemene was with the bottle-opener below deck.

Digger was run off his feet. He didn't notice the approach of Captain Palmer and Major Ellis on an unannounced inspection. Nor did the airmen. They were all much too preoccupied – until, too late, they heard Captain Palmer suddenly exclaim, 'What's that?'

'What is *what*, sir?' Major Ellis enquired loudly, as silence fell like a curtain.

'Over there!' Captain Palmer stopped short. 'I saw a boy . . .'

'A *boy*, sir . . . ?'

'. . . disappearing behind those men.'

'Perhaps you imagined it, sir.'

'No, Major Ellis, I did *not*. I saw a boy! On my ship!'

Captain Palmer was a sprightly man. He darted into the group of airmen, in time to see Digger disappear behind a wall of legs.

'Hey you! Stop! Come here!'

As the master was brought face to face with the stowaway, Les Ellis said quietly, 'I think, Captain Palmer, there is a matter I should discuss with you in private.'

So it was, half an hour later, that Tim Tovell found himself in the Captain's cabin, with orders to give a complete explanation of how Henri Hemene came to be aboard the *Kaisar-i-Hind*.

Captain Palmer was seated at his chart table, looking serious. Lieutenant-Colonel Watt appeared embarrassed, wondering how he could have missed finding the stowaway. Perhaps the troops had been *too* sober and alert! Les Ellis seemed rather chastened . . .

'I want to hear the whole story,' said Captain Palmer, reasonably. 'Major Ellis has told me something of it. Before I decide what to do, I'd like to hear it in your own words.'

He settled in his chair as Tim began to recount the tale: from the time the orphan had wandered into Christmas dinner at Bickendorf, to his discovery on the troop deck that very afternoon. He told what they'd been able to learn of Digger's background, and of the war years he'd spent in Flanders.

'It's a miracle the little fellow survived,' Tovell said. 'But he did. And, Captain Palmer, with the help of the Good Lord I hope

Henri will now grow up with my own family in Queensland.'

Just as he'd told Padre Gault in the wood at Rouelles. Tim spoke much as he had then – adding such new details as the oat sack, and the basket of sporting goods which had come aboard the *Kaisar-i-Hind*. And he told Captain Palmer about the death of Timmy, and how it strengthened his resolve to bring Digger home.

'He is not my son. But I've come to love him as if he were.' And as he struggled to control his feelings, Tovell said again, 'I can only think that, when God took Timmy from my wife and me, He sent us Digger to care for instead.'

There was silence when Tim finished.

At last, Captain Palmer, who had turned to gaze at the sea, said softly, 'Yes. Indeed. Quite remarkable.' Then, addressing himself to the senior officer, he went on, 'I don't know about you, Colonel Watt, but this seems to me an occasion where the discretion of a ship's captain might allow the young stowaway to remain on board . . . ?'

'I agree,' said the OC Troops, 'subject to certain assurances.'

'Sir, I've undertaken to meet the cost of Henri's passage,' Les Ellis broke in quickly.

'I'd be prepared to assist you in that,' added Oswald Watt, who was, in private life, a wealthy man.

'I regret the deception that's been involved,' Ellis continued. 'But there's not a man in 4th Squadron who hasn't felt affection for our mascot . . . and responsibility for his welfare.'

'Yes. That's quite obvious,' replied Captain Palmer. 'The ship's owners will have to be compensated and I accept your offer, gentlemen. You can settle the details with the Purser. That done, the lad may stay on the *Kaisar-i-Hind*, provided he doesn't go up to the saloon deck. We have Premier Ryan and his family as passengers, and I won't have them disturbed.'

'I'll attend to it immediately,' Les Ellis responded, as they prepared to depart.

Tim stood back to let the officers pass. But just as he was leaving, Captain Palmer called him back.

'Mr Tovell, you realise it's another matter altogether as to how you're going to get the boy *off* the ship at the other end . . . to obtain permission from the immigration authorities for him to land and stay with you in Australia . . .'

'I've already begun to turn my mind to it,' said Tim.

'I'm sure you have. But I don't think that's something I ought to know about. In the meantime, just keep him off the saloon deck.'

'I'll give him strict instructions.' Tim paused and then, speaking as one man to another, he added, 'Captain Palmer, let me thank you for what you've done today. I will remember you.'

The good news that the young mascot was permitted to remain on the *Kaisar-i-Hind* spread quickly through the ship. The open secret below decks became a public one upstairs – even on the saloon deck where Mr and Mrs Ryan and their two children, Jill and young Jack, quickly caught up with the gossip.

As a politician and barrister, Tom Ryan had been in London on government and legal business before the Privy Council.

Both he and his wife, Lily, had almost died from the Spanish influenza, and were using the voyage home to recuperate. Hence Captain Palmer's insistence on their privacy.

But Tom Ryan had also seen the battlefields of Flanders, and had visited Australian troops still in France. Naturally he talked to the returning soldiers on the *Kaisar-i-Hind*, and Digger's story greatly interested him. As the voyage progressed, Henri obeyed orders not to go to the saloon deck, though he often spoke to the Premier on his rounds. And every other boundary Digger stretched to the limit.

Because the troops couldn't land at Port Said, a swimming carnival was organised instead. Next morning, the sea was filled with the thrashing bodies of soldiers competing in the races. Digger nearly shouted himself hoarse barracking for his squadron. It was hot work. And when, after lunch, some soldiers decided they'd ignore the ban and swim ashore anyway, Henri went with them. The Tovell brothers saw him leap into the water from the ship's steps and climb onto the back of a waiting airman.

They had a wonderful time in the bazaars and stews of Port Said. But Henri, after ten days below decks, got badly sunburnt. When they returned to the ship, he had to go down to the hospital ward. He was there for several days recovering, making himself a favourite with Sister Ella Whiting.

'I like it here,' Digger said when Tim visited him. 'The nurses are as nice as those at Poperinghe . . . and the food is *twice* as good!'

'It's as well Captain Palmer let you stay on board,' said Tim.

'We couldn't nurse you like this, hidden on the troop deck.'

They left next afternoon, and Digger watched from his hospital porthole as the ship entered the Suez Canal: waving to the many Australian soldiers still in Egypt, who lined the banks and jeered enviously at their fellow countrymen returning home.

Serenely, the *Kaisar-i-Hind* glided through the night, her searchlights illuminating briefly the desert landscape and ships at anchor. Early next morning they entered the Red Sea, where the tropical heat and following wind made the ship unbearable.

Henri was almost grateful for his sunburn. At least he could sleep beneath a fan in the hospital ward, and not stifle on the troop decks. But he made himself get up to watch the semi-finals of the tug-o-war and a boxing match. When they anchored at Aden, and permission was given for men to go ashore for a swim, he was fit enough to join them.

Once Henri was up and about, he discovered another source of income. Since he could now appear openly on deck (Captain Palmer always seemed to look up at the sky when he spotted the boy, as if searching for enemy aircraft), takings naturally increased from the bottle business. Digger also found that other passengers wanted to take his photograph. Ever the shrewd survivor, he'd dimple his cheeks, look up with those child's eyes that had seen too much, and say, 'But of course, monsieur . . . madame . . . if you could perhaps spare a little shilling . . . ?'

Which they usually could. So Henri would pose in his uniform, or stand with Tim, looking squarely and full of self-assurance into the camera's eye; Tim in white civvies, putting on weight again after the shock of Timmy's death. In the days before the *Kaisar-i-Hind* anchored at Colombo, Digger earned more than eleven pounds from the sale of photos, which Captain Jones took care of – as banker.

They were allowed a few hours ashore. Digger wandered with Tim and Ted through the streets and markets of Colombo, crowded with people and rickshaws. It was so utterly new and exotic! The smells! The colours! The golden light! Lush gardens, vivid with flowers dripping scent, and mountains of tropical fruit in the bazaar.

'Tim! It's like paradise,' Digger cried, munching mangoes and pawpaws for the first time in his life. The wartime boy could remember only scant privation. And after the cold and snow of Europe, the island of Ceylon was a glorious steam bath.

'It's wet . . . but it's *hot*,' he exclaimed. As they were returning to the ship, they were drenched by a monsoonal downpour. The astonishing thing was that, an hour later, their clothes were nearly dry again. Not like Bickendorf!

The heavy weather continued after they left Colombo, sheets of rain dropping from the skies, followed by blazing sunshine. And the sea came up, the ship pitching and rolling its way across the Indian Ocean. It was a good thing the orchestra and the jazz band were good sailors – though the mess tables were often deserted, and the picture shows sometimes had to be cancelled.

They didn't have King Neptune's ceremony, either, when the ship crossed the equator. Partly it was because of the weather;

partly because most of the passengers had 'crossed the line' before; and partly because the authorities feared there might be unseemly behaviour. It was Sunday, and Bishop Long was preaching at Church Parade. But Young Digger, making his first voyage, insisted on being initiated by the god of the sea. So they lathered his face with soap on the mess deck, and dunked his head into a bucket of seawater. He came up spluttering and crying: 'Now your mascot is truly a *voyageur* of the world!'

The poor weather, though, didn't prevent them from celebrating the King's Birthday on 3 June with sweets and cigars. After the finals of the boxing tournament, General Glasgow distributed prizes. He got a prize himself next day, when the General's team easily won the final of the officers' tug-o-war.

Day by day the *Kaisar-i-Hind* was heading south, ever closer to Western Australia. The wireless picked up Perth on 5 June. As preparations were made for a grand farewell fancy-dress dinner, excitement was running high. Even when the rough weather put a dampener on the party (the string orchestra failed to make an appearance for the first time since leaving Southampton), their spirits weren't quenched. In a few days, they'd reach Fremantle!

'Very few people on board failed to see the sun rise on the morning of June 9,' Major Ellis wrote in the squadron's war diary, 'for with the dawn came the first glimpse of Australia.'

The rails were lined with men (and the few women on the saloon decks), straining their eyes for the distant blue smudge of land they called their own. Gulls called, and passengers inhaled faint perfumes of home carried on their sea wings.

The *Kaisar-i-Hind* anchored later that morning. She was boarded by a representative of the Minister of Defence, and by the health inspectors. After which the ship moved to Fremantle wharf, where she berthed to a huge welcome by crowds come to greet these returning airmen with bands, and garlands, and kisses, and all the overflowing joys of home.

'Leave was granted to all ranks,' Major Ellis wrote. 'As feet were once again placed on Australian soil, England, Europe and the recent strife seemed but places and incidents of the distant past.'

Tim and Ted and Digger stood by the rails watching their comrades who were leaving the *Kaisar-i-Hind* in Western Australia file down the gangway.

'I'm so excited, Tim!' Digger cried. 'I can hardly believe it!'

Nor could the brothers. Despite the odds, they'd achieved what they had planned all those months ago. They'd brought Henri back to Australia. He was safely home – or nearly so. The tragedy that war had visited upon the orphan boy belonged to that far-off place and time of which Major Ellis wrote. Digger's future lay before him, waiting with Gertie and his new family at Jandowae.

All that had to be decided was the question of how precisely he was to get there.

16: JANDOWAE

When Tim first wondered how he would land Digger in Australia, safely past the immigration officers, he developed a daring plan.

An airman who was leaving the ship at Fremantle offered to steal up to the *Kaisar-i-Hind* in a motor boat at night, smuggle Henri ashore, and send him by train to Queensland. But as they neared Australia, Tim realised it was a crackpot idea, and he discarded it. The risks were too high. He decided it was to be all or nothing. He'd take the boy with him the whole way. The Good Lord had watched over them this far – surely He wouldn't abandon them now.

So it was that Tim, Ted and Digger came to be standing by the gangway early that afternoon, at the end of the queue of men going on shore leave. They'd talked about it over lunch: whether it was better to stay on board, or whether they should try to go to Perth to get Digger some civilian clothes.

'Henri's fine on the ship in his uniform,' said Tim. 'He blends in with everybody else. But he'll stand out a mile in civvy street.'

'Couldn't we leave Digger here, and just you and I go to buy him a suit?' asked Ted.

'*Non!*' cried Henri. 'I want to go, too.'

'I know, son,' soothed Tim. 'We need you with us to make sure the new clothes will fit.'

He tipped a wink to the leave officer, and got two disembarkation passes – for himself and Digger. And even though Ted was becoming worried about the official asking too many questions at the foot of the gangway, Tim hoped their luck would continue to hold.

But luck and the Good Lord still had a few nasty surprises. Thus the customs man couldn't find the name 'Henri Hemene' on the boat roll. And as Tim and Ted began to flounder, he demanded to know, 'Who *is* this boy . . . ?'

If it hadn't been for Major Ellis coming down the gangway behind them, the diversion he created with the airmen on the wharf, and the timely arrival of Mr and Mrs Ryan with their family, Digger would have been sprung. As he'd done so often before . . . at Bickendorf, Le Havre, Hurdcott, and again on board the *Kaisar-i-Hind* . . . Les Ellis had come to their rescue.

Yet, as Tim reminded them when they slipped away to get the train to Perth, they couldn't always rely on Les Ellis to be there. They'd have to use their own wits to get Henri back on board.

So the plan arose to buy Digger a suit, like the one worn by young Jack Ryan, and have him pretend to be the Premier's son!

Now, as night fell, the return train pulled into Fremantle, and they stepped onto the platform. By the dim station lights, the impersonation wasn't too bad! In his grey serge jacket, short pants, long socks, new shoes, and a baggy cloth cap on his head, Digger looked not dissimilar to Jack Ryan. Someone, not knowing them, might mistake one boy for the other. Certainly Tim hoped so.

'Come on,' he said, clutching the brown paper parcel in which Henri's uniform had been wrapped. 'We'll soon find out!'

A cold wind was blowing off the sea as they hurried across the footbridge and along the road to the dockside. A number of other liners were in port, cabin lights winking in the evening gloom. Street lamps threw a pallid light along the wharf – enough to see by but, thankfully, not *too* much as they came alongside the *Kaisar-i-Hind*.

'Are you ready, Digger?' Whispering.

'*Oui*.'

'Good boy. And try not to laugh!'

A military policeman was waiting by the gangway.

''Evening, soldiers. Enjoy your leave?'

'Yes. But we'll be glad to sit down to our dinners.'

They presented their passes. But again, the guard suddenly looked at Digger and asked, 'Who's this?'

Tim's heart seemed to stop. He drew a deep breath. Silently asking the Good Lord and T.J. Ryan to forgive him, he replied, 'Don't you know the Queensland Premier's son?'

'Oh yes!' responded the MP. 'I saw him go ashore earlier with his parents. Good evening, sonny.'

'Goodnight, officer . . .'

The three passengers scurried aboard. And it wasn't until they were well and truly safe down on troop deck 5A, that Henri burst out: 'Was I good? Oh! That was fun, Tim! We did it! He thought I was Jack Ryan. He didn't know the *différence!*', Digger cried, putting on his Frenchy voice again!

Even Tim and Ted permitted themselves to laugh. And so did the whole of No. 4 Squadron when they heard.

The *Kaisar-i-Hind* sailed next morning. After a squally passage, they reached Adelaide just before lunch on Saturday, 14 June. And it was here, for the first time, that Tim and Henri realised something of the interest their story would create in the newspapers at home.

They berthed for only a few hours, to let ninety airmen disembark. The rest of the troops were granted 'wharf leave' only, but the YMCA put on a first-class afternoon tea and concert for them in a shed at Outer Harbour.

During an interlude, Tim and Digger were approached by a woman dressed in black, as if in mourning.

'Monsieur Tovell . . . ?' she asked nervously, in a voice that, like Henri's, revealed a French origin.

'Yes, madame.'

'And this is the *petit garçon* . . . the little boy I have heard about?'

'This is Digger.'

'*Bonjour, madame*,' he said brightly.

The woman smiled. 'Such a fine young man. He reminds me of my own . . .'

They wondered if she'd like to take Henri's photograph for sixpence. But suddenly she turned away, sobbing and hiding her distress in a handkerchief.

'Forgive me, monsieur. But my Jean-Claude is dead. He fought to defend France, as a good son should. Now, he will not be coming home . . .'

Her tears returned, as tears would return to families across Australia, year after year, for their 60,000 darling men who died in the Great War – the war, as they hoped, to end all wars.

Tim and the boy stood in silence with her; until Tovell said gently, 'Henri's mother and father also were killed, madame.'

'Then you will know I how feel! The emptiness at heart. Oh, monsieur, would you give *me* the boy . . . to bring up as my own . . . to fill the place of Jean-Claude . . . ?'

As the good barber's wife at Mons had also asked.

'Madame, I cannot do that.'

'I will give you five hundred pounds . . .'

'But that is impossible!' Tim was shocked.

'One thousand pounds, if you like . . . !'

Henri clung to Tim.

'No! I want to go to Jandowae.'

'You will like it with me . . . I promise!' The woman tried to caress him. 'We have a big house . . . my husband is rich . . . there is nothing I will not buy you . . .'

'We're going home to Gertie!' Digger shrank from her touch.

'You heard the lad, madame,' said Tim.

'Fifteen hundred pounds . . . I will pay you that much.'

You could buy several houses for that money.

'I understand your despair . . .' Tovell was getting desperate. As was the woman.

'How do *you* know what I feel?'

'Because my own son lies buried in the graveyard at home.'

'Ah . . .'

Silence dropped between them. Then she made one last effort. 'And if I were to implore you . . . ?'

'The boy isn't mine to give . . . he belongs to the squadron.'

'Fifteen hundred pounds is a lot of money.'

'Even if I would, madame, my wife would never forgive me.'

She looked at him with dying eyes, acknowledging defeat.

'Thank you, monsieur. I understand.'

She turned, and her shadow passed slowly along the wharf.

'Oh Tim!' cried Henri, when she had gone. 'You *are* going to take me to Jandowae? You won't give me to somebody else . . . ?'

'I'll get you home, son. We *will* find a way.'

That afternoon, while the *Kaisar-i-Hind* was still berthed at Adelaide, the Premier of Queensland initiated several telephone calls to the Home and Territories Department in Melbourne on Digger's behalf. In this, it would seem Tom Ryan was prompted by his wife, Lily. And Ryan was a generous man of mind and spirit – aged only forty-three, with a young family of his own. He'd seen much of Henri on the ship, and readily agreed to do what he could for the war orphan.

Ryan had been accompanied to London by the Queensland Crown Solicitor, William Webb. Now he asked Webb to contact the Commonwealth immigration authorities to obtain permission for the French boy, 'Henri Heememe', to stay in Australia.

As the ship neared Adelaide, Lily approached Tim and told him what her husband would try to arrange.

He hardly dared hope!

The Crown Solicitor spoke to J. Atlee Hunt, the Departmental Secretary, asking that Henri be allowed to land with Tovell in Sydney. Webb briefly outlined the case. He assured Hunt that Tim was a married man of good character; he gave an undertaking, on behalf of Premier Ryan, that should Tovell be unable to maintain the boy, the Queensland Government would see to his welfare.

The interview was successful.

Two days later, as the *Kaisar-i-Hind* was steaming up Port Phillip Bay, the Secretary sent a telegram to the Collector of Customs: 'No objection need be raised to lad landing in Sydney.' And on board the troopship preparing to dock at Port Melbourne, Tom Ryan received a cable from the Minister for Home Affairs: 'Permission has been given to land mascot.'

Great was everybody's rejoicing. On the saloon decks. In Captain Palmer's wardroom. In the officers' cabins. And especially below on troop deck 5A, where a small boy clung to one particular airman and wept for happiness.

'Oh Tim! It's really true. I'll really see Mum in Jandowae.'

The word falling from his lips so naturally.

'Yes, son.' And Tovell's own voice trembled at the thought of it. 'We don't have to pretend any longer. We're really going home.'

It was a cold, damp day, as the *Kaisar-i-Hind* berthed at Port Melbourne, where some 800 airmen disembarked.

There was a big welcoming ceremony. The wharf was crowded with their nearest and dearest, waving flags and handkerchiefs, and cheering themselves to a standstill. The State Commandant came aboard with greetings from the Governor-General, Sir Ronald Munro-Ferguson. Airmen from the military flying school at Point Cook were to have escorted the ship up the bay, but the flight was cancelled because of poor weather. As if to shame the military, however, two civilian aeroplanes – each carrying a lady passenger – circled the *Kaisar-i-Hind* several times in salute.

A large convoy of motor cars had assembled to bear the departing airmen in triumph to the Depot before they went home. And those travelling on to Sydney were given leave until midnight.

Young Digger and Tim took a taxi into town.

They'd said their goodbyes to the Ryan family, who were leaving the ship at Melbourne. In fact, the *Age* newspaper said Henri was seen sitting next to the Premier, with whom 'he was engaged in animated conversation'.

They'd made their farewells to Major Ellis, Captain Jones and Sergeant Wilson, who were also disembarking. And they'd given thanks for all that No. 4 Squadron had done to help them.

'You've brought me much good fortune since I became your mascot,' said Henri.

'As you have to us,' replied George Jones.

And when he gave Tim the money he still held as banker for Digger – nearly twenty pounds – Jones said: 'This isn't the end of our friendship. We won't forget you.'

To which Les Ellis added, 'Indeed not. The 4th Squadron will disband soon enough. But we'll keep our associations, wherever we are. It's a fine thing you've done . . . and will continue to do . . . for this young man, Tovell.'

'It's no easy matter to bring up a lad,' said Sergeant Wilson. 'You'll face a lot of extra expense in the years ahead. We've been talking it over, and the squadron's started a fund to help you . . .'

'The fact is, Tim,' Les Ellis went on, 'should you need further help with Henri, you know you can call on your old comrades . . .'

'Sir, I'll always bear it in mind,' Tovell replied. 'I'll let you know how the lad grows up. The important thing now, though, is to get Digger home to my wife . . . his new mother . . . at Jandowae.'

He saluted his superiors, as a soldier ought. Then, as men should who have shared much together, he shook their hands.

'I'll always remember your kindness.'

Henri, replete in the uniform he'd worn on Anzac Day, might have saluted. But the child hugged them instead.

'*Au revoir, mes amis.* Goodbye, my friends. You've made this Young Digger very happy.'

The welcoming crowds were even thicker in town than at the wharf, for the return of the AFC had been mentioned in the newspapers. Tim even saw a poster outside Flinders Street railway station, 'ARRIVAL OF FRENCH ORPHAN MASCOT'. Everywhere the airmen went, people gathered to applaud. And as Henri and Tim were going up Collins Street, looking in the shop windows, somebody called out, 'Look! There's the young Flying Corps mascot!'

At once a mob gathered, all talking and pointing and asking Digger a thousand questions.

'Look at him . . . ! Funny little chap! What's your name . . . ? What happened to your parents, sonny . . . ? Do you like it in Australia . . . ?'

Digger began to get upset. He adored being at the centre of attention – but not like this, with people pressing him and shouting. Fortunately the police arrived and, hoping to divert the crowd, they asked Tim and Henri to wait in a jeweller's shop near by.

There, Henri's eye was caught by a gold brooch, mounted with the Australian coat-of-arms.

'Tim, do we still have the money from Captain Jones?'

'Yes, Digger. Safe and sound in my wallet.'

'Do we have enough to buy this brooch?'

'How much is it?'

The shopkeeper told him the price.

'Why do you want to buy that, Digger? You're better off keeping your money.'

'I said in Perth I want to buy a present for Gertie . . . for Mum.'

'So you did, son.'

The brooch was purchased and placed in a box lined with velvet. Tim carefully put it in his pocket.

'That's a good thing you've done today, Henri,' he said.

'Will Gertie like it . . . ? Will she like me?'

'No doubt of it, son.'

Though there were always doubts.

There was still a crowd outside the shop, waiting to glimpse the mascot. Eventually the police had Tim and Henri driven in a taxi to Port Melbourne, where they went aboard the *Kaisar-i-Hind* and stayed for the next two days, safe from newspaper reporters and other nosy parkers, as the ship completed its voyage to Sydney.

They passed through the heads and entered the lovely harbour on the morning of Thursday, 19 June 1919. The *Kaisar-i-Hind* berthed at Woolloomooloo, where the 560 remaining troops disembarked. Most of them were bound for homes in New South Wales. But 160 men – Tim, Ted and Henri among them – were headed for central station and a special train for Brisbane.

There was another crowd of journalists to meet the returning airmen at the dock; and over the coming days a number of articles about Henri appeared in the Australian press.

The Melbourne *Herald* reported General Lee, the NSW State Commandant, asking Tim what he was going to do with the boy.

'Make a man of him, if he does not make a fool of himself,' was the reply. 'I suppose I will have to put him at school first; but I have a place in Queensland, and I am taking him out there with me. We will give him a horse to ride, and he ought to grow a bit more there.'

'What are you going to be, Henri?' someone else asked.

'A jockey' was the response, as the boy turned to get into a motor car.

Then there was a long article recounting THE STORY OF HENRY in the Melbourne *Age*. It said he wanted to become a farmer, and that sixty pounds had already been subscribed to the squadron fund for him.

Crowds gathered wherever Henri was recognised, people hugging and kissing him. Even after they started their train journey north, people thronged around asking endless questions, quite unconscious of the distress they might cause. And when a waitress asked Henri if he knew how to use a knife and fork, he was shocked. 'Use a knife and fork, mademoiselle? I can use a rifle!'

As the train pulled into Toowoomba at lunchtime next day, it was met by record crowds. The *Chronicle* reported that young 'Hemene Honori' in his AFC uniform 'was the cynosure of all eyes . . . When the story of the little chap became known many of the women on the platform wept, while everyone wanted to see him and hear his story . . . He is a beautiful child, though slender, but with features more like a girl than a boy. He is 11 years of age and speaks faultless English, but still retains that politeness of the French race.'

While some of the published details differed from the facts known to Tim Tovell, these articles reflected the great impression Henri's story made on the Australian people – especially women. So many of them, like the lady in Adelaide, had lost their own sons – their own husbands, brothers, fathers and sweethearts – in the war. Digger's tale of loss, of survival, of his adoption by the airmen and safe homecoming, seemed such a poignant metaphor of renewal and love arising from the ruins of war. Such a symbol of all that these grieving women had hoped might have been their own happy ending.

The train reached Brisbane central at six o'clock that night, where more crowds and reporters greeted the airmen. They drove in a convoy across river to the Depot at Kangaroo Point, where the Governor and State Commandant made welcoming speeches. The Governor was told about Henri. 'That's wonderful,' said Sir Hamilton Goold-Adams. 'I hope he'll be well looked after, and I wish him the best of luck.'

Most men were allowed to go home. But a number of them, including Digger and Tim, had to report to the Depot hospital. Henri had a sore throat, and Tim wasn't feeling very well. The doctors examined them, and gave orders to return next day. The hospital wanted them to stay for some time. Tim, in particular, had problems with his sinuses and would need an operation. But after four days waiting, he explained his situation – his need to get home because of his son's death – and was given ten days' leave.

On Wednesday, 25 June – the day Australians heard the Peace Treaty would be signed at Versailles – Tim and Henri caught the train home.

On and on they went, rattling through the western suburbs of Brisbane. Into the foothills, the train climbing all the way to the top of the escarpment and Toowoomba, where Tim and Gert had begun their lives in Australia.

Such new sights for the little boy kneeling at the window! Such a wonder, the heady smell of gum trees, and the grey-green bush spilling in a vast panorama all the way to the coast. And the plains, when at last they reached the uplands. How the paddocks and fences seemed to stretch for ever into the blue, shimmering horizon.

'Ah . . . Tim! I thought France was big. But this . . . How far to Jandowae now . . . ?'

'Not long, Digger. We have to change trains at Dalby . . .'

Dalby. Where Tim's children had been born. Where Gertie had driven on that last, terrible buggy ride with Timmy . . .

Tovell had so longed to be with her, safely home. But the nearer they got, the more anxious Tim felt, like a bridegroom again on his wedding day. Would Gertie still love him and want him as she had before? Would she forgive him for not being there with Timmy? Would Nancy know her father? And would they welcome Henri, and take the boy to their hearts, as he had? Or would they reject him, and say No, he is not one of us?

The old questions beat inside him, but no answers came. And, in truth, when the time arrived sooner than he expected, Tim realised his concerns would take care of themselves.

He'd been preparing himself for Jandowae. But halfway across the plain, at the little siding of Jimbour, the train halted. Outside, Tim saw a procession of motor cars, decorated with flags, waiting to drive them in triumph the rest of the way home. So Tim and Digger gathered their kit, buttoned their coats, straightened their slouch hats, and stepped out into the sun . . .

They were all there to meet them. Gertie, with her hair spun like a crown, smiling at Tim as she always did, and opening her arms to her love.

Young Nancy, looking shy in her coat and hat, wondered if she remembered this tall man with a moustache who everyone said was her daddy. And this boy with him . . . who was to be her brother. Not Timmy. Timmy was gone. But this one, who was dressed in a uniform like the man who said he was her father, and who called himself Henry . . .

Nancy looked uncertainly from one to the other. Until Gert, reaching down, took Henri's hands in her own, and kissed him, and said in her sweet English voice, 'So this is Digger. Welcome home, my boy.'

He looked at her and said softly, nervously, to this woman of whom he'd heard and hoped so much, 'Hello, Mum.'

The word he'd been practising, over and over again. Wondering what would she do . . . ?

Gert held his hand and turned to the girl by her side.

'And this is to be your new sister, Nancy . . .'

Tim watched them. And smiled. And embraced Gertie once more. It would be all right.

Then into the motor cars to drive the last fifteen miles. Across the black soil plain, the dust and the wind blowing through the Queensland afternoon, and into the town. Past the weatherboard houses of Jandowae, gum trees drooping beside the street. Past the bank and Mulholland's hotel. Past the police station where Sergeant Behm and his family lived. And up the road to the cottage with a tin roof and picket fence that Gertie had made home.

They went inside. And there, as the Jandowae correspondent wrote in the *Chronicle* a few days later, Tim was 'enthusiastically welcomed by his many friends'.

After they'd all been hugged and their hands shaken . . .

After the cups of tea had been drunk, the cakes and sandwiches eaten, and they'd gone outside for Gertie to take a photo of her returning heroes in the motor car . . .

After all the festivities of homecoming were over, and Emily and Ted and the guests had gone, Tim closed the door of his house upon the great world, and in the stillness of the evening drew his family to him. Gert. And his Nancy. And the orphan boy who'd come to him at Bickendorf.

Digger reached into Tim's pocket, and took out the box with the velvet lining. Pinning the gold brooch on Gertie's blouse, he said, 'This is for you, Mum.'

He put his arms around her neck. And kissed her. And Henri knew that he was home as well.

17: HOME

It seemed the happy ending that everyone wanted. The orphan boy who had been rescued from the ashes of the Great War – who had found love and hope and a new beginning with the airmen of No. 4 Squadron – now was safely home.

For the first four years after his arrival in Australia, Henri lived with Tim and Gert, as one of their own. He always spoke of Tim as his foster-father. Gert was always 'Mum'. And Henri was accepted as a bigger brother not only by young Nancy, but also by the two children who were born following the war – Edith and Ed.

The family stayed at Jandowae only briefly after the soldiers' return. Their first leave over, Tim and Henri went back to Brisbane and the military hospital, where Digger had his tonsils out and Tim's sinuses were cleared. Not until mid-September was

Tovell finally discharged from the army, and he came home for good. Henri had already enrolled at Jandowae school. He was a bright boy, and while Digger would always struggle with written English, he had a good head for figures and a technical mind. He might even achieve his wish and become an airman himself!

But for Tim and Ted, high hopes turned sour. After the war, belts were being tightened. There wasn't much work at Jandowae, and that was mostly taken by others. The Tovells did a few building jobs. They helped erect the town's war memorial. The headstone was set above Timmy's grave, with the verse his father liked:

WHO PLUCKED THIS FLOWER?

THE MASTER.

THE GARDENER HELD HIS PEACE.

'They're nice words, Tim,' Henri said, when they all went down to see it.

But the family couldn't remain. Jandowae had little to offer them. In late 1919, they moved to Cooroy, north of Brisbane, and stayed with their friends, Mr and Mrs Lee, on another farm. There, Henri learnt to ride properly. He seemed a born jockey. It was no idle boast he'd made to the newspapers! One day he lined up on a big bay mare for the main race at Cooroy show – and won it by a length. No one was more surprised than Tim and Gert Tovell. They were Sunday school people: their family didn't go in for horse racing!

A few months after moving to Cooroy, Tim bought a house in the town – a comfortable, weatherboard home, with a bow window and a verandah. Here, in April 1920, Edith was born.

Over eight decades later, Edie and Nancy could recall those years growing up at Cooroy with Digger. On the day Edie arrived, Henri ran down the yard crying, 'Tim! What do you know? I have a baby sister, and she's got blue eyes!' Only Tim had china blue eyes in that family. The little girl was not only his – she was as certainly Henri's sister . . .

There were memories of bush-walking up Cooroy mountain. Picking cape gooseberries, 'Look Edie! Here's a ripe one!' And of the family dog, his tail waving like a flag wherever the children went. For Tim kept the promise he gave Digger when they left Bickendorf. He got a German shepherd they called 'Kaiser', after the German emperor.

There was, too, the time Gert got sick after drinking bad ginger beer, and was taken to hospital in Brisbane, on a stretcher in the train. She almost died.

Then, after three years at Cooroy, Tim decided to move to Brisbane. Work was still scarce, and he was often away for days up country. Ted and Emily had already moved to the city. With Gert expecting another baby, in late 1922 the family moved to Kangaroo Point, near the river.

Concerned about the legalities of raising Henri as his own, Tim and Digger had visited the French Consul, Major H.R. Carter. He told Tim there was no difficulty with him being the boy's guardian until Digger turned twenty-one and could become a naturalised Australian. But Carter was unable to find out anything else about him. The only French surname he could find resembling the one pronounced by Henri was 'Heremene'.

It was not a name Digger ever used, and it was as 'Henry Tovell' that he enrolled at the boys school in January 1923. Tim told the headmaster something of Henri's background, but asked him to keep it quiet. Neither he nor Gert wanted the lad to be constantly reminded of his wartime years. Even so, when an ex-serviceman came to school for Anzac Day and spoke about the Flanders fighting, Henri rose to correct him on some small detail.

'Why, sonny,' asked the man, 'how do you know that? Did your father tell you?'

'No sir. He didn't need to. I was there, myself.'

By then, Henri's accent had flattened into a passable imitation of Australian speech. But the occasional French inflection was still there; and Nancy knew how upset Digger was, when walking home from school one day, that a boy had called him 'Froggie'.

'I said, "Tell Tim",' Nancy remembered. 'So Digger went and told Tim and asked permission to fight the other boy. Tim said, "Yes, you're not going to stand for that." Next day they started teasing, but Digger belted that boy up after school. It was terrible . . . The parents were going to do this and that to Digger. But Tim stood up for him. After that they left him alone. Digger gave that boy a hell of a hiding, but he wouldn't do it until Tim said he could.'

The boxing lessons from Hurdcott had stood him in good stead!

Around this time, Tim recalled, Padre Gault visited Brisbane. Henri saw his name in the newspaper, and the following Sunday they went to hear him preach at the Albert Street Methodist Church. After the service, Tim asked if he remembered the airmen's young mascot from Le Havre. Padre Gault certainly did.

'I've often wondered what became of the little fellow.'

'Well, here he is!' And Tim beckoned Digger forward.

The Padre's astonishment was complete. He shook hands, and laughed, and asked a thousand questions, and finally had Henri stay with him for three days. Asking, what was the boy going to do with the rest of his life?

The subject, in fact, was concerning them all.

Officially, Henri turned fifteen at Christmas 1922. While Tim and Gert believed he was younger than the Bickendorf doctors reckoned, he was reaching the age when most boys started work. With Nancy at school, Edie a toddler, and the new baby due in May, the growing teenager was becoming a burden on the family budget. Tim was just beginning to establish himself as a builder in Brisbane, and wondered if he could afford to apprentice Henri himself. But when Digger saw an advertisement for young men to join the recently formed Royal Australian Air Force as mechanics, he decided to apply.

Tim wrote to Sergeant Wilson – now Pilot Officer Wilson of the RAAF – in Melbourne. The result was a proposal from the Air Board that the Minister give special authority to enlist Henri. This was necessary because recruits had to be eighteen – whereas Digger's age was now estimated at 'about sixteen'.

But a problem arose. As Henri was still a French citizen, the Consul-General in Sydney, M. Campana, refused permission. It was contrary to French law to enlist a citizen in a foreign defence force, and Henri could be penalised. His hopes seemed dashed. Yet the airmen were nothing if not resourceful. If their former mascot couldn't be a serviceman, what about civilian employment? Hec Wilson and his wife, Mary, agreed to look after him.

Thus the Secretary of the Air Board, Major Patrick Coleman, wrote to Henri in June, offering him a job at two pounds a week. Tim replied as a father might, 'He is a good lad, and I sincerely hope that the step he is taking will lead him to success . . .'

Young Digger Tovell was leaving home, going back into the wide world. But his heart would always remain with Tim, and Gertie, his mum. On the night before he left Brisbane for Melbourne, the orphan boy wrote in Tim's autograph book a verse from his Bible:

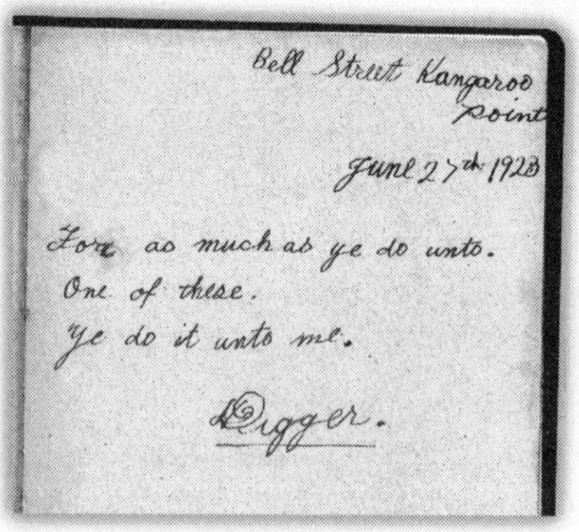
Bell Street Kangaroo Point

June 27th 1920

For as much as ye do unto.
One of these.
Ye do it unto me.

Digger.

Henry Hemene Tovell began work as a temporary junior assistant – a messenger boy – in Major Coleman's own office at Victoria Barracks. It was new and interesting work – at least to begin with. Indeed, surrounded by so many air force officers in their new blue uniforms, it felt almost like old times again.

Henri settled in with Hec and Mary at Lantana Road, Gardenvale. Every morning he caught the train into the city, and walked to the office. It was a long day, and he often didn't get home until late, because three times a week Henri went to night school. He had to improve his education if he was to qualify for an apprenticeship. For Digger was determined to get a *proper* job with the RAAF, and eventually move into the single men's quarters at No. 1 Flying Training School and Aircraft Depot, Point Cook.

It wasn't that Henri was especially unhappy with the Wilsons. They helped him buy a pushbike. He joined the scouts. The house was comfortable and welcoming, and the talk around the dinner table was of aeroplanes and airmen, Hec's promotion to Flying Officer, and their old friends from No. 4 Squadron. Digger was even given an ex-serviceman's badge.

But it just wasn't home. Nor did Henri ever see Hec and Mary Wilson as his family. They had no other children. Tim and Mum and the young ones were in Brisbane, and Henri missed them. Increasingly, he chafed at the thought of having to stay a messenger until he turned twenty-one and could join the RAAF as a naturalised citizen. In late 1925 Digger wrote asking to come home. He was getting nowhere in Melbourne, he said. Couldn't Tim help him?

Tovell replied. And in December, Digger sent a letter of resignation to Major Coleman. '. . . I consider that now I am eighteen years of age it is time I was learning a trade and as I cannot see any prospect of an early advancement in my present position my only hope is to return to Queensland where my Father is prepeared [sic] to have me apprenticed.'

Major Coleman was a perceptive man. He'd taken a real interest in Henri's welfare, and could see there was justice in his complaint. The lad was offered a civilian apprenticeship at Point Cook – a rare thing for the RAAF. But Digger seemed determined to leave. Coleman wrote to Brisbane. 'Bearing in mind the circumstances under which Henry was sent to Melbourne', he asked, did Tim want the boy to sever his connection with the RAAF?

Tovell was dismayed. He told Coleman he'd offered to apprentice Henri only if there was no prospect of his learning a trade where he was. Tim had since written suggesting Digger accept the RAAF offer, and felt confident he would do so. 'He has never complained previously, and has always spoken in the highest terms of his treatment at the hands of Mr and Mrs Wilson.'

Tim proudly told Major Coleman he hoped that Henri would eventually make a name for himself in the RAAF. But he added, 'Should he at any time prove unworthy of his position, I am prepared to re-assume responsibility for his support and welfare. This I consider my bounden duty.'

Henri withdrew his resignation. In March 1926 he started at the Point Cook workshops as an apprentice fitter and turner. A few months later, he was given leave to go home.

Like all good holidays, it was too short. There were special teas and outings; endless talk with Tim and Gert, and games with the children; there were visits to see old soldiers in the military hospital at Kangaroo Point, and to say hello to the vicar, Mr Perry, at St Mary's church. Henri met Vera Schaffer, a girl about his own age, who promised to write to him. And before Digger went back, Gert took their photographs in the garden: the four children as a group; then Tim and Digger together, in their suits and service badges, the lad standing with his hands behind his back, just like his father.

On the reverse someone wrote, 'Dad and Digger, last time he was home.'

Digger returned to the Wilsons, who had moved to Werribee, nearer Point Cook where Hec was the armament officer. The holiday didn't improve the lad's homesickness. Nor did Vera write – even though Henri asked Gert to plead his cause.

He soon had other distractions. Henri bought a Harley Davidson motor bike, which he rode to town most weekends. He'd waited long enough for one, he wrote. But it was expensive. 'Mum I am sorry I cannot send the children a pound this year for buying this bike has set me back terribly but they will not be deprived of all of it for I am incloysing [sic] ten shillings with this letter that will buy them some sort of a present for Christmas. I am sorry, but you can't make money go any feather [sic] than its value can you.'

In February 1927, his OC, Wing Commander Cole, gave

Henri a glowing report. 'He is diligent and progressing satisfactorily in his trade.' By March, he'd got his wish and moved to the single men's quarters on the base. But away from Hec Wilson's steadying influence, things began to go wrong. Henri grew disinterested in his work, his studies, and on parade. He'd much rather go riding on his motor bike, or bird shooting in the salt marshes. Digger became moody and difficult, writing home about his loneliness and boredom, and telling Gert he'd made up his mind to return to Brisbane when his time was over. '. . . Home for me, Mum, Home Sweet home . . .'

In all of this, Digger probably was no more restless than other adolescents. Given his background, he could have had many more problems! And he was, in reality, much younger than his official age and the other apprentices. But the growing pains of one teenage youth were of little consequence to the staff at a military air station, trying to knock a whole intake of recruits into shape. And the boyish cheek, which had so charmed the airmen at Bickendorf and Hurdcott, was regarded at Point Cook as little better than insubordination. The NCOs thought Henri was 'quite a trial'.

Certainly Wing Commander Cole gave him a very *un*satisfactory report in February 1928, and recommended against a pay rise. But he noted that Henri had shown recent improvement, mainly due to Leading Aircraftsman Robert Sanderson, who'd been asked to take care of him. And in the 1927 RAAF Christmas card he sent home, Henri pasted a photograph of an airman descending by a parachute, as if to say 'Happy landings!'

'From Digger with best of love to all' he wrote, with the wish that *Many Happy Years be thine full of Golden Hours.*

And indeed the family would treasure that card always.

For some reason, RAAF records gave Henri's birthdate as 1906. Whether it was an error or an attempt to make Digger appear even older, is unknown. But by the beginning of 1928 Henri had officially turned twenty-one – old enough to apply for naturalisation.

Early that year Major Coleman visited Tim and Gert at the house they'd just bought in George Street, Kangaroo Point, to discuss Digger's future. They agreed he should become naturalised and finish his apprenticeship, whether or not he eventually enlisted with the RAAF or returned to 'Home Sweet Home'.

Major Coleman and Hec Wilson helped Henri fill out the papers, insert the newspaper advertisements, sign the certificates, and complete his statutory declaration. He gave his age as 'approximately twenty-one' – born 25 December 1907, the date fixed at Bickendorf. But then as Digger acknowledged in a supporting statement, 'It is impossible to give a definite statement of my accurate age. I was too young to remember and no knowledge of my date of Birth, or my parents' names . . . if there is anything that requires further explanation, I will do so if in my power.'

The authorities didn't need anything else. By his own admission, Henri was born in 1907 and therefore was still only twenty. He received a letter dated 16 May 1928, telling him to apply again next year and advising him to obtain documentary evidence about his age and parents, 'which are doubtless on record in France.'

Everyone was dismayed – especially Digger. He was planning to go to Brisbane by ship for his holidays in mid-year, with his naturalisation certificate. Now, all that work had been a waste of time! His restlessness returned, but it wasn't as easy to escape Point Cook. He'd sold his motor cycle, and had to rely on lifts or borrowing a machine when he wanted to go to Melbourne – which had become rather more frequent.

For Henri had acquired a new girlfriend, who lived in the city. She was helping to steady him and encourage pride in his appearance. The last photographs sent to Tim and Gert 'From your loving son Digger', show a handsome young fellow in his felt hat, silk shirt and scarf, blazer, flannel trousers and patent leather shoes. No wonder he couldn't afford to run a motor cycle.

The pain of having his naturalisation deferred must have cut deep, however. Henri doubtless sought any chance to go to town, and have his new young lady soothe his injured feelings with her sweet kisses.

So it was, on the afternoon of Wednesday 23 May, that Henri went to Melbourne. By one account, Digger was asked to deliver some documents to Victoria Barracks. Borrowing a motor bike, he set off on the sixteen mile journey. His despatch delivered, Digger went to visit his girlfriend. But, as Major Coleman afterwards told Tim, she wasn't home. Instead, Henri had dinner with her father, and it was late when he left the city for the return trip.

It was there that the accident happened.

A taxi, driven by Alfred Shocbridge, was making a U-turn in Spring Street, outside the Windsor Hotel, when Henri ran into it just before midnight. Whether he saw the cab or not, no one could tell. Witnesses said the motor bike had a bright headlamp, but the cab's headlights were dimmed and its parking lights were on.

The motor cycle crashed into the taxi's left rear mudguard, flinging Henri onto the road.

Constable John Duffy called an ambulance and had Henri taken to the Melbourne Hospital, where Doctor Fairley treated his cuts and fractured skull. Hec Wilson's address was found in Henri's pocket. He drove urgently to the hospital, and sat through the night with Digger. Doctor Fairley saw him again, but Henri was already in a coma, beyond help or hope.

It was 24 May. Empire Day. And at half past five in the morning, Young Digger died.

He was, it seems, only eighteen.

Major Coleman's telegram was sent to the wrong address, and it wasn't until mid-afternoon that Gertie got the news. She was devastated. Her daughter, Edie, remembered that day with the utmost clarity, over seven decades later.

'I came home from school. My mother had an English friend, Mrs Eldridge, visiting for afternoon tea. I said, "Hello Mrs Eldridge", and she said, "Your mother isn't well." I thought, My mother's never sick, but Mrs Eldridge said, "She's had some sad news. Digger is dead." I can remember, when I was told that, everything stopped. I was a child and I was told, your big brother's dead. That was the first death I'd ever known. Well, mother came in and – oh – she looked . . . I can still see it. She was heart-broken. And of course they'd gone to get Dad to come home. Mrs Eldridge stayed with Mother until Dad came in, and the two of them were just distraught.'

Tim had a return telegram sent:

HEART BROKEN OVER HENRYS DEATH
SEND US ALL PARTICULARS T W TOVELL

But he stayed in his house of mourning. It had been such a happy home. Their young son, Ed, had turned five only the day before. Nancy had started work as a shorthand typist. Tim was building a new kitchen, and fixing the sleep-out for Digger when he came home for his holidays. And now . . .

'I loved my father very dearly,' Edie said. 'He came to me when I had gone to bed. He knelt by me, and he put his head in my lap. It broke his heart, because mother was so upset . . . and I was so close to Digger. I can remember that man crying his heart out, and I was only eight years of age . . .'

Digger was buried the day after he died. Many stories about the wartime mascot appeared in the newspapers; but Tim Tovell, far away in Brisbane, was given no chance to attend the funeral. He had to pour out his grief in a letter to Major Coleman, finding it almost impossible to believe that, even as he penned the lines, Henri was being laid to rest in Melbourne.

'It is comforting to us to know that you are there Sir to see the last of him on this earth. Our minister has just called and Mrs Tovell and I knelt with him in solemn prayer in the little room where only a few weeks ago you sat with us, and we discussed his future bless him . . . I remember when he and I arrived home from France, we stood by the grave of my Dear Son, and read on the headstone these words, Who plucked this flower, The Master, the Gardiner [sic] held his peace. And he said, they are nice words Tim, I hope that these will some day be placed at the head of his own Dear Grave.'

Before he left for the Fawkner Cemetery, Coleman wrote to Tim, '. . . What an end for a lad who had been through what he had and just at a time when things were looking brighter for him – it is indeed sad . . . I know how you and Mrs Tovell must be feeling for the poor lad, but it is thankful to know he knew no pain, and you both at least have the satisfaction that you did all in your power for him whilst he was alive. I think you know how appreciative he was of your kindness . . .'

They couldn't bury Henri with full military honours. He wasn't formally enlisted in the RAAF. But Major Coleman arranged what he could.

Henri's coffin was draped with the colours of the old Australian Flying Corps. Uniformed airmen were his pallbearers. An RAAF wagon and trailer carried him to the cemetery.

But there was no volley of shots fired over him. And there

was no bugler to play the Last Post as he was lowered into his grave. Nine AFC veterans were there: Captain Roy King, Hec Wilson, and others exchanging memories of their mascot. The Reverend Rowlands paid tribute to the lad who had 'lived more intensely in his short span than most who have reached three score and ten.' As earth rattled on the coffin, a woman threw a tiny French flag into the grave. Henri's little sweetheart was there, sobbing bitterly, said the *Argus*.

Hec Wilson received more than 200 condolence messages, and there were many wreaths at the graveside.

Among them was one that read, 'A tribute to a real soldier laddie from the Padre'.

A week after the funeral, a large crowd attended a memorial service for Henri at St Mary's church, Kangaroo Point. To those who mourned the war orphan, the Reverend John Perry urged them to be thankful they'd been privileged to rescue him.

'He might have become just a piece of human driftwood without hope and without happiness in the world,' Perry told them. They'd given him at least a few years of comfort and joy. 'Let us rejoice, even in our sorrow, in the knowledge that he is once again united to those who loved him most upon earth, and that family circle so tragically broken in the years of war has, by this last tragedy, been made one again.'

Tim found the words reassuring, and wrote to Major Coleman asking him to send every scrap of news about Digger.

There was much that Coleman might have told him.

The inquest on Henri's death was held on 28 May – a mere four days after his death. The haste was extraordinary. Digger died on Thursday; was buried on Friday; and the coronial enquiry held on Monday. But not until weeks later was Tim told about the hearing on the lad who had taken his name. It must have cut him to the heart. He couldn't even attend Henri's inquest. It was a brief, straightforward affair, however, and the coroner found that he died 'from injuries received in an accidental collision.'

The other news was that the *Argus* had started a fund to raise £150 to build a memorial over Henri's grave, and subscriptions were coming in quickly. Again, very strangely, nobody bothered to tell the Tovell family. Tim found out about it at a meeting of Brisbane ex-servicemen. And no one said what would happen to Digger's personal belongings.

The only other letter Tim received from Melbourne in the weeks after Henri died was a rather painful one from Hec Wilson. It seemed to deal mainly with the lad's faults and failings – which Tim felt no longer mattered much. But it stung him into writing bitterly to Major Coleman in July, complaining that he and his wife had been treated with indifference. '. . . Whatever Henry may or may not have been to others, he was more than a mere passing fancy to us.'

Coleman replied, enclosing some press clippings about Henri's death and inquest, and advising that his effects would be auctioned. As he'd left no Will, the proceeds would be paid to the Curator of Intestate Estates who'd been told that Henri was Tovell's adopted son. Coleman went on to say that the memorial fund had already closed, and a committee of old No. 4 Squadron men was choosing the design. He then added, 'I don't know why subscriptions were called from Brisbane, as the fund went really well from the start and if necessary much more could have been collected.'

Major Coleman appeared oblivious to the wounding import of his words. He didn't ask Tim to offer a view on the headstone for the lad whom he and his wife regarded as a son. Tovell's request to use the words from Timmy's grave wasn't acknowledged. Indeed, these officers arranging matters in Melbourne were surprised that Tim and his Brisbane friends had even been asked to contribute to the memorial!

The Major said he would advise Tim of further developments. Yet this would seem to be the last official letter he sent Tovell – for whom the pain of indifference went on and on. 'It was all taken out of his hands,' Edie remembered, 'which broke his heart, I must confess. I think my father was never quite the same after that.'

The auction of Henri's effects raised nearly seventeen pounds, to which was added over twenty-three pounds in outstanding pay and arrears. After deducting funeral and canteen expenses, it would appear the balance was forwarded to the memorial fund.

Henri's RAAF uniform and equipment were returned to stores, and his private correspondence was handed to Hec Wilson, who had recently been promoted to command No. 2 Flight at Point Cook. What became of the papers is unknown; but Wilson sent back Henri's ex-serviceman's badge to the Returned Sailors' and Soldiers' Imperial League of Australia (RS & SILA), together with a letter published in *The Duckboard* magazine.

Whatever Wilson said that so pained Tim Tovell, he wrote kindly enough about Henri to *The Duckboard*.

'It gave my wife and myself great pleasure in looking after him, and to do our best to place him in the position to be a respectable citizen, so as to uphold the wonderful tradition of the AIF. I have no doubt he would have been a credit to the old comrades of the 4th AFC if he had not met with such a tragic death.'

The Duckboard helped with fund-raising for Henri's memorial in Fawkner Cemetery – though it took longer than expected to complete the project. It wasn't until July 1931 that Coleman and the Wilsons approved a final design by the sculptor, Wallace Anderson.

The monument was very handsome, such had been the public response.

At the head was a tall freestone plinth, on which stood a bronze sculpture of a refugee boy, two feet six inches high. In ragged shorts and shoes, he appeared much as Henri had when he first came to the airmen at Bickendorf.

On the plinth, beneath the AFC wings, was engraved in gold letters:

> ERECTED BY PUBLIC SUBSCRIPTION
> TO THE MEMORY OF
> HENRI HEREMENE TOVELL
> A NAMELESS WAR ORPHAN
> ADOPTED BY NO. 4 SQUADRON
> AUSTRALIAN FLYING CORPS
> IN FRANCE DURING THE GREAT
> WAR 1914–18 TAKING THE NAME
> OF HIS SELF-APPOINTED GUARDIAN
> AIR MECHANIC T.W. TOVELL
> OF BRISBANE HE RETURNED TO
> AUSTRALIA WITH THE SQUADRON
> AND LIVED WITH HIS GUARDIAN
> UNTIL 1923 WHEN FLYING OFFICER
> H.A. WILSON ASSUMED
> RESPONSIBILITY FOR HIS WELFARE.
> ACCIDENTALLY KILLED AT
> MELBOURNE 24 MAY 1928
> AGED ABOUT 21 YEARS

The words from Timmy's grave, that Henri so liked, were not included.

18: EPILOGUE

Henri's memorial was unveiled at Fawkner Cemetery in February 1932. Tim and Gert were not present: neither of them visited Melbourne again. The 1930s were depression years. Then came the Second World War. And after that, well, they were getting on and it was a long way to travel. But their family went from time to time, and sent back photos of the statue looking out across the dead.

It was there until at least the later 1950s. Edie remembered it turning dark with patination over the years, so that it was sometimes known as the 'black boy'. Then, one day, it disappeared – presumably stolen and melted down – and the grave was vandalised. Tovell's children were able to have the gravestones restored, but the statue was never replaced. They couldn't afford it; though they kept the news from Tim and Gert, in case it distressed them.

Yet what could a bronze statue signify? The boy's living presence was still so close to them . . . his miniature uniform hanging in the wardrobe; the oat sack out in Tim's workshop with THE DINKUM OIL; the photographs; their memories . . .

A number of articles appeared over the years, giving versions of Henri's story: in the squadron history written by Lieutenant E.J. Richards; in *Reveille* magazine and newspapers. There was a chapter, *Henri*, based on conversations with Tim, in Norman Ellison's 1957 book, *Flying Matilda*. The family didn't like it much, as it made Tim sound broadly Australian – whereas he kept his Englishness to the last.

But as for the man himself, Tovell seemed too close to his subject to write Digger's life as he wished. He put together some short articles for *The Whiz-Bang* magazine in 1928 and 1929; but every attempt to pen a complete account for the Australian War Memorial ended in failure. At last, in 1932, Tim spoke to a neighbour, Professor Cumbrae-Stewart of Queensland University, who wrote a full version based on Tovell's recollections. It was a basis for most subsequent accounts – including one written by the war historian, Arthur Bazley, when Tim died. Echoing words used by the Brisbane *Daily Mail* after Henri's death, Bazley said it 'revived memories of one of the most extraordinary incidents of the First World War.'

The years, in fact, were gathering them all in.

Hec Wilson retired from the RAAF in 1929, and went on the

reserve list. When the Second World War broke out in 1939, he re-enlisted as a Flight Lieutenant, serving at training schools. Wilson left in February 1945 with ill health and died in September 1949, just after his sixtieth birthday.

Major Ellis was a businessman in civil life, but kept close links with the AFC Association and the reserve, moving to Sydney in 1929. During the war, he was OC of the large RAAF station at Bradfield Park. He was appointed Wing Commander in 1941, and Group Captain the following year. He died suddenly in January 1948, aged fifty-three, survived by his widow, Kathleen.

Captain Jones rose higher in the RAAF than any of them, becoming an Air Marshal. He was appointed Chief of Air Staff in 1942, and served as head of the RAAF for ten years. Sir George Jones was knighted in 1953, continued his interest in civil and military aviation, and died in August 1992 aged ninety-five.

For the Tovell family, life in the years following Digger's death continued somewhat more sadly, but they were still involved in the world around them. Their son, Ed, was apprenticed to Tim as a builder. With the outbreak of war, Ed joined the RAAF in the family tradition, serving gallantly as a pilot in Britain and Europe, earning the Distinguished Flying Cross and being mentioned in dispatches. After the war, Ed continued as a civil aviation pilot and investigator in Australia.

In Brisbane, during the war years, Nancy was a driver for the United States forces, delivering the cakes and pies Gertie always cooked for the men. The home in Kangaroo Point became open house to Australian and American servicemen and women. Tim tried to enlist again, was refused, but was seconded to the United States Army anyway, working in a military lumber yard. Indeed, Tim and Gert wanted to act as foster parents to one of the refugee children being brought out from Europe.

Nothing came of it. Perhaps they were considered too old. But at least the incident showed how deeply the experience of nurturing Young Digger had touched their lives. Tim would still bring out the little uniform on special occasions. He'd talk to his grandchildren about the war and the orphan boy who'd wandered into the mess at Bickendorf that Christmas Day, and of the great adventure when they smuggled him home.

Tim retired as a builder, but he still made fine inlaid walking sticks and picture frames in his workshop. He still worshipped at St Mary's, and grew his roses (though he could barely smell them). He went to soccer on Saturdays, and marched every Anzac Day carrying the AFC wreath. Until, in the fullness of time, he died at home in August 1966, at the age of eighty-eight.

Gertie survived him for another seventeen years. She lived in the house at George Street (now renamed Pearson Street) for as long as she could. But increasingly, in old age, she became forgetful and disturbed. Sometimes the past seemed too painful to bear. Letters and photographs were kept, yet other things were destroyed without telling anyone. Thus the family learned that Gertie had burnt Digger's miniature uniform in the fire under the laundry copper, believing it to be moth-eaten. Even THE

DINKUM OIL, the oat sack, and the gold brooch Digger gave her disappeared in time.

At last, Gertie went into a retirement home, where she died in August 1983, aged ninety-four.

So, as the Reverend Perry suggested in his eulogy for Digger, these family circles in France and Australia that had cherished the boy known as Henri Hemene Tovell, were made one again before eternity. His grave is still in Fawkner Cemetery, though somewhat in need of repair. Perhaps one day it might be restored. Maybe another statue of a ragged war orphan will again stand on the headstone.

And it would be nice to think that eventually Young Digger's tomb might bear the words Tim Tovell sent from Hurdcott, and which can still be seen on little Timmy's grave at Jandowae:

WHO PLUCKED THIS FLOWER?

THE MASTER.

THE GARDENER HELD HIS PEACE.

Then the story would really be complete.

APPENDIX I

APPLICATION FOR NATURALISATION

Statement by Henri Hemene Tovell

(AWM93 37 – official records)

(Spelling and grammar as written)

R.A.A.F.
Point Cooke,
Melbourne
28th April 1928
The Secretary,
Home and Territories Department

Sir,

I hereby forward my application for naturalization under the Commonwealth Nationality Act 1920–1925.

These warriors, so bold and proud. Digger, Ted and Tim on Anzac Day, 1919. Note Tim's weight loss. [AWM P00867.001]

Australian soldiers, with bayonets fixed, passing the Prince of Wales taking the salute in The Strand, London, Anzac Day 1919. [AWM H16106]

Full of self-assurance – Digger, with Tim in civvies (left) and another soldier, on board the *Kaisar-i-Hind*. [AWM A03679]

The growing teenager. Henri in Melbourne with Hec Wilson kneeling, c. 1924. [Courtesy Nancy Elliot]

Safely home. Gertie's photograph of Henri with Tim and Nancy, in the car that drove them to Jandowae, June 1919. [Courtesy Nancy Elliot]

Henri apprenticed at Point Cook. He has signed the photo and marked himself with a cross, standing on a ladder looking into the cockpit of a seaplane. [Courtesy Nancy Elliot]

Tim and Henri at Brisbane, mid-1926. On the back of this family photo at the AWM, someone has written, 'Dad and Digger, last time he was home.' [AWM H13597]

Henri in Melbourne not long before he was killed in 1928, a handsome young fellow in his silk scarf and blazer. [AWM A03680]

Henri at Point Cook on a mate's AJS motor cycle. Tim Tovell wrote on the back of one print, 'He was riding this machine when killed.' [AWM P00867.003]

Henri's headstone at Fawkner Cemetery, Melbourne, with the bronze statue of the orphan boy (now missing). [AWM A03681]

My Case is rather complicated to my mind than that which you have previously dealt with.

In the early part of January 1915 (no knowledge of actual date) my Peoples House in Lille, France was blown up by enemy shell fire, the Occupants Mother and two others being killed. My Father was previously killed in action. When the incident happened as far as I can remember I was some distance along the Street. I approached the scene, and immediately seemed to realise my position. My definite age not known, would consider that I was within the vicinity of 6 or 7 years old. From that day onwards I roamed all over France, attaching myself to various British Regiments during the years of War, I was twice wounded slightly by enemy shell-fire – once attended to by an English Casualty clearing Station for a few days.

During the latter days of the War I advanced towards Germany with a Royal Flying Corp Squadron, until that unit definitely was stationed at The Bickendorf Aerodrome, Cologne, Germany in December 1918.

The 4th Squadron Australian Flying Corps being stationed on the Bickendorf Aerodrome I seemed to have unofficially attached myself to that unit, and remained with them until I disembarked at Brisbane, Queensland in June 1919. When the 4th A.F.C. was stationed at Cologne, a Mechanic of that unit (whom I now claim as my Foster-Father, having adopted his name since I arrived in Australia – the name I am also desirous of, if permitted to be naturalised as, so will use the name Tovell on the forms) named Timothy Tovell acted as my Guardian right through the piece.

The Commanding Officer of the unit Major L. Ellis was in approval of me remaining with the Unit. I was clothed very suitably by the generosity of the members of the 4th Squadron by a collection taken up. About March 1919 the Unit moved off from Cologne by road transport to England. I was attached to Mr Tovell until we reached Lille, the idea being if no trace of relatives or information regarding me were discovered I was to be the Mascot of the 4th A.F.C. The complete convoy of transport and personnel remained in Lille during Saturday and Sunday [*actually Mons*], and Major Ellis arranged that a thorough search and inquiry be made in Lille and the locality in which I resided prior to the War. This inquiry failed to reveal any information whatsoever regarding my relatives or knowledge of them, due principally to the heavy casualty of that area which was subjected to long and consistent heavy artillery fire.

It was then decided that attempts be made to take me with the unit to Australia as their Mascot. I was in the Camp with the unit at Le Harve for 1 week awaiting transport across the Channel. I then arrived at Southampton, then entrained to Hurdcott Camp Salisbury Plain England.

I think it was the morning of the 6th May 1919 the Squadron moved from Hurdcott to Southampton to embark on "The Kaiser-i-Hind" for Australia, I being conveyed to the troopship in a Chaff-bag. (Please find enclosed copies of photos taken that morning). The troopship moved out from the pier at Southampton late in the afternoon of the 6th May 1919 I still being kept under cover. Early morning of the 7th May 1919

I was released from my captivity, I was walking along the deck when the Captain of the Kaiser-i-Hind approached me, and discovering I was not on the boat roll, he stated that he was to return to port and have me put ashore, but thanks to the timely assistance of the late Premier of Queensland Mr Ryan who was aboard, and the late Colonel O. Watt O.C. Troopship discussing the question with the Captain, they stating that they would be responsible for my presence on the Vessel if he continued, this persuaded the Captain to continue the journey with me aboard. I have a faint recollection of the trouble and discussion due to my presence on the boat.

I disembarked from the boat at Brisbane Queensland and proceeded with Mr Tovell to his Family and Home. There I resided for a period of 4 years, until my presence became a burden domestically to Mr Tovell. He communicated with Mr Wilson of Garden Vale, Melbourne, who is an Officer in the Air Force, and was also a Member of the 4th A.F.C. (that I remembered at the time.) Mr Wilson and Major Coleman the Secretary of Air Board arranged with the Air Board for me to come to Melbourne and be employed as a Junior Messenger in the RAAF. Major Coleman communicated with the French Consul, that arrangement being Official. I have no knowledge of the facts only that I was employed by the R.A.A.F. in a temporary capacity, and am still as such learning a trade Fitting and turning in the Workshops at Point Cooke. When I left Queensland in 1923 I resided with Mr and Mrs Wilson 2, Lantana Road, Garden Vale, Melbourne for 3 years. I attended night school when residing with them for 3 nights a week for $2^{1}/_{2}$ years.

It is impossible to give a definite statement of my accurate age. I was too young to remember and no knowledge of my date of Birth, or my parents names. The unit I came to Australia with allotted Xmas Day as my Birthday and I have regarded that day ever since.

I trust I have fully explained my case, also that I have to make approximate statements due to my age at the time, if there is anything that requires further explanation I will do so if in my power.

Yours respectfully, H.H. Tovell

[*The Application was supported with certificates signed by Patrick Eugene Coleman, Hector Allan Wilson, and Sidney Edward Dunslow JP of Anzac House, stating that Henri Hemene Tovell was known to them as a person of good repute and had an adequate knowledge of the English language.*]

APPENDIX II

ARTICLE FROM THE BRISBANE DAILY MAIL
21 June 1919

(Reprinted with permission)

FRENCH ORPHAN SMUGGLED TO AUSTRALIA 'LIVED FOR DAYS IN A BAG'

An extraordinary story of the smuggling of an eleven-year-old French lad many thousands of miles from Germany to Brisbane, was unfolded last night when the troop train drew into Central station.

Leaning out the window of a carriage was a bright-faced youngster who had waved his hand and shouted to the gathering of cheering relatives on the platform. He was Henri Heememe, a French orphan. In charge of him was Air Mechanic Tovell of the 4th Flying Squadron, who enlisted at Toowoomba. Before he enlisted he was a builder and undertaker at Jondowae, Dalby.

Little Henri shook hands with the 'Daily Mail' representative, and said, 'Will you see me a little later; I will tell you the story of my life. I'm told it is very interesting.'

A couple of minutes later he was seated in a motor car and, between Air Mechanic Tovell and his brother, who belongs to the same unit, was driven to Kangaroo Point hospital. While seated at tea he attracted the attention of the Governor, Sir Hamilton Goold-Adams. 'Who is the boy?' asked the Governor. When told that he was a French orphan and had been wounded in the line in France, the Governor said, 'That's wonderful. I hope he will be well looked after, and I wish him the best of luck.'

THOUGHT IT WAS LILLE

'I don't know where I was born,' said Henri, 'but I suppose it was Lille, from what I have been told. My father was killed in the war – during the first week – and my mother a short while later. I don't know a lot about my past, but I had no brothers or sisters. I know I am glad to be here. The Aussies have been very kind to me all through, and I never want to leave their country.'

THE CHRISTMAS DINNER

'Henri came to us on Christmas Day,' explained Air Mechanic Tovell, 'in very amusing circumstances. We were near the German city of Cologne at the time and the lads of the Squadron decided to spend the day in style. We arranged a really capital Christmas Day dinner. There was poultry, roast beef, and pudding. It was served by German waiters, and the dinner was eaten to the strains of a German band, who played quite voluntarily "God Save the King" and "Rule Britannia." I have photographs of the band and the waiters Well, while the dinner was at its height, little Henri came into the hut from the English lines. He said the smell of the poultry made him desert the English troops. He did not want to do so but he liked the smell of the poultry. Having lived on beef and biscuit for years, a lad of his age was a bag of bones. The lads jumped at the chance of making the lad happy, and he had his best dinner since childhood. From that time onwards he was never away from the Squadron, and we unofficially transferred him from the "Tommies!" He had been with the Royal Field Artillery and an English Flying Squadron.

BLOWN INTO A DITCH

'How they came to get him was this way: during the retreat from Mons he was placed in a motor car and driven away, but a shell wrecked the car and he was blown into a ditch. An English officer adopted the lad and made him the mascot of the regiment. He remained with the English artillery until the middle of 1916, when he was wounded in the line near Ypres. The majority of the gun company to whom he was attached was killed. Henri was wounded in the knee. After he had been treated in hospital he was taken back by the artillery, but four days after joining up again he was blown up, and the officer who had adopted him was killed. He then joined the English Flying Corps, and during the advance that was made in 1917 [*1918*] he was taken through the district where his father used to own a brewery. Enquiries were made by the English troops, but the brewery, his father, and all his friends had disappeared. He then joined us on Christmas Day at Cologne, as I have described.

'IN A SACK'

'On February 27 last, the squadron left Cologne for England. We got Henri as far as Le Havre, but the difficulty then arose of finding means to get him to England. We thought of all sorts of schemes, and finally decided to place him in a sack branded "Oats". He was placed aboard the steamer *Lorina*, and landed at Southampton. Tied up in the sack, he lay on the wharf for hours, but never moved. As an Australian officer said at the time, "He displayed all the qualities which saved his race from extermination at Verdun" [*French fortress, 1916 battlefield*]. At Hurdcott camp in England he was a great favourite with the men of the 4th Division.

'IN A BASKET'

'All went well until the day came for us to embark for Australia. We had no excuse for having an oat bag on the ship – the *Kaisar-i-Hind* – and for a time we were in queer street. There were all sorts of bets made among the men as to whether we would land him on the transport, and those who bet the squadron could do it won their wagers. We got a large basket and branded it 'Sporting materials'.

'We fitted him into the basket and got him aboard. At the top of the gangway the embarkation officer asked: "What is in that basket?" An Australian officer replied, "Only boxing gloves". The basket was passed by the embarkation officer and stowed below. Three days after the ship had sailed the lad was produced to the amazement of the majority of the troops.

COMMANDER AND THE LAD

'When the commander of the ship passed him on deck, he used to look up at the sky as if searching for hostile aircraft. The commanding officer, Colonel Watt, of Sydney, a wonderfully brilliant flyer, said nothing severe about our smuggling trick, and the Premier, Mr Ryan, was good enough to send a wireless message to Queensland [*cables from Melbourne*] arranging for the lad to land. He often used to chat with the lad, and told him he would do all he could for him in Queensland. Henri was the pet of the ship but was not spoiled. Every night he said his prayers. He is a lovely lad, and will do well. I am adopting him.'

MET QUEEN OF ROUMANIA

The lad talked with pride of Anzac Day in London, when he marched in the procession, of his presentation in London to the Queen of Roumania and other notabilities. 'I did not meet Billy Hughes [*Australian Prime Minister*]' he added, 'but I was too afraid.'

Travelling through from Wallangarra yesterday on the train, a young lady serving luncheon asked, 'Can you use a knife and fork?' Henri was shocked, and replied, 'Use a knife and fork! I can use a rifle.'

He is dressed in A.I.F. uniform, wears a wound stripe on his left cuff, and looks a very fine lad. He was adopted in Cologne by Air Mechanic Tovell the day his son died in Queensland, but at the time he had not received the sad news.

[On 25 May 1928, the day after Digger died, the Daily Mail published an article and photographs, saying Henri's death 'revived memories of one of the most extraordinary incidents of the war.' It reproduced substantially the same material as the 1919 report, but with these final paragraphs presumably based on an interview.]

Strangely enough, Mr Tovell announced his intention of adopting Henri in a letter to his wife from France just at the time of the death of his eldest son in Brisbane [*Dalby*]. 'One more in the family will not matter' he wrote, unconscious of the loss he had sustained. So the little French orphan took the place of his son, and became as one of the family.

There were others, however, who were eager to care for him, as instanced by the case of a lady in Adelaide, who had offered to give Mr Tovell £1500 if he would hand the orphan over to her. Mr Tovell's refusal was immediate. He had become attached to the lad, for whom in the lines he had often saved his own meals and himself gone hungry.

LIFE IN BRISBANE

Henri was educated at St Mary's Church of England school, Kangaroo Point, where also he attended the Sunday school of which Mr Tovell is the superintendent. His schooling over, he became a fitter and turner. Still he retained the enthusiasm of his earlier years for the air force, and it seemed but a natural development of his inclination that three years ago he should go to the Point Cook aviation headquarters to join the air force as a mechanic. There he was about to qualify as a flying officer when the end came.

About midnight on Wednesday last he was riding a motor cycle in Melbourne when there was a collision with a taxi, and Henri fractured his skull. He was hurried to the Melbourne hospital, but died yesterday morning. When he was notified of the tragedy by the Air Board Mr Tovell broke down under the burden of his grief. The funeral will take place today.

All his friends knew young Henri as 'Digger' though, as Mr Tovell explained, 'when we adopted him he told us his name was Henri Heemene. So we called him Henry Hemene Tovell, and judged that he was about 11 years old.' On that reckoning, Henri would have been 21 years of age next Christmas. But fate had numbered his years a little sooner.

Endnotes

Note: AWM photographs may be accessed through the Collection database at www.awm.gov.au

Chapter 1

Disembarkation pass. Ellison p 15.

Miniature uniform. Ellison p 10. See AWM photograph P00867.001.

Boat roll. While Henri's presence was known on the *Kaisar-i-Hind*, nowhere does his name appear among four thick files of military papers relating to the voyage. On board were 174 officers, 1393 other ranks, fifty-seven civilians (including ten children) and 321 crew: 1945 souls altogether (plus Henri). Lt Col Watt's diary, Papers of HMT *Kaisar-i-Hind*.

Kaisar-i-Hind. The name apparently means 'Lioness of India', a title adopted by Queen Victoria.

AFC. The military passengers included Nos 2, 3 and 4 Squadrons and Nos 5, 6, 7 and 8 training squadrons, Papers of HMT *Kaisar-i-Hind*. No. 1 Squadron sailed from Egypt in March 1919, Cutlack p 385.

Customs officer. Ellison p 15 calls him the 'disembarkation officer'. I assume he was an on-shore civilian present with the military. See Hunt's cable Ch 16.

Ellis's help. Ellison p 15. The diversion is imagined. Tim says merely that, as Major Ellis was explaining about Henri, 'we do a get'.

Captain Palmer. Ellison pp 13–14.

Premier Ryan & family. Ellison p 15.

Perth. Ellison p 15 says Tim and Henri went to Perth to buy clothes.

Chapter 2

Bickendorf. Description of Christmas dinner is based on Richards p 42, Ellison, and No. 4 Squadron's AIF war diary. For decorations see AWM photograph P00826.227.

No. 4 Squadron. No. 4 Squadron is used in the narrative voice, and interchangeably with 4th Squadron in conversational form, as was usual at the time. 4 Squadron is modern usage.

Football matches. Richards p 42.

Imshie & Henri's reply. Ellison p 4.

Menu, toasts & music. In AIF war diary.

Ellis & Jones. Ellison p 4 and Bazley (1967). Jones is not in the photograph, but neither is Tim. Jones born 22 November 1896; Ellis 14 October 1894.

No. 43 Squadron. A key assumption. Richards p 71 and Bazley (1967) say Henri was with No. 43 Squadron. Nos 79 and 48 Squadrons were together at Ste Marie Cappel in October 1918, later at Rekkem and Nivelles (Halley). The only time No. 43 Squadron shared an aerodrome with either of them was at Bickendorf. I assume Henri went to No. 43 Squadron there. Interestingly, No. 206 Squadron, one of the seven RAF units at Bickendorf, was also at Ste Marie Cappel in April and October 1918, but is not mentioned in any account of Henri.

Honoré. I believe this to have been the orphan's true name. He signed a photograph and postcard from Cologne 'Heememe Honoré', with surname first. There is a photograph among the H.H. Tovell Papers signed 'Honoré Heememe'. The Toowoomba *Chronicle* 21 June 1919 gives his name as 'Hemene Honori'. No such surnames, including 'Heremene' (memorial) or 'Hermene' (inquest), appear in 2001 regional telephone directories. There are many families called 'Herman' or 'Hermann', see Author's Note and also note Ch 17.

Children visited by war. See AWM photograph H08572, also *The Times* reference for refugees.

Young Digger. Nickname in the *Argus* 25 May 1928.

Photograph. A keyed photograph is in the AIF war diary where the boy's name is given as 'A/Cpl Honoré (mascot)', and also captioned in AWM photograph P02658.004. Ted is in the back row, fifth from the left.

The Aussies will do me. Tovell's postcard in H.H. Tovell Papers, see Ch 12.

Officers' Christmas party. Richards p 42.

Lt Johnson. Also close to Henri, see skating reference Ch 6.

Sleeping quarters. Ellison p 4 says Henri slept in Tim's hut on Christmas Night. Bazley says he returned to RAF squadrons, reappearing in the Australian lines next morning.

Duty officer. A literary device to give some necessary background.

Joe. Photograph of Henri captioned 'Joe' is in Richards facing p 36, also National Archives of Australia (NAA) Papers.

Napoleon & Tricolour. Ellison p 4.

Chapter 3

Wounds. Ellison p 6, Richards p 71, Bazley (Cumbrae-Stewart). The artillery officer is nowhere named, see note Ch 9. Appendix I says Henri was in hospital for a few days, Ellison and Richards say two months.

Tim's gassing. Family recollection. Mentioned 1953 in Tim's files with Department of Veterans' Affairs (DVA).

Jam tin. The *Age.*

Stone throwing. Ellison p 4.

Maman. Ellison p 7, also Bazley (including Cumbrae-Stewart), and see Appendix I.

Rifle. Ellison p 5.

Rat-catcher. Ellison p 5, and AWM photograph P00826.151.

Dog. Ellison pp 5–6. 'Roy' is invented.

Chapter 4

Royal visits. Richards p 43, and p 41 for the 11th Wing squadrons and their planes at Bickendorf. They were: Nos 4 (Snipes), 29 (SE5s), 43 (Snipes), 48 (Bristol Fighters), 70 (Camels), 79 (Dolphins), 149 (FEs), 206 (DH9s).

Uniform. Ellison p 6 and the visit to the tailor. Jones bought the boots: Ellison says in England, but Jones G p 25 says the sheepskin was made up in Cologne.

Snipes. Cutlack pp 397–420 for aeroplanes in WWI.

Prince Edward 'Just like one of us!'. Tim writing on postcard in H.H. Tovell Papers.

Cap. Ellison p 6.

Figures in garden. Henri's statement Appendix I.

Duke of Clarence. Author interviews with Nancy Elliot and Edith Lock. No record of the incident survives in the Royal Archives.

Tim's history. Elliot and Lock interviews. Work book and photographs in family collection.

1912 voyage to Australia. Diary and autograph album in family collection.

Lille. Bazley. Ellison p 6 says Henri was found by the British at Lens; but Lille appears in most other accounts.

Chapter 5

Foundation Day. Richards p 44, AWM photograph P00826.145, AIF war diary. *Squadron formation.* Richards p 7.

Lille raid. Richards p 26, Cutlack pp 346–348, Newton p 27.

Activities at Bickendorf. Richards p 44. Visits to Cologne, fraternisation prohibited, restrictions on buying food, Orders 4 January 1919, AIF war diary.

Foundation Day Dinner. AWM photograph H13878.

Henri's age. Ellison p 7.

Skies above Bickendorf. Richards pp 42–43.

Joy ride. Imagined. The *Age* says Henri was taken on two secret flights. The two-seater LVG used to fly visitors, mentioned by Jones G p 25 (and ms), is a reasonable guess. Second flight Ch 7 is imagined. From January No. 4 Squadron also had a two-seater German Rumpler machine for intelligence work, AIF war diary.

Parachutes. Cutlack p 376.

One more in the family . . . Daily Mail 25 May 1928 Appendix II for direct quote; also Ellison p 6 for variation, '. . . one extra in the family wouldn't make that much difference.'

Chapter 6

Snow. AWM photographs P00826.154 and 180.

Wheedling food for Germans. Ellison p 5.

Influenza. Richards pp 44, 69. *Tim's pleurisy.* WWI Personnel Records, NAA.

Fire. Richards pp 44–45.

Car wrecked by shell. Brisbane *Daily Mail* Appendix II, Bazely (Cumbrae-Stewart). *'Uncle'.* Account possibly by Major Coleman, NAA Papers. See also Henri's statement Appendix I.

Skating. Richards p 44, AWM photograph P00826.235.

Postcard. Family collection. See note Ch 2 on Honoré.

School. Ellison p 7, author visit to Ste Marie Cappel, November 2000.

Jandowae. Tim's work book, poems, photographs of hotel, house, buggy, family, Tim and Ted in uniform, family collection. Elliot interview. The pub is now the Club Hotel.

Enlistment. WWI Personnel Records for Tim and Ted Tovell. The brothers transferred to the AFC in March 1917, went to Laverton (Victoria) in June; and sailed for Britain in HMAT *Aeneas* in October. They were at various UK training schools until 18 October 1918, when they were posted to France and No. 4 Squadron.

Family. Elliot and Lock interviews.

Chapter 7

Orders. Richards p 45, AIF war diary.

Jones's nightmares. Jones G p 24.

150 enemy planes. Cutlack p 385.

Losses. Richards pp 69–70.

Taplin. Richards pp 29, 23.

Death of Red Baron. Cutlack pp 249–252, Air Council history p 299 for British version. Goering, of course, became one of Hitler's inner circle, commander of the air force, head of the Gestapo, and director of the German economy during WWII. Committed suicide 1946.

Silhouette. Postcard in family collection.

Joy ride. Imagined. See note Ch 5.

Tovell's authority. Ellison p 5, full text in Bazley.

The Dinkum Oil. Ellison p 5. It was in Tim's workshop for years.

Final parade. Richards p 45.

Chapter 8

Return journey. Details in Richards pp 45–47, AIF war diary and Lt J Ellison's monthly reports as Equipment Officer. Visit by author November 2000. *Farewell from Bickendorf.* AWM photographs P00826.086, 088, and 091 for the Kaiser's statue.

Perth teashop. The incident is imagined.

Planned trip to Paris & breakdown. Jones G p 25, AWM photograph P00826.107 of Crossley.

Wrong way to tickle Marie. Nettleingham p 23, with variations from www.ingeb.org/songs. Nettleingham, an RFC officer, also has a ruder version (*It took a long time to get it hairy/'Twas a long time to grow*, referring to the airmen's moustaches).

Namur. Richards pp 38–39 and AWM photograph P00826.261; *Eupen*, AWM P00826.259; *Liège*, P00826.260; *Mons*, P00826.129.

Nivelles etc. Aerodromes used by RAF squadrons, Halley.

Mons. Sunday stopover, Richards p 47 and AIF war diary. The barber in Bazley (Tovell's 1928 narrative). Angels story in Mons War Museum brochure and other accounts, eg Graves.

Saint-Symphorien. The scene is imagined, serving as literary catharsis. Henri's flashbacks were real, however, see Ellison; and the cemetery is as lovely as described. The two Allied soldiers killed on 11 November 1918 and buried at Saint-Symphorien were Private George Price of the Canadian Infantry, and Trooper George Ellison of the 5th (Royal Irish) Lancers.

Chapter 9

The restaurant. The meal is wholly imagined, to draw together the differing versions of Henri's story. The account, possibly by Major Coleman, in the NAA Papers, has a tantalising but inconclusive paragraph:

'. . . an interesting occurrence is the fact that on the way to the embarking place in France an Imperial SM [Sgt Major] recognised the boy and practically confirmed all reports about his origin and career prior to being attached to the Australians. He also gave 2nd AM Tovell the name of the battery which picked the lad up after his parents were killed and his home destroyed, but this document has subsequently been lost.'

No other account mentions this incident. Tovell's family does not recall the document, but it strengthens my reliance on his version. A letter from Tim to Coleman on 21 June 1923 offers to send details of Henri's history, NAA Papers.

Brewery. Account in NAA Papers, Bazely (Cumbrae-Stewart), Appendix II.

Seclin. The *Argus*, 25 May 1928.

French battery. The *Age*, 24 June 1919.

Car. See note Ch 6.

Poperinghe. Based on author visits to Ypres, Poperinghe, the brilliant In Flanders Fields Museum, Talbot House, November 2000.

Hospital & artillery officer. Ellison p 6. *Ypres.* AWM P00247.002

Balloon unit. Bazley, see note above.

Balloons. See Cutlack pp 284–286, Jones H, vol IV pp 150–151.

Sainte Marie Cappel. Bazley. *Nuns.* Ellison p 7, author visit November 2000. Aerodrome near the village, see Halley.

Chinese Labour Company. Ellison p 7, also *Army Service Corps.* See reference Controller of Labour BEF.

Sims, Palliser. Jones G p 23.

RAF Squadrons. Moves, Halley. *Henri.* Bazley papers. The Royal Flying Corps (RFC) and the Royal Naval Air Service merged to become the Royal Air Force (RAF) in April 1918, the world's first separate air defence service.

No. 43 Squadron. Assumed. See note Ch 2.

Chapter 10

Lille enquiries. Bazley, Henri's statement Appendix I. *Roads.* Lt Ellison's reports in AIF war diary.

Accident. Richards p 47. Tim's back injury, Elliot interview and his DVA file. I assume it happened here.

Béthune. See AWM photograph H13588.

Tim's adventure. Elliot interview. Similar story Richards pp 34–35. The Tovells joined No. 4 Squadron as riggers on 19 October 1918, Ted posted to A Flight, Tim to B Flight, AIF war diary.

Rouelles. Author visit November 2000. Base photographs AWM H01076, H01078, H01111.

Padre Gault & stunts. Gault pp 50, 60, 74–75 for 'Watch Your Socks!' and description of AIF Base. See AWM photograph

H15641. Gault's obituary in the *Argus* 2, 4 February 1938.

Henri's health certificate. Text in Bazley (1967).

Gault & Tovell. Ellison pp 7–8.

Chapter 11

The oat sack. Ellison p 8, including the wooden box and jam tins. See also the Brisbane *Daily Mail* Appendix II. The *Age* says a sugar bag was used, the *Argus* May 1928 a bag of official records, and Richards a kit bag. The Hurdcott photographs plainly show the bag marked *OATS 100 lbs.* Reconstructing the operation, it is clear how important both brothers were.

Napoleon. I assume the flag and statue were left behind. The family does not remember them.

Gault's card, Major Ellis. Bazley (1967 and Cumbrae-Stewart).

Smuggling. Ellison pp 8–9, and Bazley. Some accounts say Tim left his kit bag behind, but surely not! I assume Ted brought it.

Le Havre harbour. See photo AWM H11820.

The hold. The accounts are unclear: 'hold' is the word used, but they don't usually have seats. I have made it a locker room 'like a small hold'.

Departure. Richards p 47. *Timings.* Bazley (Tovell 1928), Ellison.

Tim's dark dream. Elliot interview, put here for dramatic purposes. Ellison p 6 states Tovell learned of Timmy's death at Hurdcott.

Jam tin. Ellison p 9.

Orange and bread roll. Ellison and Bazley.

Rivulet of pee. Lock interview.

Timings & Henri's reappearance. AIF war diary, Bazley (Tovell 1928), Ellison p 9.

Chapter 12

'The wonderful smile'. Bazley (Cumbrae-Stewart).

Massage. Ellison p 9.

Verdun. See Appendix II.

Fovant. Author visit 2000. See publications by the Fovant Badges Society. AWM photograph of Hurdcott sports, H00304. *Quartermaster's store.* AWM photo D00300.

Photographs. They are AWM H13589, H13591, A03056. Some captions say they were taken in France, but the buildings and grounds are identical with known Hurdcott photographs – see Henri boxing and in his 'British Warm' (under Uniform below). Others suggest they were taken as the squadron *left* Hurdcott, but this cannot be correct, see Ch 14. Also note Henri is wearing his Cologne clothes, not the tailored London uniform.

Squadron fund. Tim's notebook in family collection.

Timmy's death. Based on Elliot and Lock interviews; the *Courier* weather report 31 January 1919, and funeral Toowoomba *Chronicle* 5 February; author visit to Jandowae and Jimbour July 2000; interview with David Russell QC, whose family has owned Jimbour House since 1924. The buggy trip is clear in the family memory, but the details have been imagined.

Who plucked this flower? The words appear in varying forms on epitaphs and in newspaper death notices. See Stevenson 'Home Book of Quotations'. Origin unknown, possibly inspired by the Resurrection scene in *John 20 v 15–16*.

Tim's verse. Tovell wrote the following verse in his notebook:

The Masters Message
Lift up thine eyes, My Son.
Pausing awhile
Rest thou on Me.
Thy way to see.
Stretch forth thy hand, My Son,
That way to know
And calmly stand
Till I command
I am the Orphans Friend
Presence Divine
Still at thy side
Whate'er betide.

Visit to Princes Risborough. Both Nancy Elliot and Edith Lock recall Tim saying he visited his family living at Princes Risborough during this time in England.

Horseferry Road YMCA. See AWM photographs H01300 ff, and the Aldwych H01255.

Uniform. Ellison p 10. See AWM photograph H13592, and A03678 for Digger in his 'British Warm'.

AFC colour patch. A pale blue triangle, with dark blue centre stripe and red side stripes.

Postcard. Found in papers of H.H. Tovell. I thank the AWM conservators who carefully removed the newspaper clipping pasted over the handwritten message.

Queen Marie. Bazley (Cumbrae-Stewart), Ellison p 10, Appendix II.

Acting Corporal. Keyed photograph in AIF war diary see note Ch 2, the *Age* (which called him a lance-corporal).

Chapter 13

Johnson. WWI Personnel Records, and AIF war diary.

Henri's behaviour. Ellison p 9.

Two-up school. Ellison pp 10–11, the *Age*, The Australian Encyclopedia for description of game. 'Swy' is from the German word *zwei* meaning two.

The Dinkum Oil. Ellison p 11. Henri deprived of his stripes, the *Age.*

Toys. Ellison pp 11–12.

Salisbury & walk home. Ellison p 12. Author visit 2000.

Boxing. Photograph of Henri & Ted at AWM P00867.004.

Anzac Day March. Richards p 48 and photograph AWM H16106. Photographs AWM P00867.001 of Tim, Ted, Henri on Anzac Day (note Tim's weight loss), and Henri singly in AWM H13592. Note also Henri's swagger stick and service ribbon.

Cobby's stunt. Cobby pp 102–103.

Chapter 14

Leaving Hurdcott. Major Ellis's final report in AIF war diary.

Ellis's proposal. Ellison p 12.

Wagers & terms. The *Argus* 25 May 1928 says Ellis placed a £25 bet with the 'transport officer' – assumed to be Lt Ellison, responsible for transport. I have added Jones, Ellison p 13. Again, reconstructing the operation, it is clear how important the officers' compliance was for its success.

Basket. Ellison p 12, also the *Daily Mail.* Bazley (1967) mentions the pierrot outfits. Pierrot photograph see AWM P01939.001.

Nos 2 and 3 Squadrons. See AIF war diaries AWM 4. Also Papers of the voyage of HMT *Kaisar-i-Hind* and Lt Col Watt's diary.

Jones. Ellison p 13 and Bazley both say Jones tossed down his cabin number on a piece of paper. The bag and key are imagined. Jones G is very circumspect in his autobiography p 25, 'We took Henri back to England with us, and managed to smuggle him aboard a troopship bound for Australia . . .' Bazley says Tim carried the basket to Jones's cabin. Ellison p 13 says Tim went down to Jones's cabin later, which seems more likely. The *Daily Mail* Appendix II is somewhat different again.

Kit bag hide. Imagined. Ellison p 13 says only that Henri was 'safely planted' as the ship left the dock

Departure. See Ellis's final report in AIF war diary, Watt's diary.

Chapter 15

Voyage. All details of events, weather, food, sports, mess-deck competitions, Mr Sparkes' report, 'dry ship' policy, are from Papers of HMT *Kaisar-i-Hind*, Watt's diary, and Ellis's final report AIF war diary. Ship photograph AWM P01147.001.

Henri's bottle and photo money. Ellison p 14, amounts in Tim's notebook, see Ch 12. Bottle money appears from 7 May.

Elgood. Watt's diary, Ellis's final AIF war diary entry, Papers of HMT *Kaisar-i-Hind*.

Discovery. It is a little uncertain when Captain Palmer discovered Henri. Bazley says Port Said, 16–17 May (Cumbrae-Stewart and Tovell 1928), and money from 'photos' appears in Tim's notebook from 20 May. I have adopted this. Ellison does not give the date, but says Henri gained acceptance at Port Said, p 14. Henri suggests he was found the day after sailing (Appendix I), and the *Age* says Colombo.

Captain Palmer. Ellison pp 13–14. The *Argus* 25 May 1928 and Henri (Appendix I) say Watt (and Premier Ryan) helped. Ellis's presence may be inferred from Ellison. See also Appendix II.

Tom Ryan. Murphy pp 404–426. See Appendix II, and the *Age* for Henri and Ryan 'engaged in animated conversation.' Ellison p 15 says Henri didn't go to the saloon deck. Weakened by the Spanish influenza, Ryan was to die of pneumonia in 1921.

Sunburn. Ellison p 14 and *Jones the banker*, p 15.

Captain Palmer looking skywards. The *Daily Mail* Appendix II.

Shipboard photograph. See AWM A03679.

Colombo. Bazley (Cumbrae-Stewart).

King Neptune. Papers of HMT *Kaisar-i-Hind*. Henri's private dunking is imagined.

Fremantle. Ellis's final report AIF war diary, Watt's diary.

Chapter 16

Tim's plan. Ellison p 14, and *Jack Ryan impersonation*, p 15.

Adelaide. The French woman offering £1500, Ellison p 15, the

Daily Mail Appendix II. I have assumed she lost her son in the war. It is unclear how she heard about Henri: little had appeared in the Australian press to this point. Photograph of ship at Adelaide AWM H13879.

Ryan's help. Lily, Ellison p 15. Whether Lily was asked to approach her husband by Digger, by some other person, or whether it was her own idea, is unclear.

Records of conversation and cables by Webb and Hunt. Department of the Interior file. Murphy does not mention Ryan's intervention. *Minister's cable.* Ellison p 16.

Port Melbourne arrival. The *Argus* 17 June 1919, Ellis's final report in AIF war diary, the *Age* for Henri seen talking to Ryan and the £60 subscribed for Henri by the squadron.

Collins Street. Bazley (Cumbrae-Stewart), Ellison p 16 also the gold brooch. The brooch has disappeared.

Newspaper reports. The *Herald* Melbourne 20 June, the *Age* 24 June. The *Herald* oddly referred to Henri as 'little Piou Piou'. Some details in the *Age* report differ from those given by Tovell. It appears to be based on talks with returned AFC airmen, but strangely it says Digger came to No. 4 Squadron at Lille – Cologne and Christmas Day aren't mentioned. See Brisbane *Daily Mail* 21 June Appendix II, for Tovell's account.

Henri's distress. Bazely (Cumbrae-Stewart). The Toowoomba *Chronicle* 21 June uses similar name Henri wrote on the card from Cologne with his surname first, 'Hemene Honori' (actually Heememe Honoré).

Knife and fork. Appendix II.

Brisbane welcome. The *Courier* 21 June, which gives Henri's age as eight, *Daily Mail* Appendix II. *Hospital.* Ellison p 16.

Arrival home. The *Chronicle* 2 July says Tim and Henri were met at Jimbour and motored into Jandowae on Wednesday 25 June.

Hello Mum. Ellison p 16, also gold brooch.

Chapter 17

Hospital. Henri's tonsils Ellison p 17; Tim's sinuses, DVA file. Ellison says Tim was 'a cot-case . . . for seven months', but his records show he was discharged from the army on 17 September 1919. Perhaps Ellison meant seven weeks.

School. Jandowae school enrolment 4 September 1919, Qld State Archives. Both Nancy and Henri left in October 1919.

They're nice words, Tim. Tovell letter to Major Coleman 25 May 1928, NAA Papers.

Move to Cooroy. Elliot and Lock interviews; author visit to Cooroy July 2000.

Horse race. Ellison p 17.

Gertie sick. Elliot interview.

French Consul. Ellison p 18, also account possibly by Coleman in NAA Papers, which include correspondence with Carter and Campana. After Henri's death, Major Carter unveiled Digger's photograph in the Brisbane club rooms of the RS&SILA.

Heremene. The boy who signed himself Heememe Honoré in Cologne in January 1919, acquired yet another version of his surname. Even that would change. Heememe is used in the

Webb-Hunt correspondence; Henri used Hemene in his naturalisation application; Heremene appears on his memorial; and Hermene in the inquest papers. It's curious the surname 'Herman' or 'Hermann' didn't suggest itself to the French Consul, for the pronunciation is very similar to Heremene. See note on Honoré Ch 2.

Brisbane move. Elliot interview; Cooroy school register, Qld State Archives. 'Henri Heememe' enrolled 27 January 1920, left November 1922.

Headmaster. Ellison p 19; Kangaroo Point boys school register 29 January 1923, Qld State Archives.

Fight. Elliot interview, and similar story Ellison p 18.

Gault. Ellison p 19 puts the visit in 1922. I could not confirm it.

RAAF advertisement. Ellison p 20. The RAAF was formed in March 1921 as a separate defence service.

Wilson letter. Henri's statement Appendix I. Ellison says Tim initially wrote directly to Coleman, but it seems unlikely. Coleman had not served in the AFC.

Coleman letters. To Henri and Tim; also to Carter and Consul-General, with replies, NAA Papers.

Henri's message. Tim's autograph book, family collection.

Air Board. Coulthard-Clark p 370, Henri's employment NAA Papers.

Wilson. Service records. Author visit to Lantana Rd, No. 2 has been demolished.

Night school. Henri's statement Appendix I.

Henri's ex-serviceman's badge. The *Duckboard* 2 July 1928.

Resignation. NAA Papers, also for Coleman's letter and Tovell's response. Note in file says Henri began at Point Cook on 1 March 1926.

Holiday. Note in NAA Papers says Henri was due for 18 days recreation leave on 14 July 1926. Vera Schaffer, Elliot interview. See AWM photograph H13597 and P00867.002.

Henri's letters. Family collection letter 8 November 1926; H.H. Tovell Papers, letters 17 December 1926 and 12 June 1927.

Single men's quarters. Note on file NAA Papers. At this time the single airmen probably still lived in Nissen huts, see Coulthard-Clark pp 121–122.

Henri's behaviour. Coulthard-Clark p 127.

Wing Cdr Cole's reports. NAA Papers. The February 1928 report states: 'Trade progress not satisfactory. Conduct not satisfactory. Diligence not satisfactory. Attention on parade not satisfactory . . . In accordance, I cannot recommend that the annual increment due, be given to the temporary junior assistant.' But see below, Auction of Henri's effects.

1927 Christmas card. Family collection. It is unclear if the parachutist is Henri.

1906. Coleman note in NAA Papers.

Coleman in Brisbane. Tim's letter 25 May 1928, NAA Papers.

Naturalisation. Department of the Interior file, Henri's statement Appendix I.

Plan to go home by ship. Lock interview, Ellison p 20.

Sold bike. On back of photograph in family collection Henri has written, 'On my (own) bike before I sold it at PC.'

Girlfriend. Coleman's letter to Tim 25 May 1928, the *Argus* 26 May. She is not named. Possibly the daughter of 'Mr Fiske of Westgarth Street North Melbourne' (actually James Fisk of North Fitzroy) who is named in NAA Papers as one of three people having an interest in Henri's future (the others are Wilson and Tovell). Nancy Elliot and Edith Lock recall Jack Fisk, of Stanthorpe, as a wartime friend of Tim's. Possibly he was related to James Fisk.

Henri in civvies. See AWM photo A03680.

Despatch. Mentioned by Rev Perry in his eulogy 3 June 1928.

Death. Based on Coleman letter to Tim 25 May family collection, and Proceedings of Inquest. The motor cycle belonged to Aircraftsman Grade 1 Duncan Cameron of the Point Cook Workshop Squadron, NAA Papers. And see photo of Henri on a mate's racing TT model AJS motor bike annotated by Tim, 'He was riding this machine when killed', AWM P00867.003.

Telegrams. In NAA Papers, also letters; Lock interview; newspaper reports as cited.

Tim's letter. 25 May NAA Papers.

Funeral. The *Argus* 26 May, which gives Henri's age as eighteen.

Memorial service. Brisbane *Courier* 4 June. *Perry's eulogy.* H.H. Tovell Papers.

Tim's letters. NAA Papers.

Inquest. Proceedings of Inquest, the *Argus* 29 May 1928. The speed with which everything was done is astonishing. Tovell was given no opportunity to attend the funeral or even the inquest upon the young man who regarded him as his foster-father.

Coleman letter. Dated 17 July, NAA Papers.

Auction of effects. NAA Papers. Despite Cole's February report, Coleman recommended Henri's estate be paid his wage rise.

Curator of Deceased Estates. It is unclear what happened to the balance of Henri's estate. A note from Cole in NAA Papers suggests it be paid to memorial fund.

Wilson. Letter to *The Duckboard* 2 July 1928.

Memorial. NAA Papers; photograph with statue of orphan boy AWM A03681; the grave is D632, Methodist portion, Fawkner Cemetery.

Epilogue

Statue. Lock and Elliot interviews with author. The memorial, erected on 3 February 1932, cost nearly £300, NAA Papers.

Cumbrae-Stewart. Tim's correspondence with AWM in T.W. Tovell Papers. I was unable to locate Cumbrae-Stewart's original ms, but a (partial) copy is in Bazley collection.

Wilson. Service papers. Death notice the *Age* 20 September 1949.

Ellis. Obituary *Wings* March 1948; *Who's Who* 1947.

Jones. Autobiography. *Who's Who* entry 1992.

Tovell family. Interviews with Nancy Elliot, Edith Lock, Ed Tovell.

ACKNOWLEDGEMENTS

Shortly after completing *Soldier Boy*, I was lunching with my friend, Ashley Ekins, Senior Historian at the Australian War Memorial, when he pushed an envelope across the table. 'Here's your next book, Tony.' A moment reading the few press clippings about the orphan mascot, *Young Digger*, was enough to convince me. The stories of the two boys, James Martin and Henri Tovell, stand as powerful metaphors on either side of the history of Australia's involvement in the Great War – Anzac and the Armistice – like a pair of bookends. My gratitude to Ashley Ekins, is enormous.

Through the resources of the AWM, I was able to contact the family of Timothy Tovell. His daughters, Mrs Edith Lock, Mrs Nancy Elliot and her children, Marilyn, Rick, Rob and Sally generously shared their memories with me, and gave access to family photographs, letters and other memorabilia which enhanced, authenticated and enriched the narrative. I am deeply grateful for their assistance. Tim's son, Edward Tovell of Brisbane, also kindly helped with my enquiries.

My friends, Dr Chris Coulthard-Clark, Dr Michael McKernan and Lieutenant-Colonel Rod Webster read the manuscript and gave invaluable assistance and advice on military history. I am very grateful to them, although naturally any errors of fact, inference or interpretation are solely my responsibility.

My research for the book involved not only the national institutions in Canberra, but also visits elsewhere in Australia, Britain and Europe. Many people and organisations assisted me at every stage of the journey, and I express my sincere thanks to every one. In particular, I acknowledge the help given by the following:

Canberra: The ACT Cultural Council and the ACT Government; the Director and staff of the Australian War Memorial, in particular Ian Affleck, Peter Aitken, Ian Kelly, Michael Nelmes, Joanne Smedley and the always helpful members of the Research Centre; Janet Beck and staff of RAAF Historical Records; HE the Ambassador and staff of the Embassy of Belgium; Brian Buckley and staff of the Department of Veterans' Affairs; Verona Burgess; Dr Chris Coulthard-Clark; my friend, Dr Alan Cowan, who gave valuable medical advice; the Department of Defence for permission to use the AFC wings in the chapter headings; HE the Ambassador and staff of the Embassy of France, and also of the French Consulate in Sydney; Anne-Marie Gachet, Kenneth and Nadia Kuhlmann who kindly helped with the

French translations; Dr Michael McKernan; Neil Wynes Morse, who researched the verse *Who plucked this flower?*; the National Archives of Australia; the National Library of Australia, and staff of the reading room and newspaper and microform section; Bob Towns, Pat and Robin Wain of the Fyshwick Antique Centre.

Victoria: Staff of the Fawkner Cemetery; my sister Vanessa Harrison, who provided accommodation and transport; my daughter Jane Hill, who undertook much record searching; Neil Follett; Reg Jardley and members of the RAAF Association; staff of the Public Record Office of Victoria; RAAF Museum Point Cook; the Victorian Branch of the RSL; Lieutenant-Colonel Rod Webster who helped identify motor cycles, cars and aeroplanes, and advised on military matters; Eddie Young and members of the Melbourne Sub-branch of the RSL at Duckboard House.

Queensland: Marilyn Elliot; Nancy Elliot; Rick Elliot; Rob Elliot; Sally Elliot; staff of the Club Hotel, Jandowae; Museum of Australian Army Flying, Oakey; Queensland State Archives; Brisbane Sub-branch of the RSL; David Russell QC, whose family has owned Jimbour House since 1924; the Director and staff of the State Library of Queensland and the John Oxley Library who very kindly searched the Toowoomba newspapers for me; Edward Tovell; David Tucker and members of the Albert Street Uniting Church.

Western Australia: Peg Wooldridge of the Western Australian branch of the Australian Railway Historical Society.

England: Oliver Everett, Assistant Keeper of the Royal Archives, Windsor Castle; staff of the Imperial War Museum,

London; Edith Lock; Edward and Gail Mann who provided accommodation and loving family hospitality; staff of the Museum of Army Flying, Middle Wallop; staff of the RAF Museum, Hendon; parishioners of St Mary's, Princes Risborough; Pauline Story of the Cross Keys, Fovant; staff of Wilton House.

Germany: Staff of the Information Bureau, and the citizens of Cologne who kindly showed me the way to Bickendorf Aerodrome (no longer used for flying and now being redeveloped), helped me when I got lost, and directed me to Stadtwald gardens; Nicole Friegel who generously helped with translations.

Belgium: The Commonwealth War Graves Commission; staff of the Information and Tourism Bureaux at Liège, Mons and Ypres; the ground staff of the beautiful military cemetery at Saint-Symphorien, near Mons; Sainte-Waudru's Collegiate Church, Mons; staff of the War Museum, and the Musée du Centenaire, Mons; Laetitia Brouwers who provided generous hospitality and transport at Ypres; staff of the brilliant In Flanders Fields Museum, Ypres; Simon Wearing and Kurt Debacker of Flanders Battlefield Tour, Ypres; the congregations of St Martin's Cathedral, St George's Memorial Church, and the buglers of the Ypres Fire Brigade who made Armistice Day 2000 – and every night at the Menin Gate – a moving experience beyond words; staff of Talbot House, Poperinghe, who continue Tubby Clayton's tradition of making everyone welcome.

France: Professor Annette Becker of Lille; staff of the Tourism and Information Bureaux at Lille, Armentières, Arras,

Amiens and Le Havre; the Commonwealth War Graves Commission; Martine Blavier and staff of the Préfecture du Nord Cabinet, Lille, who made many enquiries about the orphan known as Henri Hemene Tovell on my behalf, alas without success; Monsieur Paul, Lionel Defontaine, and the residents of Sainte Marie Cappel who helped me find the house where Henri stayed with *les soeurs*; the staff and splendid young visitor guides at the Canadian National Vimy Memorial; the tour guides of the underground tunnels at Arras, used by soldiers and medical teams during the Great War; staff of the Franco-Australian Museum at Villers-Bretonneux, and of the Australian National Memorial beyond the town; the Musée Malraux, Le Havre; staff of the municipal offices at Rouelles; and the people of the seaport of Honfleur, who made my last afternoon in France so memorable.

I wish to acknowledge, once again, the faith shown in my work by my publisher Julie Watts, and editor Suzanne Wilson. This book is the result of a genuinely creative partnership.

Last, as she is also first, I thank my dear wife, Gillian, for her constant support, encouragement and advice. Truly, she sustains all.

Anthony Hill

References and Further Reading

AIF War Diary, No. 4 Squadron AFC, July 1918 to June 1919. AWM 4 reel 133, includes menu, musical selections and keyed photograph for Christmas Day at Bickendorf, Foundation Day 1919 sports programme, daily entries, orders and monthly reports by OC, Equipment Officer etc.

Air Council, *A Short History of the Royal Air Force*, (Air Ministry, London, 1929), especially pp 418–421 on kite balloons, and p 299 for British account of the Red Baron's death.

Australian Encyclopedia (The Grolier Society, 1981 edition).

Bazley, Arthur, papers relating to Timothy Tovell and Henri Hemene Tovell, AWM 3DRL/3520 Item 119. The material includes photos, ms article about Henri by Bazley based on accounts written by Tim Tovell in 1928–29 (see *The Whiz-Bang*), Professor Cumbrae-Stewart in 1932, Richards and Ellison.

Cobby, A.H., DSO, DFC, *High Adventure* (Kookaburra Technical Publications, Dandenong, 1981 ed). See pp 102–103 for the Anzac Day 1919 fly past in London and farewell from England.

Coleman, Major Patrick Eugene, Secretary of the Air Board 1921–39. See under National Archives of Australia. Coleman died in 1950.

Controller of Labour, British Expeditionary Force, Extracts from War Diary 7 October to 11 November 1918, AWM 26 468/10. For further descriptions of the work and manpower of the Labour Companies in France, see also AWM 45 29/79–80.

Coulthard-Clark, C.D., *The Third Brother, The Royal Australian Air Force 1921–39* (Allen & Unwin in association with the RAAF, Sydney, 1991), see pp 370 ff for Major Coleman's office, and pp 120–127 for life at Point Cook in the 1920s and a recollection of Henri.

Cumbrae-Stewart, Prof. F.D., extracts from 1932 account of Henri based on notes from Timothy Tovell, see under Bazley. The copy of his ms deposited with the AWM Library could not be located.

Cutlack, F.M., *The Official History of Australia in the War of 1914–1918*, Vol. VIII, *The Australian Flying Corps in the Western and Eastern Theatres of War*, (Angus & Robertson Ltd., Sydney, 1935). See pp 214–215 and 249–252 for the Red Baron, pp 284–286 for balloons, and p 376 for parachutes. Also entries for Cobby, Ellis, Jones, King etc., the excellent appendices for types of WWI aircraft, trades, use of incendiary bullets, and glossary.

Department of the Interior, Papers relating to the life of Henri Hemene Tovell, mascot of No. 4 Squadron AFC, AWM93 37 (official records), includes correspondence between Hunt and Webb allowing Henri to land in Australia 1919, Henri's Application for Naturalisation 1928, photographs.

Elliot, Mrs Nancy, Timothy and Gertrude Tovell's eldest daughter, b July 1913. Interviews with the author at Brisbane 17 April and 21 July 2000, 12 February 2001, transcript deposited at AWM. Her sons Rick and Rob, and daughters Sally and Marilyn, were present at various times, contributed family memories and kindly gave access to family collections.

Ellison, Norman, *Flying Matilda, Early Days in Australian Aviation*, (Angus and Robertson, Sydney, 1957). Chapter 1, *Henri*, in which Tim Tovell tells the detailed story.

Fovant Badges Society, Fovant, Salisbury, Wiltshire SP3 5LJ, England; and see Internet site.

Gault, Chaplain Lt Col James A., *Padre Gault's Stunt Book*, (The Epworth Press, London, 1920s). Padre Gault died in February 1938.

Graves, Robert, *Goodbye To All That* (1929, The Folio Society 1999). A classic and caustic account of WWI by a British infantry officer, fighting on the ground over which No. 4 Squadron AFC flew. See Ch XV for a sceptical footnote on the angels of Mons.

Halley, James J. *The Squadrons of the Royal Air Force & Commonwealth 1918–1988* (Air-Britain Historians Ltd, Tonbridge 1988). Gives details of the aerodromes used by, among others, Nos 43, 48 & 79 Squadrons RAF during WWI.

HMT *Kaisar-i-Hind*, Papers of voyage departed Southampton 6 May 1919, arrived Sydney 19 June 1919. AWM 7 *Kaisar-i-Hind*, (four folders), see especially Folder 3 for Lt Col Watt's diary and associated papers. Nowhere is Henri's name or presence noted among the fifty-seven civilian passengers on board (including ten children).

Jones, Air Marshal Sir George, KBE, CB, DFC, *From Private to Air Marshal* (Greenhouse Publications, Melbourne, 1988). See pp 22–26 for end of war, Cologne, Henri, and voyage home. Also ms *Autobiographical Memoir*, AWM MSS0738 (and later version MSS1027) for the LVG commandeered at Namur.

Jones, H.A., *The War In The Air, Being the Story of the part played in the Great War by the Royal Air Force*, (Oxford, 1937). See appendices pp 150 ff, for locations of RAF Squadrons at the Armistice, vol IV pp 150–151 on co-operation between artillery and balloon observers.

Journal of the League of WWI Aviation Historians, *Over The Front*, Spring 1991, pp 36 ff for location of aerodromes on the Western Front.

Laffin, John, *Guide to Australian Battlefields of the Western Front 1916–1918*, (Kangaroo Press & AWM, Sydney, 1992).

Lewis, Cecil, *Sagittarius Rising* (1936, The Folio Society edition,

1998). The classic book by a WWI airman. Lewis spares none of the fear and horror. The reader is in the cockpit with him. But his prose also soars to reach transcendent moments of the human spirit. See the epigraph to this book, and also the reference under Saint-Exupéry.

Lock, Mrs Edith, Timothy and Gertrude Tovell's second daughter b April 1920. Interview with author at Chipping Norton, England, 25 September 2000, transcript deposited with AWM. Mrs Lock also kindly gave access to family collections.

Macfarlane, Sandy, & Kingham, Chris, *Princes Risborough Past*, (Phillimore & Co Ltd., Chichester, West Sussex, 1997).

Murphy, D.J., *T.J. Ryan, a political biography* (UQP, Brisbane, 1975, 1990). Thomas Joseph Ryan (1876–1921), was Premier of Queensland 1915–19. See pp 404–426 for the trip to Europe and return in the *Kaisar-i-Hind*. Murphy does not mention Ryan helping Henri to land in Australia, but see Department of the Interior reference.

National Archives of Australia, Papers relating to Henri H Tovell Memorial, series A705 file 202/3/334, includes correspondence to and from Major Coleman 1923–1933, an unsigned account of Henri's background possibly by Coleman (mid-1920s), Henri's application to resign in 1925, employment as civilian apprentice at Point Cook in 1926, death in 1928, auction of his effects, public memorial subscription and erection of sculpture by Wallace Anderson at Fawkner Cemetery 1928–33. WWI Personnel Records for Timothy and Edward Tovell, Joseph Ellison, Norman Ellison, Norman Johnson and Hector Wilson.

Nettleingham, 2nd Lt Frederick Thomas, *Tommy's Tunes, A comprehensive collection of soldiers' songs, marching melodies, rude rhymes, and popular parodies, composed, collected, and arranged on active service with the B.E.F.* (Erskine MacDonald, London, 1917). Australian wartime songs and parodies can also be found in Warren Fahey's *Digger's Songs* (1996) and Graham Seal's *Digger folksong and verse of World War One* (1991).

Newton, Dennis, *Australian Air Aces, Australian Fighter Pilots in Combat*, (Aerospace Publications, Canberra, 1996). See entries for Cobby, King, Jones and McCloughry.

Proceedings of Inquest upon Henri Hermene Tovell, Melbourne Morgue, 28 May 1928, Daniel Berriman, Coroner, Public Record Office of Victoria, VPRS 24/P unit 1134 file 675/1928.

Queensland Post Office Directory 1918–1919, Jandowae, Jimbour.

Queensland Public Records. State school enrolments for Henri Tovell: Jandowae 4 September 1919; Cooroy 27 January 1920; Kangaroo Point (boys) 29 January 1923.

Reveille, 30 April 1931, article by C. Smith *Digger's Mascot: War Orphan's Fate.*

Richards, Lt E.J., *Australian Airmen, History of the 4th Squadron, Australian Flying Corps*, (undated, early 1920s). Lt Edward John Richards was a pilot with No. 4 Squadron.

Saint-Exupéry, Antoine de, *Wind, Sand and Stars* (1939, The Folio Society edition 1990). A French aviator of the 1920s and 30s, he flew in South America and The Sahara. Killed during WWII. The Folio Society edition has a fine introduction by

Cecil Lewis *qv*, about early morning take-off during WWI. Saint-Ex, as he was known, is famous for his children's story, *The Little Prince* (1943), which tells of an airman and a star child, but is really about the mystery – even mysticism – of the air, known to those early pilots.

Stevenson, Burton Egbert, *The Home Book of Quotations*, (Dodd, Mead, New York, 10th edition 1967). See p 384 No. 5 for verse.

The Age, Melbourne, 24 June 1919, 'The Story of Henry'.

The Argus, Melbourne, 16–24 June 1919, homecoming; 25–26, 29 May 1928, death and inquest; 2, 4 February 1938, Padre Gault.

The Chronicle, Toowoomba, 5 February 1919 for Timmy's death; 21 June and 2 July for homecoming.

The Courier, Brisbane, 31 January 1919; 21 June 1919.

The Daily Mail, Brisbane, 21 June 1919, 25 May 1928 Appendix II.

The Duckboard, Official Organ of the Melbourne Sub-branch of the RS&SILA, 2 July 1928 letter from Hec Wilson.

The Herald, Melbourne, 20 June 1919.

The Times History of the War, (London, 1920). Photographs of refugees: Vol II p 463; Vol III p 444; Vol XVIII pp 102, 190; Vol XX pp 115, 333. Scuttling of German fleet at Scarpa Flow 1919: Vol XXI pp 22–23.

The Whiz-Bang, Official Organ of the Brisbane Sub-branch of the RS&SILA, November 1928–February 1929. A series of short articles by Tim Tovell telling Henri's story, similar to Bazley.

Tovell, Edward John DFC, Timothy and Gertrude Tovell's son,

born May 1923. Interviews with author by telephone May 2001.

Tovell, Henri Heremene, Papers, AWM PR87/199, includes photographs in uniform at London and Hurdcott, Tim's postcard, grave, Rev John Perry's sermon 3 June 1928, letters home 1926–27, Tim's letter from Panama 1917. For Application for Naturalisation 1928 (Appendix I), and official correspondence allowing him to land in Australia 1919, see under Department of the Interior. For RAAF employment, see National Archives of Australia.

Tovell, Timothy William, Private records of Henri Hememe Tovell, 'Digger', AWM93 12/11/4801 (official records), includes correspondence with AWM on narrative by Cumbrae-Stewart *qv.* For correspondence with Major Coleman 1923–28, see under National Archives of Australia. Photographs, letters, notebook from Hurdcott and the *Kaisar-i-Hind*, work book 1898–1913, diary of voyage to Australia 1912, memorabilia, birth and marriage certificates etc, in family collections. See also *The Whiz-Bang*, and Ellison. WWI Personnel Records, National Archives of Australia, also for Edward John Tovell.

Watt, Lt Col Walter Oswald, OBE, diary as OC Troops, see HMT *Kaisar-i-Hind.* Sadly, Watt drowned in 1921.

Who's Who in Australia, (Herald & Weekly Times, Melbourne, 1947), entry for Group Captain A.W.L. Ellis.

Wings, 1 March 1948, obituary on Group Captain Ellis.

Photographic Credits

Every effort has been made to trace copyright holders of photographs. The publishers would appreciate hearing from any copyright holder not here acknowledged.

FRONT COVER, BACK COVER AND SPINE: Photograph of Young Digger with Tim Tovell courtesy of Nancy Elliot (photo taken at Béthune: see p 110); poppies picture courtesy of Getty Images; photograph of Sopwith Snipe planes courtesy of Australian War Memorial, Canberra (Australian War Memorial negative number P00826.156); replica of Australian Flying Corps colour patch (as seen on back cover) courtesy of Bob Towns.

INSIDE FRONT COVER: Photograph of Young Digger courtesy of Nancy Elliot.

INSIDE BACK COVER: Postcard courtesy of Nancy Elliot.

AUTHOR PHOTO: Copyright © Sandy Spiers.

AFC wings: Courtesy of the Australian War Memorial.

PICTURE INSERTS: The following photographs are from the Australian War Memorial.
Photographic Collections: AWM H08572; AWM P02658.004; AWM P00826.151; AWM P00826.136; AWM P00826.086;

AWM P00826.263; AWM P00826.107; AWM P03638.001; AWM H13589; AWM A03056; AWM H13591; AWM P00867.004; AWM P00867.001; AWM H16106; AWM A03679; AWM H13597; AWM A03680; AWM P00867.003; AWM A03681.

OTHER PHOTO CREDITS: Courtesy of Nancy Elliot. Facsimiles of Young Digger's handwriting and postcard appearing in text courtesy of Nancy Elliot.